SAVING DAVE

Life can change in the blink of an eye.

Richard Grainger

First Edition Published in Great Britain 2021 by
Otterdene Publishing
Richard Grainger asserts his moral right to be
identified as the author of this book.

ISBN pbk: 978-0-9561341-3-4
ISBN ebk: 978-0-9561341-4-1

Copyright © Richard Grainger 2021
Formatted by Bee-Edited.com

This book is a work of fiction and, except in the case of
historical fact any resemblance to actual persons, living
or dead, is purely coincidental

This book is
dedicated to Jake,
an inspiration to us
all.

"There are no words
to express the abyss
between isolation
and having one ally."

Gilbert K. Chesterton

PROLOGUE

ONE YEAR AGO – THE ACCIDENT

Perhaps it was no great surprise that the first word Dave said was 'fuck'.

And the fact that this utterance occurred some eighteen years, two months, three days and seven hours after he was born caused considerable consternation, not least of all to Dave.

In fact, it caused so much consternation that the three other people who heard it imagined that they had heard it. Indeed, they thought that there must be some logical explanation as to why they all thought that they had heard it. And this was because there was as little likelihood of Dave saying anything – let alone 'fuck' – as there was of the object that had just struck him reciting the entire works of William Shakespeare.

PART ONE

BEFORE THE
ACCIDENT

ONE

DAVE

The truth is often boring.

Someone once said that a lie can go around the world in the morning before the truth has put his trousers on.

What I'm about to tell you is the truth and I don't think it's boring because it's my life, and although you may well end up feeling sorry for me – or again, you may not – it's the best life I can have so I just have to make the most of it, even after everything that's happened to me.

When you've finished reading this, you can make your own mind up about whether I've been lucky or not.

But who knows what the future holds?

Do any of us?

***

Okay, so I'll begin to tell you about myself.

I was born around eighteen years ago, a healthy baby. Of course, I don't remember anything about this – does anyone? But from what I've found out over the years, listening to the parents' conversations, this is what happened.

About two and a half years into my life, they figured out that something was wrong. Most babies, I believe, progress from crawling to walking by their first birthday, but by the time I'd passed my second birthday, I was still crawling across the carpet like a slug on a lettuce leaf.

And that's a pretty good comparison because, apparently, I was shaped like a football, so when crawling became rolling, and then forward and sideways movement finally stopped altogether, the parents decided they ought to investigate. I don't know why it took them so long to notice this because I can't remember that far back. But it doesn't really surprise me, cos they've always found more important and interesting stuff to do than pay much attention to me.

It took a doctor, who I think is called a paediatrician, about three nano-seconds to work out that both my hips were dislocated, and that without surgery to fix this I had as much chance of walking as a baby seal.

So I had both hips broken and reset, but I never got to walk anyway because, after the operation, there was some sort of 'complication'. And then, after they'd got that under control, one of the nurses in the ITU went for a fag break, during which time I stopped breathing.

By the time someone noticed and the resuscitation team did their stuff, I was so totally fucked that not being able to walk was the least of my problems.

So let me tell you about the list of ailments I was left with: I was blind, I couldn't speak, but I could make noises – noises which most people find very irritating, which is pretty much why I make them ... actually, no, that's not entirely correct. I make them because everybody makes their own noises, so why should mine be any less important than anyone else's? It's my way of expressing myself, and just because nobody can understand me shouldn't make what I have to say any less important. It's like when the father hears something on the radio and says, 'He's talking utter shit.' This doesn't mean that there is actual poo coming out of his mouth; it just means that the father doesn't like or agree with what he's saying. So that makes my noises better than 'talking shit' because nobody can dislike or disagree with what I'm saying, because they can't understand it. For me, what I'm saying is perfectly clear, and just because I can't make it understandable shouldn't make it any less valid ... should it?

Anyway, that's got that off my chest.

Where was I?

Oh yeah, my ailments.

I have no control over any of my limbs – I think this is what's known as quadriplegic. I'm supposed to have epilepsy ... okay, hands up – well, not up in my case – I fake this because I learned how to do it, and a convincing epileptic episode at least guarantees me some attention. A seizure is the correct term, but the father refers to it, mainly to annoy the mother, as a fit. And I also quite like the medicine. It tastes okay and sends me to sleep, and being asleep is by far my favourite time. It's a time when no one can be horrible to me.

And to make all of this worse I've worked out from what I've heard on BBC Radio 4 – which the mother leaves on in my room all the time because she likes to listen to it and she probably assumes that I would too; which, actually, I do – that I have what is called locked-in syndrome.

Yes. Read that again ... Locked. In. Syndrome.

The trouble is that I was the only person to have figured this out.

As you might understand, this was really frustrating, but I've sort of got used to it by now ... well, most of the time anyway. I can be quite negative, bitter and resentful about what happened to me, but I usually try to be positive. Sometimes, though, it makes me, I don't know ... maybe angry, when I think about how the parents have used my shitty life to their own advantage. Although, if I'm honest, I can remember the mother caring for me in a maternal kind of way before she found something better to spend her time on than looking after a fuck-up like me.

By the way, I need to warn you that there is going to be some strong language in this narrative. The person who is writing it for me – Sarah – is called a ghostwriter. She's writing this for me because I can't read, I can't write, and although I know some quite complex vocabulary because of BBC Radio 4 (like psychopath, for example) I'm not confident that I understand other words well enough to use them. That's because I can only learn words that I hear being used, and unless I hear them on BBC Radio 4, I don't have much chance of increasing my vocabulary.

7

I've told her not to use words that I can't understand because, when she reads this back to me, I want to be sure that this is what I wanted to say and not some work of literary fiction.

So those are my disabilities, but you're not allowed to call them disabilities any more because we all have abilities, don't we? Even fuck-ups like me.

And just what are these? you're wondering.

I have control over the movement of my right eye. Nobody knew this, of course, other than Scooter the dog, so this skill set had fairly limited value.

I have an incredible memory. If I hear a word, even a really complicated word, I always remember it. But if I don't know what a word means, I can't ask anybody so I just have to guess, and sometimes I get it wrong. And I never forget people's names or numbers ... especially numbers. I can tell you how many people there were on the *Titanic* (one thousand, three hundred and sixteen passengers, and nine hundred and thirteen crew, making a total of two thousand, two hundred and twenty-nine) and how many survived (seven hundred and thirteen) when it hit an iceberg, although I'm not completely sure what an iceberg is or why it hit it in the first place.

And I have fantastic hearing. Well, it isn't really fantastic, because to hear everything isn't as cool as it sounds and, in any case, it only keeps me awake. And I can control movements of my head, which I do to follow the direction of sounds.

But when I began to understand what people were saying, listening to what they said about me was, at first, quite distressing. They say things about me because they think I can't understand what they're saying. But then I got used to it, and over the years it simply became boring. Same old, same old.

At least, that was the case until around a week ago – I can't remember exactly when because I don't have much concept of time, and unless I try really hard and pay attention to the radio, I get confused.

So let's just say it was a week ago. One day the father came back from the pub and was, for once, not particularly unpleasant to me. In fact, after he'd drunk some more beer, he came into my bedroom, kissed the top of my head and told me that he'd had a call from his – actually *my* – lawyer, and that I was going to be worth something after all.

TWO

ROGER

Roger scratched his testicles and stretched.

Warm sunlight danced particles of dust across the cove of the bay window and dragged him reluctantly into another gloomy day.

His mind began to calculate just how he might possibly avoid wasting it. Wasting it ... supervising the twins and babysitting Dave.

This he considered to be Gill's job. But she had asked him a week ago to keep today free, as apparently she had an appointment; she'd reminded him of this as she leapt out of bed. A leap, Roger considered, somewhat excessive for the mundane promise of her day.

'And this is going to take the entire day, is it?' he'd asked at the time.

'Yes, Roger, it will take the entire day,' she'd replied in a manner that suggested further investigation would only serve to fracture the fragile peace that existed between them at present.

Gill hadn't been well recently. No, that wasn't right, he corrected himself – Gill hadn't been herself recently. There was a difference here. Okay, she'd had some sort of breakdown that resulted in her seeing a shrink twice a week, but that couldn't be classed as illness, could it? He wasn't aware of any diagnostic labelling that had been formally attached to her. Gill was always having 'breakdowns'. Like the time she got up from the dinner table, screaming how much she hated this fucking family, and then disappeared for two days, only to return acting as if nothing at all had happened. NFG, Roger had remarked to the twins. Normal For Gill.

Or the time, he recalled, when the twins were aged about four, that she scooped one under each arm, grabbed her bag and car keys, stormed out and left him to look after Dave for six hours. Probably the worst six hours of his life, and certainly the only six hours he had ever devoted entirely to Dave.

Roger grimaced at the thought, particularly the 'bonding process' with Dave that had consisted of an aborted attempt to feed him: a task he undertook only because he could find no one else to do it. This had resulted in Dave spraying the food, in projectile fashion, over a relatively new and hitherto clean T-shirt. After Roger had cleaned up and calmed down a bit, he'd repaid Dave by banishing him to his beanbag with televised cricket for company. And in between these two events the real bonding had taken place, wherein he had informed his eldest son (then aged seven) that he was a blot on humanity, the worst thing that had ever happened to him, and that if he didn't die of natural causes pretty soon, then he would think of a way to assist him with the process.

Dave had turned his head despondently to the left, and other than making what Roger referred to as 'one of his mooing noises', had nothing further to say on the matter.

***

This particular day started with no hint of abnormality. It was going to be neither worse nor better than any other wasted day, he thought.

The bright morning sunshine eventually pulled Roger into a sluggish and reluctant wakefulness. Gill, as she did every day – whether he wanted it or not – had left him a mug of sweet, milky tea at six-thirty before she took Scooter – the acrimonious, malodorous mutt of indeterminate ancestry who had duped them into adoption from rescue kennels nine years ago – for his reluctant run.

And as was the case every day during Roger's holidays, the tea was ignored and he drifted back into some sort of slumber in which he dreamt of a life in which things were very different, and one in which he wasn't facing the fact that the family home would be repossessed unless he could find an imminent solution to his current financial crisis.

He glanced at his phone. There were no messages, of course; he expected none, and social media held no interest for him. A phone was a phone, Roger often remarked. It was for making calls and for telling the time and the date. And this particular function informed him that it was Wednesday 17 July, which Roger's brain calibrated as the third day of the second week of his summer holiday; the precious six weeks that spanned the abyss of time he wasted teaching SMSC (Spiritual, Moral, Social & Cultural Education – including careers) to semi-literate primates at Wiley Hall Academy, whose only interest was to avoid any form of learning other than that which kept them at the top of the food chain on their own feral council estates.

Roger was quick to point out, to anyone willing to listen, that if you held the belief that academy status was no longer a governmental strategy for improving failing schools, then you knew nothing about state education. Because they were, and for Roger, the trick was to get through the day without the enactment of threats of violence from pupils, or giving grounds for HR to haul him over the coals for an inappropriate verbal or even physical response to said threats.

But things, he reflected, hadn't always been this bad, and the fact that this was as bleak a phase of his life as he could remember was, Roger would reluctantly admit, totally his own fault.

Roger was forty-six years old and the only child of elderly parents who had died shortly before his fortieth birthday, leaving him over two and a half million pounds to squander. The manner of their death was not without mystery, but the coroner concluded that the failure of their car to stop at a major traffic light-controlled junction was down to 'natural causes'.

And this was undoubtedly due to the fact that Hempsall senior had inadvertently taken around four times the recommended dose of Sitagliptin – a drug he took to control diabetes – and, as a result, had suffered acute heart failure. And whether it was his heart's failure or being T-boned by a Tesco eighteen-wheeler that had killed him was purely conjectural, concluded the coroner. The fact of the matter was that John and Eileen Hempsall were now dead and there was no blame to be attached to this event; therefore, the executors of their wills were free to distribute their estates to the beneficiaries – there was only one – as prescribed.

The salient outcome of this was that it had allowed Roger to retire from teaching, an occupation he had come to hate, but one which he would privately admit at least meant that there were only two months of the year in which he had no holiday. And Ashley Grove Preparatory School, with its middle-class, middle-England values, and punters who were happy to shell out the best part of twenty-five grand a year for boarding education, suited Roger's somewhat elevated perception of his own social status.

Also, teaching put some distance between himself and Dave.

But by his forty-fifth birthday, the inheritance money had all but gone – fast cars, doomed business projects and an escalating gambling addiction being the principle money pits.

Thus, Roger had been forced to return to teaching. But the doors of Ashley Grove Preparatory School were firmly closed to him. Noel Sprockett, the long-suffering headmaster, had heaved a gigantic sigh of relief upon receipt of Roger's written notice to quit, and welcoming Roger back was about as appealing as an unannounced OFSTED inspection coupled with having to actually leave his study and teach. Sorry, Roger, no vacancies, no ... not even on a part-time basis. Let you know if anything comes up, old boy.

So it was the state section to which Roger was reluctantly forced to turn, and after six months of fruitless applications largely due to a) Sprockett's less than complimentary reference, and b) the fact that state institutions are not renowned for their warmth of welcome to those

13

from the 'other side' of education, Roger eventually managed to land the job at Wiley Hall.

But it paid a pittance.

The cars had long gone – his beloved Aston Martin had been replaced by a ghastly little Japanese runaround and an adapted van for Dave's transportation. But worse still, Gill had been forced to return to work, and this was a double whammy as a) blame for this was firmly laid (justifiably, Roger had to admit) at his door, meaning sex was as rare an occurrence as a fulfilling and enjoyable day at work, and b) he had to spend more time childminding Dave.

Added to this dismal scenario was the fact that an escalating amount of sick leave, ditto seeing her shrink, had resulted in a severe reduction of income from Gill's employer, and the threat of this – like sex – drying up altogether loomed closer by the day.

So all in all, Roger thought, pulling his mind away from the quagmire of his recent past, on this bright and beautiful July morning, reasons to be cheerful were few and far between.

And as he had, against Gill's advice, opened a third bottle of wine last night, even the prospect of alcohol later in the day did little to brighten his mood.

But then something flashed across his bleary consciousness that began to dissipate the shadows of gloom: the phone call he'd received yesterday evening. Yes, there *was* one thread of hope, one faint half-chance that could change all of this. And yesterday evening's call, which he'd received on the way to the pub, had turned that thread into a rope; indeed, almost a rope bridge that crossed the chasm between poverty and wealth.

About three years ago, when the money mountain was starting to look like a small slagheap, something had happened.

Dave had a minor accident at his school which resulted in a short stay in hospital, and following this, Roger persuaded Gill to talk to a lawyer.

The lawyer concluded that while they were likely to win the case, what they (Dave) would be awarded by the court would barely cover his costs.

But have you ever considered, he'd said, investigating how Dave got to be, hmmm – and here he paused, searching for more appropriate words than 'totally fucked'.

Roger had, in fact, considered this on many occasions but had failed to persuade Gill of his altruistic motivation for this course of action. Gill was a nurse, and nurses do not sue the NHS, do they? she'd said. And in any case, she'd told Roger, your only interest in this is that you see Dave as a potential cash cow.

But the lawyer, a Mr Charles Cuerliez, a senior partner of a firm named Gottemby, Short & Cuerliez, was very convincing.

It's not about the money, he'd said. Well, it *is* about the money, but it's only what Dave is entitled to, and what is going to happen to Dave in the future? Hmmm? Besides, *you* are entitled to compensation for justifiable expenses in connection with Dave's needs over the past, let me see ... fourteen years.

Dave had been present at the initial meeting, for the simple reason that on this occasion there was nowhere else to leave him, and at this point had made one of his 'mooing' noises – not dissimilar, most people thought, to utterances made by Chewbacca. Noises that no one – other than Dave – was ever able to attribute any meaning to. But on this occasion it meant agreement.

What, continued Mr 'Call me Charles' Cuerliez, if neither social services nor the NHS were able to provide an appropriate home for Dave in the future? What if Dave – due to lack of funding – were to be shoved into an old people's home and left to lie in the corner on a (pissstained) beanbag, with wholly inadequate care from lowpaid Eastern European staff who couldn't give a tuppenny fuck (not his exact words) about his welfare? Hmmm?

So Gill had been persuaded.

And then, a week ago, Mr Cuerliez had made a hugely significant discovery. The ITU staff roster from Monday, 14 June 2004, showed that there were insufficient staff on duty.

Cuerliez had struck gold.

According to the Paediatric Intensive Care Society's recommendations:

'In summary, the minimum number of qualified nurses required to staff one Level 3 critical care bed is, therefore, a minimum of 7.01 WTE.'

The roster showed that there were only three nurses on duty, and at the precise moment of Dave's 'incident', one had gone out for a fag break – of course, this was referred to as 'on administrative duties' – and the other two were responding to an emergency affecting the only other patient in ITU, who was registered as Level 2 critical.

And as Dave was a Level 3 critical patient, that made it four-point-zero-one nurses short of a full posse.

The North-Eastern Health Authority was understandably reluctant to hand over the relevant documentation, but when they were eventually persuaded to oblige, and 'Call me Charles' discovered that one page in the roster from Monday 12 May had been crudely doctored and another was missing.

Gotcha.

All Mr Cuerliez, his team of barristers and a top QC, whose name held no interest for Roger, had to do now was to persuade the North-Eastern Health Authority that the game was up and to settle out of court. But although one battle, he'd told Roger on the telephone yesterday – maybe a tad pessimistically – had been won, they were still a very long way from winning the war.

Roger had no idea what the spoils of this particular war might be, but he knew the sum coming their (Dave's) way would be sufficient for him to tell the head of HR at Wiley Hall to shove her letters of complaint where the proverbial sun doesn't shine.

And with that thought, he heard the back door open, Gill's voice yell, 'Come here, you mangy old bastard,' (presumably, he thought, at Scooter) and decided it might be as good a time as any to get out of bed.

THREE

GILL

DIARY ENTRY: Friday, 20 July 2001

Dave came into this world at 03.57 last Monday morning.

I'd love to say that he just popped out, but he didn't.

He's my son, my first-born, and I love him, but I can tell that something isn't quite what it should be – I just know that nothing is going to be plain sailing. I don't know how ... call it a mother's instinct.

It was an obstructed labour, or what is called 'labour dystocia', and this meant that my uterus was contracting normally, but the little blighter refused to come out through my pelvis because it was physically blocked.

And guess what was blocking it?

Dave, of course; he had a birth weight of nine pounds and fifteen ounces and was classed as a large or abnormally sized baby.

And this meant an emergency C-section – or if we're splitting hairs, an unplanned C-section – because the doctor considered that Dave's life wasn't in danger, whereas the midwife thought it was as there was a significant chance that he wasn't getting enough oxygen; and even in my state, as a nurse myself I know that lack of oxygen results in either severe brain damage or death.

Put like that, I'd say his life was in danger.

On the positive side, I'd already had one epidural, so I had what is called a combined spinal-epidural anaesthesia, and I felt nothing.

And when I say nothing, I mean nothing.

17

I suppose, if I'm honest, what I did feel was relief. Relief that the ordeal was over, but none of the joy and euphoric bullshit the second-time mums had eulogised about in the prenatal classes.

I will always remember holding him and feeling a strange sensation of disappointment. I had this, I suppose ... premonition that the complications of his birth would be surpassed by the complications that his life would bring. I put it down to the fact I was exhausted and alone. No Roger – I can't remember what his excuse was, and frankly the only interest he had shown in my pregnancy evaporated after the conception.

I had this weird conviction that here was an unremarkable baby – size apart – who would stumble through an unremarkable childhood and an unremarkable youth into an unremarkable adulthood, and, at best, his life would be a litany of complication and disappointment.

And so I passed him back to the midwife and fell into a deep, dreamless sleep.

FOUR

DAVE

The best part of being forced to constantly listen to BBC
Radio 4 is that occasionally you accidentally learn something that might be of use.

Okay, so I'll admit, you probably *can* learn something
every day if you are minded to do so, which, incidentally,
I'm not.

Take the news, for example.

This is what is going on in the world, but how it's supposed to interest most ordinary people is, well ... beyond
me. Most of it is boring because it's about things called
markets and politics. Although I actually like the news,
because sometimes there are really interesting stories,
most of it is just irrelevant information, isn't it? What interests the people who report the news – I think they're
called the media – is the reaction to these events ... the
crying mothers, the screaming children; maybe, if they're
lucky, smoke or a scene of total destruction they can describe in the background; the overexcited eye witnesses
– sad losers given a chance to talk to an audience for the
first time in their lives. That's good reporting, though;
giving a total randomer his fifteen minutes of fame,
somebody once called it, or so John Fucking Humphrys
told me. Actually, more like fifteen seconds.

By the way, I don't think this is his real name, but this
is how the father refers to him, so perhaps it is? Although
on the radio they don't seem to bother with his middle
name. I wish my middle name was Fucking instead of Nigel because that would be really cool.

There was an American politician called JFK who was shot, and I wonder if his middle name was Fucking as well? Perhaps that's why people always use his initials when they refer to him.

So I think in future when I want to talk about John Fucking Humphrys, I'm going to call him JFH because it's neater and I'm not sure whether he likes his middle name being used anyway.

I don't know much about people, but I do know that they are only interested in things that affect them. And as a mass murder in a Texas church has no bearing on the cost of beer, mortgages or petrol, it isn't what most people would call newsworthy. But of course it *is* newsworthy because I don't think mass murders occur very often in this country, so that means this country is supposedly a safer place to live. Unless I've missed something … which is entirely possible.

Aren't I lucky?

But mass murder in itself interests me. Not mass murders in which random people get killed, but mass murder where the killer targets a very specific group of people.

Like, for example, his family.

FIVE

GILL

DIARY ENTRY: Monday, 10 May 2004

Tell me why I don't like Mondays?

I'll tell you why I don't like Mondays.

I don't like Mondays for a very good reason, and that's because shit always seems to happen on a Monday.

It's the most shitprobable day of the week.

Dave being born on a Monday? I'm not sure if that slides seamlessly into the shitistical set of shitty events but, let's just say, if Dave hadn't been born with DDH – that stands for Developmental Dysplasia of the Hip – then last Monday wouldn't have happened, and this Monday – the biggest shitstorm of all – wouldn't have happened either.

Not that it makes the slightest jot of difference, but the paediatrician who diagnosed Dave's DDH seemed to think that he wasn't, in fact, born like this, that it happened during his first year of life and – hear this – that it was actually our fault!

So just how could this have happened? I asked.

It could have happened, he replied, due to excessively tight swaddling whereby Dave's hips and knees were habitually straight. Quite common really, and you mustn't feel guilty, he added with a syrupy smile, just to ensure that guilt was all that I will ever feel.

Guilty?

I didn't even know what swaddling is and – because I didn't want to appear stupid – I didn't ask him and googled it when I got home. Stupid, wasn't it? I'm accused of a procedure that led to the dislocation of my baby's hips and I don't even know what it is. Worse than that, I don't even *say* I don't know what it is.

But I'm a Senior Staff Nurse, you see, hardwired to accept the decree of the Gods of the White Coat without query. If he says I did it, then I did it.

I'm not stupid. I know how the game is played.

Let's just say that Dave's hips *had* been dislocated at birth. This is – according to my research – by far the most probable occurrence (eighty-five per cent of babies with DDH are born with it). This being the case, someone should have flagged this up; if not at the time of his birth, it should have been picked up at a postnatal clinic within the following month.

And as this wasn't flagged up, this means blame. And where there's blame, etc.

So last Monday Dave underwent surgery to correct his hips. It was an eight-hour operation, and we were told that it had been successful. He sailed through it. When I say *we* were told, *I* was told because Roger was at work. No complications ... period of convalescence ... intensive physio ... get him moving as soon as possible ... blah-de-blah.

But there were complications.

On Wednesday I was woken in the middle of the night and told that Dave had been rushed into surgery. Blood clots had formed and there was some other complication – a problem with his lungs, they told me – and although I didn't fully understand, I did understand that Dave's condition was life-threatening.

After this particular bout of surgery he was admitted to the ITU and classed as Level 3, which meant that he was one step away from needing mechanical ventilation to keep him alive.

I couldn't believe this was happening.

Roger didn't help, claiming that he couldn't get time off work because he was needed for Sports Day, and anyway, he couldn't leave the dog. And even if he could, he wasn't 'great' in hospitals anyway.

Bullshit.

I felt so alone. I wasn't managing the situation; it was managing me. What information I did get had to be dragged from the ITU doctor – a Dr Sullivan – as if she was breaching the Official Secrets Act, the Hippocratic Oath, the Famous Five's code of conduct or any combination of the above.

And along with the loneliness, the isolation, the increasing sense of institutionalisation, I became aware of a creeping sense of dread.

It was like I was in a horror movie where the tension builds gradually. As does the paranoia; it builds and builds ... and builds.

And then it happened.

Dave stopped breathing.

SIX

DAVE

Mass murder.

It's been on my mind a lot recently.

To be honest, I think of little else, and I can't help wondering whether ... if I could ... would I?

Would I what?

Would I murder my parents? And my brothers? Get them all out of the way at the same time?

Of course, being as totally screwed as I am, it's impossible. A pipe dream. But that doesn't stop me fantasising about it, particularly as there's nothing much else to fantasise about. I know there's something called sex that's supposed to kick in at about my age, but as there's as little prospect of that as walking on the moon, there's not much point in fantasising about it, is there? Anyway, I don't know much about sex but I'm learning quite a lot about mass murder. I think it's probably more my sort of thing than sex, but I could well be wrong.

Why would I want to do this, you're probably wondering?

That's easy enough to answer. Because the dysfunctional (I think that's the right word?) family that I had the misfortune to be born into constantly make my life hell with emotional abuse and neglect, and by the fact that they – yes, even the mother – seem to be in some sort of denial about my existence and my circumstances. Hello ... look at me, I'm fucked and can't do anything for myself. I didn't ask to be like this: a retard in a wheelchair, capable of nothing but understanding everything.

Can't you just see that? No? Well, maybe try looking a bit harder.

It would be so much better if I was braindead ... if I didn't have a clue about what was going on around me. But I'm not.

What makes it worse is that everyone – including the doctors ... no, especially the doctors – think that my brain is totally sizzled and that there's as much going on between my ears as, I dunno, something with nothing between its ears. Maybe someone who plays football? Because I've heard footballers interviewed in the sport section on BBC Radio 4 and I think they may also suffer from some form of brain damage, but nowhere near as bad as mine.

There's nothing wrong with my brain; it's just, like I said, that everything's locked in, so communication is impossible. Well, at least it is until I can figure out a way to do it. In fact, I think I'm probably quite intelligent. I think I'm way more intelligent than the parents and light years ahead of the ginger twats that are called my siblings. By the way, I've worked out what a twat is. It actually has two meanings: the first is a person regarded as stupid or obnoxious, and the second refers to a woman's genitals ... that's her sex bits. When the father refers to the twins as 'ginger twats', I'm fairly sure that he's referring to the first meaning. Of course, they may have some resemblance to a woman's genitals, but if they did, I don't suppose he'd want to draw everyone's attention to it.

So why do I think I'm way more intelligent than the rest of my family?

Because I very much doubt that any of them could come up with the totally foolproof plan that I've come up with.

A plan to murder them all and get away with it.

SEVEN

ROGER

Gill stood by the Aga and scooped porridge into a bowl.

'I don't know how you eat that stuff,' said Roger. 'It makes me want to heave.' The toaster clicked, and he deftly extracted both slices with three fingers and applied a thick layer of butter followed by a blanket of Marmite. 'And it reminds me of boarding school and all the misery that came with that particular internment.'

'I don't know how you eat *that* stuff,' she countered. 'Makes *me* want to heave. Anyway, boarding school didn't cause you any lasting damage, apart from oddness and social inadequacy. And they compensated you pretty well for it.'

Roger guessed she was referring to his rapidly diminishing inheritance but let the comment go. Best to keep off the subject of money this morning, he thought.

'Your plans for the day?'

So occupied had he been with weighing up the balance between another mountain of money potentially coming his (Dave's) way and the other side of the coin – which hardly bore thinking about – that he hadn't really thought this through.

'Not really got any. Might see if there's a game on at Headingley. Take the boys over there.' He could see where this was going. Gill never asked him about his plans unless she had plans of her own.

'By boys, I do hope you're including Dave in that?'

'Well ... I wasn't, actually. I assumed you'd be here to look after him.' He knew what the answer would be, but it was worth a try.

'No can do. I told you, Martin asked if I could change my Thursday appointment to today. Then I'm going shopping and having lunch with a friend.' She put her bowl into the sink and began to give Dave his breakfast – Ready Brek, same thing every morning.

'I told you a week ago *and* this morning, or have you forgotten already? You're on holiday. It's about time you did a bit more with Dave anyway.'

'Martin? Who the hell is Martin?'

'Don't be obtuse, Roger. You know very well who Martin is.'

Dave squeezed a mouthful of Ready Brek out of his mouth; it slid down his chin and into the plastic drip tray from where Gill scooped it up and pushed it back into his mouth.

'Nope, doesn't ring any bells,' replied Roger. 'Your secret lover?' Gill blushed. 'Oh ... did I touch a nerve there?'

'Fuck off, Roger. You really can be a total wanker sometimes.'

'Put it down to a boarding school education, my dear,' he replied. Avoiding controversy was the course to steer, he thought, if he stood any chance of a day without Dave. 'And so much for your policy of not swearing in front of Dave.'

Gill ignored this.

'Martin Maynard is my counsellor. You know that very well.'

'Oh ... your shrink? We're on first-name terms now, are we?'

'What's wrong with that? It hardly violates the doctor–patient relationship, does it?'

'Tiny oak trees lead to little acorns. I think I may have that the wrong way round, but you know what I mean. No smoke—'

'Anyway, don't the staff at Wiley Hall all call the head Gary?'

'I don't. I call him Mr Cunt, which is what all the pupils – sorry, "students" – call him.'

'Oh, for God's sake, Roger.'

'Well it's not my fault his surname is Cant, is it? I think he may have some Chinese ancestry. He looks a bit ... I don't know ... anyway, don't think I'd have gone into teaching if I'd been him.'

'You wouldn't have gone into teaching if you'd been able to do anything else,' Gill countered.

Roger felt the customary cloak of inevitability drape over his shoulders and knew that, as usual, he wasn't going to win this battle.

Bloody shrink ruled their lives now, he thought. Twice a week? It'd soon be twice a day the way things were going, and not only that; he'd recommended that Gill enrolled on an anger management course – attendance requirement: two evenings a week.

'Can't you take Dave with you?' He already knew what the answer would be. 'You know how the twins feel about going out with him?'

Gill continued to shove Ready Brek into Dave's mouth as if trying to force an overlarge package into the intransigent entry slot of a post box. Dave continued to moo and turned his head to the side to coincide with Gill's next lunge with the spoon, resulting in an earful of Ready Brek.

'Oh, for fuck's sake.'

Perhaps, Roger thought, the anger management course wasn't such a bad idea.

'I can't really blame them. I mean ... people are always giving him looks, what with all his bloody noises. If it weren't so obvious that he's totally buggered, everyone would be constantly telling him to shut up.' Roger put a fist to his mouth, miming a megaphone. 'You ... you boy, yes ... the one in the wheelchair over there ... STOP MAKING THOSE BLOODY NOISES! YOU'RE DRIVING EVERYONE MAD.'

Gill finished removing Ready Brek from Dave's ear, and for a moment, it looked as if she would put it into his mouth. She didn't.

'That's not funny, Roger.'

'At least that's the one good thing about Dave. One look tells you all you need to know.' Roger placed another slice of bread in the toaster and clicked it down. 'God knows how parents of kids with Tourette's cope. I really couldn't handle that.'

'And you handle Dave's condition so very well, don't you?' Dave's moo this time would have been translated as a plea to Gill to take him with her, but for reasons Dave understood, and Roger had yet to learn, this was never going to happen.

EIGHT

THE TWINS

Hillcrest, in its current guise, was a six-bedroomed residence with three bathrooms set in an acre or so of garden, paddock, and passably well-tended lawns with a tennis court whose fence and playing surface had seen better days.

The garden showed signs of fairly recent unenthusiastic attention but was a hop and a skip away from being reclaimed by nature.

Built in 1906, it began life as a rectory, and from the outside, the vast bay windows, the grim, grey granite facia and the four-potted pillared chimneys did little to suggest any warmth of welcome for the unfamiliar visitor.

It was a house that promised only gloom.

Around thirteen years ago, a family of three had moved in. Not long after, they were blessed with twins and – to the casual observer – there was little to convey more than a hint of dysfunctional decrepitude, other than the fact that the eldest child – now on the threshold of manhood – had clearly suffered a severe and debilitating handicap.

Little money had been spent on the dwelling and it showed.

And to the casual observer, this was clearly a matter of choice rather than affordability, for one of the outbuildings had housed an Aston Martin Vantage while the other contained a Ferrari Testarossa. But recently a

Nissan Note had replaced the Aston, while the other out-
building now lay vacant.

And should the same casual observer know anything
about the value of these cars, he would have understood
that the amount the owner could have obtained from the
sale of these iconic vehicles would have been more than
sufficient to knock the entire house down and rebuild it
as a manifestation of contemporary lavish architecture,
banishing the lingering aura of Presbyterian parsimony
that the residence still exuded.

Hillcrest, as the name would suggest – but is not always the case – was positioned on the crown of a gently
sloping knoll, south-facing towards the village – perhaps
better referred to as a hamlet – of Rising Bucklebury, a
settlement that could be traced back to the ninth century,
and one that owed its continued popularity to the proximity of the more substantial village of South Cave, the
metropolis of Hull and – perhaps of greater importance –
the A63, which morphs into the M62, thus giving access
to the North, and indeed – should one want it – the rest
of England, and even Scotland.

But quaint as it was, there was little to interest anyone other than those seeking peace and isolation in Rising Bucklebury. There was a church, within whose grave-
yard the souls of the dead outnumbered those of the living by roughly ten to one. A post office that doubled as a
Spar minimarket and sold cards, alcohol and a smatter-
ing of basic groceries. A village square once hosted a
long-abandoned cricket ground. The peel of church bells
in the nineteen sixties coincided with the last sound of
leather on willow.

And in this idyllic but terminally boring setting,
Dave's twin brothers, Axel and Boris, occupied bedrooms
at opposite ends of Hillcrest, sentenced to pass the dull
hours of the summer holiday with little to do other than
to make life for Dave – who they held responsible for this
confinement – as miserable as humanly possible.

To the twins, everything was Dave's fault.

It was Dave's fault that they rarely had a family holiday. Gill had made it clear to the twins that looking after
Dave at home (with minimal help from your father) was

enough of a trial without dragging his wheelchair around some bloody airport and forcing food into him by the side of a swimming pool with everybody gawping at them. Besides which, she'd said, he hates hot weather and his skin would burn to a crisp. Who would that be a holiday for ... hmmm? Certainly not me.

It was Dave's fault that they were left to their own devices, bored, feckless and ultimately reckless, abandoned to explore, exploit and contaminate their neighbourhood during the vast swathes of the summer holidays.

And it was Dave's fault that when they discovered an activity that their parents found less than wholesome (mainly terrorising the neighbours) they – generally Gill – reacted with what they considered to be excessive and disproportionate retribution. This overreaction was generally prefixed with the diatribe 'As if my life wasn't difficult enough already', and proceeded along the lines of 'You should just try looking after Dave for one day and you would see what a hell my life has become'.

In short, this was not a family that, to the keener observer, could be viewed as functional in any sense of the word. And as their final year at Ashley Grove approached, the twins had suggested to Gill and Roger that it could be in everyone's interest if they were to continue their senior education at the local comprehensive rather than an expensive boarding school. And to this Gill had replied that had Roger not wasted a fortune on cars and failed business projects, an expensive boarding school would be precisely where they would be headed. But now, thanks to Roger, she'd said, it was unlikely that in a year's time any form of private education would be on the cards, let alone boarding school, so the comp it would have to be.

The twins had heaved a collective sigh of relief.

Then to darken the holidays further, a week ago Roger had announced that they were shortly to be packed off to a residential cricket course at Sedburgh School, and although they disagreed about many things, they shared the view that this was almost as bad a punishment as having to attend Ashley Grove during term time.

So it is against this dismal backdrop that Boris made his way to Axel's room across half an acre of threadbare and mite-encrusted landing carpet – carpet that had likely first been trodden by the last rector of this parish.

The prime reason for Boris's trek was because Axel's room occupied a position above the kitchen, and during summer months, when windows on both floors were open, it was almost impossible not to overhear all conversations from below.

'What's she doing today?' asked Boris. 'Heard anything of interest?'

'Going to see her shrink.'

'What? Again?'

'Rog isn't happy. Was talking about dragging us to cricket but she said he'd have to take Dave cos she can't take him with her.'

'Fuck,' said Boris. 'In fact, double fuck. Means we'll be stuck with him all day. Got any fags?'

'Nope.'

Pause.

'What did he say about going to cricket? He won't take *him*, will he? Cos that means he'd have to feed him. He's only done that once before and it was a disaster, or so she keeps tellin' him.'

'Nah, she said his physio's coming at eleven anyway and she's asked her to give him his lunch.'

'Who's his physio? Thought he had physio at that place he goes to they call a "school".' Boris underscored his cynicism for the institution charged with catering for Dave's educational needs by making speech marks with his fingers. '"The North-Eastern School for the Totally Fucked", isn't it called?'

'Well, this one's new, apparently. I'm not sure she's an actual physio, not that it matters. Some bird called Molly.'

'Molly? Who the hell would call someone Molly? She must be bloody ancient.'

With this, Boris noticed that his brother was more absorbed with his laptop than their conversation, and instead of asking him what he found so interesting, he lunged forward and prised it out of his hands.

'Oi—!'

'What have we got here then, bruv?' he said, hoping it was what he was expecting it to be. 'Hardcore porn?'

It wasn't.

'What the heck are you looking at this for?'

Axel shrugged.

'Thought it might be interesting to give Rog some ideas as to what twelve-year-olds from normal families do during the holidays.'

Boris read from the screen:

'"The next time your preteens start complaining about not having anything to do, try out some of these stimulating activities to do with kids.

'"Set up easels and paint pictures outdoors. Visit your local science museum. Learn how to knot friendship bracelets. Go to a coffee shop and write poetry. Put on an impromptu play." Jesus. People actually *do* this shit? And I thought *our* holidays were bad enough.' Boris laughed, then stopped when a thought hit him. 'He ... maybe the impromptu play isn't such a bad idea. What part could we give Dave?'

'Well, a non-speaking part—'

'Obviously. I know! How about Frankenstein? And we could get him to fall in love with Molly the Old Maid!'

They spent the next few minutes plotting scenes for an impromptu play that both knew would never have a curtain call.

'She's not old,' said Axel.

Boris handed him his laptop back.

'Who isn't?'

'Molly.'

'How'd you know?'

Axel was without doubt the more intelligent, sensitive and perceptive of the twins. It would have been clear to the casual observer, were there to have been one, that Axel was the brains of the outfit, while Boris was – at best – the brawn, as in how A preceded B.

'Because,' replied Axel, whose radar was seldom bypassed, 'I heard her tell Rog. Actually ... it sounded like more of a warning.'

'Well, get on with it. Do I have to drag it out of you? Tell him what?'

'She told him about Molly.'

NINE

GILL

DIARY ENTRY: Wednesday, 12 May 2004

It's been a nightmare two days.

I've hardly slept or eaten, surviving only on coffee. Oh ... and the odd cigarette. Actually, quite a lot of cigarettes. I haven't smoked since I found out I was expecting Dave, but isn't it great how readily nicotine creeps back into your life like an old friend and asks you, with a forgiving voice, why you haven't kept in touch?

Dave's still on the ventilator. His status is referred to as a prolonged state of unconsciousness, better known as a coma, as he is totally unresponsive to his environment.

Dr Sullivan has been her less than forthcoming self, and I can't help thinking that this is because she's not optimistic about Dave's prospects, which makes her fearful because of my status, my knowledge of procedures and the system, and the increasing possibility that someone has screwed up.

I don't care if someone has screwed up. I would defend my colleagues to the bitter end if I were in her shoes. I just want some accurate information and my little boy to come back to me.

No one knows, I realise this; how can they? You can be in a coma for days, weeks or even years. I try not to think about the fact that Dave was a normal, strong, healthy – albeit obese – and responsive baby until two days ago. And I try not to think about the possibility that

I may have been responsible for whatever Dave's out-come will be.

So even if someone in ITU has screwed up, if I had been more attentive about how I 'swaddled' Dave, had been even vaguely aware of the potential harm I was causing him, none of this would have happened. If there's any blame, then it rests on my shoulders, and I will have to live with the consequences.

TEN

DAVE

I want to tell you about my school.

Technically it's a school, but really it's not.

And as much as I hate the bastard, I have to admit that Boris's definition is pretty accurate: it is 'The North-Eastern School for the Totally Fucked', and there's nothing that you could actually call education that goes on there.

That's not to say I don't like it.

I have a swimming lesson three times a week. It's called hydrotherapy and it's different from swimming lessons because it involves special exercises that you do in a pool with very warm water. I like the pool because it's almost like a bath. I really try not to poo in it, but sometimes the warm water and the freedom gets me so excited that I just have to let one go. Of course I wear a nappy or the pool would be full of turds, but it still pisses off my therapist because she has to get out and change me.

You couldn't call it a swimming lesson because there's as much chance of me staying afloat as a corpse ... actually, I think corpses *can* float and that's why the murderer always fills their pockets with stones, according to a play I heard on BBC Radio 4, but they can't swim and that's the point I'm trying to make.

I also like my physio sessions, although sometimes it can be hard work; and if the male physio does it and the weather is hot, as it has been recently, sometimes he sweats over me and his sweat smells and tastes of stale beer. I know it's stale beer because the father smells the same.

The woman physio is better. She is gentler and doesn't work me so hard. I know it's important for me to have physio because if I don't, my body will just stop working completely and will end up in an odd shape, particularly as I spend so much time either lying down or in a wheelchair. Also, because I'm inactive I have a lot of problems with my chest and lungs, so physio cuts down the number of times I have chest infections – which, by the way, are hell.

Sometimes the woman physio – her name is Lucy – has a helper, a younger woman called Jane who is on something called work experience. I like it when Jane comes because they talk about interesting things. Lucy is married and Jane has a boyfriend and both these men are wankers. I'm not quite sure what a wanker is but I think it must be really cool to be a wanker because women talk about you all the time. Like, when Jane asks: 'Do you know what the wanker did next? Go on, guess.' Although I'm not sure how Lucy could guess, unless there's something that wankers do all the time that's actually quite predictable. What Leon – that's the wanker we're talking about – did next was to go to the pub, so I guess that must make the father a wanker as well. But as he couldn't be described as cool, maybe that devalues the badge of wanker a bit. Anyway, I need to find out more about it.

Apart from that, school isn't great. It's just a place for me to go so that other people have to look after me for a few hours, then I get sent home again.

Oh ... that's one of the best bits. I like the journey. This man called Bob, who's always cheerful, picks me up, and he either sings or whistles all the way to school and all the way back home. He's not really that good at it but it makes a change from BBC Radio 4. There's me and another girl called Alice on the bus, and I think she likes his singing too because she used to cry when she got on to the bus but now she doesn't.

I'm not going to bore you with what we do at school but I will tell you about art, which is my favourite subject. This is where we have a tray of paint and the teacher puts our hands in it and then we put our hands on this big piece of paper and wiggle them about a bit. I used to like to suck my thumb and I once did this with paint on it and I was sick for ages, so now I only do this if I want to be sent home. And as school isn't as bad as home, I don't do it very often.

Our artwork gets sent back with us, and the father once said that I was the new Picasso. Then he got told off by the mother for putting his beer glass down on it and leaving a ring.

We also have subjects called humanities and comparative religion and English and maths. My teacher knows how pointless this so she just puts on the TV or a video or something and goes to the kitchen at the back of the classroom to drink coffee with other teachers and people called classroom assistants. Their conversations are sometimes more interesting than the videos – apart from the ones about comparative religions – and sometimes they talk about wankers too.

I don't like the food at school. In fact, I don't like most of the food I'm given because I'm only given food that's basically liquid and is easy for people to feed me.

At school my teacher isn't very good at feeding me, so she just says that I'm not hungry and gives up. That's part of the reason why I'm so skinny.

I've heard of a place called McDonald's that everybody goes on about, where the food's fantastic, and I wish I could go there some day. Actually, I'm not that ambitious – who would be in my condition? Although I do have one ambition ... maybe two if I include killing my family. But that would be my dream holiday – to visit McDonald's. I dunno – do people go there on holiday? Maybe just for weekends?

Anyway ... back to school.

Well, actually, not back to school, because school's finished now. I don't know if I said, but it's the summer holidays and that means there's no more school. Only because I'm now eighteen I'm not supposed to go back to school in September because people of my age either go to university, get a job or do something called a gap year, which according to the father means they basically fuck about for a year at their parents' expense.

Well, I don't think I'll be going to university – I mean, is there a 'University for the Totally Fucked'?

And I doubt I'll be getting a job either.

The father sometimes talks about what I could do as a job. I'm not sure what a crash-test dummy is but I don't think I like the sound of it. And as for working for NASA and being sent to Mars on a one-way mission, well, I'm not so sure about that one either. It would have to pay really well, but it *would* get me away from this family.

But, like I said a moment ago, I do have one ambition. I would like to be a journalist.

Yes, read that again ... I'd like to have a job being a journalist.

There's this journalist called Gary O'Donoghue who worked for BBC Radio 4 for a while, and I really liked listening to him. He's not on BBC Radio 4 any more, though, because he now works in television (which I'm only stuck in front of when the father wants to watch cricket and then forgets to move me or turn it off when it finishes) and I think he's the top journalist in Washington... that's in America. In fact, I think he's more of a legend than JFH because he has a disability: he's blind, like me. Okay, his body isn't totally fucked like mine, but if you're blind it must be really hard to be a journalist. I heard him once on BBC Radio 4 say that on his first day he was asked to bungee jump off Chelsea Bridge, which is in London. That's almost as scary as being made to do a parachute jump if you're blind ... I'll tell you about that in a minute. As far as I know he is the only blind reporter who works for the BBC, and this is something I would really like to do cos I'm interested in finding out about stuff and I can remember it really well; in fact, I think I could be brilliant at it. But I know I'm never going to be a journalist because ... well, because although he once said that the BBC have what he called 'fantastic diversity and anti-discrimination policies', I don't think I could do what he did and go to Oxford University, no matter how many quotas they have.

41

So what's going to happen is that the mother is trying to get the school to keep me on, probably until I'm about thirty, and I don't really mind. Especially if I can't be a journalist.

I'd rather be anywhere than around my family, and I'll tell you more about why this is in a bit.

ELEVEN

GILL

DIARY ENTRY: Thursday, 17 June 2004

I was right.

Dave's been in a coma for almost six weeks now.

I've been living in a small room near the ITU ward, reserved for parents whose child is in a critical state, since Dave was admitted, and this morning Dr Sullivan paid me a visit.

She was very calm and started by asking me how I was bearing up and if I had everything I needed, blah-de-blah. But I could almost smell her anxiety, which even an excessive application of Sensi Giorgio Armani failed to conceal. And this apprehension transferred to me so that my heart was beating like a drum even before she said what I knew she was going to say.

'We need to talk,' she said, with a hint of a smile.

'Of course we do,' I replied, although why I said this I don't really know.

'I think it would be better if you could arrange for your husband' – she looked through a sheaf of papers on her clipboard – 'Roger ... he's a teacher, isn't he? Anyway, I think it's really important that he's here. When we talk.'

'Of course,' I replied. 'I'll call him.'

I felt sick to the pit of my stomach. It was how I'd always imagined I'd feel if I had a visit from the police and they told me that there'd been a terrible road accident ... but could I possibly make them a cup of tea and ... oh, maybe some nice biccies, you know the chocolate ones, before they elaborate?

'I'll call him,' I repeated, managing to stop short of asking her whether she would like a cup of tea and some nice biccies, you know the chocolate ones, first. 'I'll ask him to come in his lunch break. That's around one. Would that suit?'

She consulted her clipboard again, tapping it with a fingernail. Her hands were expensively manicured and each of her nails – short because of the risk of infection attached to acrylic or gel, but still elegant – was either an individual colour or was painted with some kind of glitter that resembled a coat of arms or something. Anyway, a lot of thought had gone into them and they were much nicer than my nails, which don't benefit from anything much other than my teeth.

She's an attractive woman, Dr Sullivan. I'd not noticed before. Why would I with everything else? Early forties and a little taller than me – maybe five-seven? Black hair cut in a bob touches her shoulders, ending in a provocatively seductive curl. Full lips, straight nose … perfect facial features. Lucky her. She's not as skinny as I am (I know I'm too skinny, by the way) but she's what you might call curvy, and if I were offered a body swap, I'd jump at it.

Oh my God! I felt beads of perspiration on my brow, and to my horror I sensed moisture spread elsewhere. My eyes were drinking her in. Okay, I've felt attracted to women before, but not like this. I really wanted her to desire me like I craved her body, her face, her scent, and everything about her, so I pulled my eyes away, embarrassed and guilty. My son is at death's door and here am I indulging my bi-curious fantasies.

She looked at me and blushed. She knows. Her smile – more of a pout and almost too fleeting to register – made my heart beat faster.

'I'm sorry Mrs Hempsall—'

'Gill, please.'

'Gill then. I have an appointment at one, and I'm afraid it's something that I can't alter at short notice.'

Can't be her nails again; surely not. Maybe hair?

'How about three-thirty? Roger can get away at three.'

'Three-thirty's fine.' She placed a hand on my shoulder and held my gaze with almost hypnotic green eyes. God ... I would have given anything for her to pull me hard against her breasts and kiss me. Roughly.

She didn't.

'I'll see you both in my office at three-thirty then.' Again the pout – no, that's my overactive imagination; it was only a smile ... it was only a smile. 'You know where it is, don't you?'

I nodded.

She turned.

She left, closing the door softly behind her.

I burst into tears. I'm not quite sure why, but it seemed like the best thing to do at the time, and for so many different reasons.

TWELVE

DAVE

I'm in my room as usual, by the way, in case you were wondering.

The mother wheeled me in here, put on BBC Radio 4 and said she'd see me later. But I know all about this anyway because they were talking about it over breakfast.

My room is next door to the kitchen where the parents are still eating breakfast and arguing about all the usual stuff and, of course, the father is still trying to get out of 'looking after' me.

I also heard every word of the conversation upstairs. You know, the one between the ginger twats. I'm pretty sure my understanding of the word 'twat' is correct because the father calls Boris Johnson and Donald Trump twats and I think JFH called Nicola Sturgeon this as well once, although perhaps I might have imagined it.

I don't know anything about this Molly. It's news to me and I must admit I'm quite looking forward to it. I like it when someone new comes along because they are generally really nice to me to begin with until I do something they find irritating, like screaming in their ear, and then they're just like everyone else.

Everybody else, that is, except for my family. Okay, the mother doesn't hate me – at least, if she does, she manages to disguise it – but the other three do and try to make my life as miserable as possible.

Let me give you an example of this.

A couple of years ago – remember, I'm not very good with time, so that's just a rough guess, but I think we've had two Christmases since then – they made me do a parachute jump.

Yes ... read that again: A. Parachute. Jump.

This was the twins' idea. Someone's dad at their prep school who the father knows – some macho-type who was in the Marines or something – was doing this for charity and persuaded the father to do it too.

That's when the twins got to work.

They started this rumour that I was going to do it with him and an instructor or somebody who steers the thing would be strapped to me, and then everyone was saying what a fantastic idea and how brave I was and shit like that.

Brave? Like I was even asked about it.

I'd been on a plane once before and I literally crapped myself.

I was quite young, and nobody had bothered to explain to me that we were going to leave the actual ground and exactly how we were going to do it. I mean, I'd probably worked out that we were going travel through the air, but did we go straight up gently, or what? It would have been nice to have been told this.

So I had no idea that we were going to be flung down this thing I think's called a runway, and then suddenly the plane was at a different angle and I don't know if this is what was supposed to happen or not? I've never been so scared in my life, even when Boris tied my wheelchair to the quad bike and dragged me backwards round the garden for half an hour. This was worse, much worse.

I didn't even know exactly what a plane was at the time but I'd heard on BBC Radio 4 about one crashing recently – EgyptAir Flight 804, if I remember correctly, and as I've told you, my memory's usually pretty good – and everyone was killed, so when one of these things crashes, that's it. You're dead.

So then it levelled off and it was quite smooth for a bit, and that wasn't so bad.

The father was sitting next to me. He'd had quite a lot of beer at the airport and now he asked for some more from someone he said loudly was called a 'trolley dolly', but before he got his beer the plane started jerking around and everyone was told to go back to their seats, put their seatbelts on, and that the toilets would be out of use until we had flown through something the pilot called turbulence.

The trouble was it went on like this for the whole flight – maybe sometimes not quite so bad – and as I was in this booster seat sort of thing that wasn't secured properly, that made it even worse. I was sure we were going to die, and that's probably the first time in my life that I've felt I would rather live a bit longer – even with my family – than die from getting flung out of the sky.

I managed to scream so much that I made myself have an epileptic fit – at least that's what a doctor who was on the plane and was called to help out said it was. I screamed for most of the flight until I passed out. I screamed so much that the father tried to gag me and told me if I didn't shut up, the plane would have to land and we would be kicked off. I don't know why he bothered because, as I've already said, he thinks that I can't understand anything, but maybe that's how desperate he was for me to shut up. I would have liked to have shut up but I was terrified.

Someone behind us heard what he'd told me and said that this wouldn't happen as we were going over the sea at the moment and it was unlikely that the pilot would attempt to land on water just to kick us off.

And when we did land, the pilot came out from the front and said to the father – very quietly, but I could hear it clearly – that if he ever brought me on to his fucking plane again, he would personally open the door at thirty-five thousand feet and throw me out. I'm not sure if that's a very good example of customer service, particularly as he didn't say this to some women at the back of the plane who were very drunk and – in my opinion at least – had been more of a nuisance than I was.

So the father replied that it was all the mother's idea, and if she ever persuaded him to take me on a plane again, he'd open the door at thirty-five thousand feet and toss himself out first. Of course the twins thought it was hilarious.

The mother had to take me home on a train, but I quite enjoyed that because the train stayed on the ground the whole time.

So that's what I think of flying and everyone in my family knew this, especially the father, so when the parachute jump was mentioned I couldn't believe that they were actually intending to go through with it.

Maybe they have very short memories.

Even the mother didn't object to it, but when I look back at it now, maybe this was because she had other things on her mind.

THIRTEEN

GILL

DIARY ENTRY: Thursday, 17 June 2004

Roger finally showed up late. Of course. At three-fifteen.

We arrived at Dr Sullivan's office to find her waiting for us with the door open.

There was an uncomfortable-looking settee opposite her desk where she motioned us to sit. She sat in an easy chair, and I noticed she'd removed her white coat to reveal a plain mid-thigh-length black Chanel dress. A little too stylish for work, I thought, although it suited her and looked fantastic. But my moment of madness at our earlier meeting had long since been replaced by anxiety.

'I'm afraid,' she began gravely, crossing her slender legs, 'that I have to give you some bad news.' Roger shifted uneasily. This had better be bloody important, he'd said when I'd told him his presence was required. Great support, Roger, I'd said, but then what would I expect from you?

'There's no easy way to say this, but there is a significant chance that your little boy ... Dave, may have suffered a brain injury as a result of his seizure – possibly a severe brain injury. But we won't know until he comes out of the coma.' She cleared her throat nervously, flicked an imaginary speck from her dress. 'If, that is, he does come out of the coma. I'm afraid that's an eventuality you need to prepare yourselves for.'

Somewhere in there the word 'seizure' was buried. I picked that up amongst the rest of the horror story that our son's life had become, and Roger did too.

'What seizure would that be?' asked Roger, quite aggressively. 'I wasn't aware he'd had a "seizure". We were told that he'd stopped breathing.'

Dr Sullivan managed a half-smile; unconvincing, but at least she tried.

My eyes were drawn to the NHS identity card attached to a lanyard around her neck. Her name is Judith. Judith Sullivan. It has a nice ring to it. She's probably called Jude, or isn't that a boy's name? And talking of rings, she wore none. Despite myself, I will do anything to divert my mind from what I know she's going to say next, even with my guilty secret: I have a crush on her.

'We're probably talking semantics here, Roger. Whether he stopped breathing and this triggered the seizure, or whether he had a seizure which impaired his ability to breathe, frankly, we shall never know. But we do know that he's still in a coma and we have no idea when – if at all – he will come out of it.'

'Hang on,' said Roger, 'this isn't about saving Dave, is it? It's about saving your arses.'

'Roger, let's just hear what Dr Sullivan has to say. Please?'

'I don't want to go into technicalities—'

'Please do,' Roger said. 'Please go into technicalities.'

'Okay.' She took a deep breath and continued. 'There's something called the Glasgow Scale. It assesses eye-opening, verbal responses and voluntary movements in response to a command. Most people in a coma will have a total score of eight or less. A lower score means someone may have experienced more severe brain damage and could be less likely to recover.'

There's silence.

'And Dave's score?' asked Roger.

'Dave's score is three.'

FOURTEEN

DAVE

Oh yes.

The parachute jump.

Somewhere on the wall in my room there's a certificate with my name on it saying that I'd completed a 'two-mile-high tandem skydive'. Actually, there are quite a lot of certificates on my wall, although I get so many certificates, mainly from school, that the father usually just puts them in the bin. Anyway, he's quite proud of this one and he's got one too. He's also got a T-shirt, although I think that was probably part of the package, but I didn't get one.

A while ago, the father bought me this other T-shirt that I really hate but thankfully I'm not made to wear it very often. Apparently, it has a picture of someone like me in a wheelchair and says: 'I'm only in it for the parking', which is a bit stupid cos I don't even drive.

Anyway, back to the jump.

I knew when it was going to happen because they'd been talking about it for days.

So one day – I think it was a Saturday – we were loaded into the car they call the Davemobile, which is a wheelchair-adapted vehicle that the father says looks like the car the Pope rides around in, and we set off to a place called Durham. I couldn't believe this was happening. I mean, how could someone as fucked as I am be allowed to be flung out of a plane at ten thousand feet and fall halfway to the ground at one hundred and twenty miles an hour before this parachute thing opened … if it *did* open? I'd heard on BBC Radio 4 about someone in the army being killed when his parachute didn't open and he was a soldier and wasn't even handicapped. This was going to be way, way far worse than the last time I went in a plane, and the parents seemed to think that this was a good idea? I mean ... I was seriously bricking it.

There's no need to worry, I told myself, because I was sure I'd get out of it on what's called medical grounds. But when we got to the centre the man in charge said as long as I was sixteen years of age and under fifteen stone (I'm only six and three-quarter stone because I don't eat very much) all the father had to do was to sign something called a medical consent form.

The man then read out a long list of medical conditions.

He said, 'Does your son suffer from diabetes, epilepsy, fits, recurrent blackouts, heart or lung disease, mental illness or asthma?'

And you know what the father replied? Silly question because you couldn't really.

'Pretty much all of those and a few more I could add. Is being a total pain in the arse on your list?'

The man didn't think this was very funny. Instead he said that I must be really brave and told me how much I was going to enjoy it. Really?

All the father had to do was sign this form and that was it. I couldn't believe it.

Then we went to the café, and the father and the mother had bacon butties and I had some water and then we met the instructor who told us that there was absolutely nothing to worry about and that he'd handle everything. He then started giving instructions to the father but I kind of switched off a bit because I was too busy crapping myself (sorry) and the mother took me away to change my nappy so I missed most of it.

Would the pilot throw me out of the plane if I started to scream, like the other one said he would? I suppose if he did, at least I'd be attached to someone with a parachute, and as we were going to be thrown out of the plane anyway, it wouldn't really matter.

Then we went out to the plane. I was pushed in my wheelchair, but when we got there I was lifted into it and strapped to the instructor we had met earlier and the father was attached to a separate instructor.

The plane wasn't what I was expecting. It felt like it was much smaller than the other one I'd been on and I didn't have to wait for a ramp to lift me in my wheelchair up into it. In fact, we didn't even take my wheelchair, but it turned out that I wouldn't need it anyway.

So by now, as you can imagine, I was totally, totally cacking it and I would have done anything to get off that plane. Actually, there's not much I could have done, but you may know what I mean.

And that's when two things happened.

First, I was about to start screaming, but something changed in, like, my head? So I decided not to. And I'm pretty sure this is the first time I ever experienced something called anger. And this anger, which I know is an emotion, was even stronger than my fear, which is also an emotion. If I was going to die, I was going to die with something I think's called dignity. And if I lived, I was somehow going to pay the bastards back – the parents and the ginger twats – for what they'd put me through. I had no idea how I was going to do this, but the fact that I'd decided I was going to do it gave me some sort of, I dunno, inner strength? Maybe even something called motivation?

And the other thing that happened was that I knew my first bit of payback was going to be very effective and also easy for me to do.

Because I have a very particular skill ... a skill which I have acquired over a short career, and a skill I will tell you about in a moment, that makes me a nightmare for people like my family. I didn't make that up, by the way. I heard someone called Liam Neeson talk about this when he was interviewed once. He has such a cool accent that I missed hearing what his special skill actually was.

But right now there's something I really want to listen to on BBC Radio 4.

FIFTEEN

GILL

DIARY ENTRY: Thursday, 17 June 2004

'Three?' said Roger. 'Jesus ... Christ.'

There was silence in the room. Somewhere a clock ticked, reminding me that time was still moving, seconds passing that didn't even begin to eat into the eternity of hell that lay before me. My life as I knew it was over. I had never been exactly what you might call carefree, but life with a mentally handicapped child? This was a prison sentence for both of us. And probably a prison sentence that had been caused by me.

'What exactly does three mean?' asked Roger.

'Let me try to explain. Although the Paediatric Glasgow Coma Indicator is not a precise predictor for children as young as Dave, and in any case, its efficacy is sometimes questioned, it does generally provide a fairly accurate insight as to a patient's prognosis. As I said, there are three elements to it: visual, verbal and motor responses, and these are graded in the PGCI on a scale of one to six.' She paused to let us digest this, and the clock ticked on.

'Dave's response to stimuli for each of these was at Level 1: his eyes did not open, he gave no response to verbal cues, and there was absolutely no motor response.'

Silence.

'But he might ...' I said, 'surely he might come out of the coma and be okay. I mean, there is a chance, isn't there?'

Dr Sullivan took a deep breath, releasing it slowly. It reminded me of how a smoker might breathe. Was she a smoker? I wondered. And then I remembered that I was now a smoker.

'Of course, there's always a chance. You're a nurse, Gill, you know that. But from my experience and from those of my colleagues, one of whom – a senior paediatric neurologist – has examined Dave, we feel it is only right that we should prepare you for the worst.'

There was nothing more to be said. Another long, uncomfortable silence hung in the air before she spoke again.

'I think' – she looked at Roger – 'you have to prepare yourselves for the possibility that he may not come out of the coma. And the longer he spends in a vegetative state, the more likely it is that, should he regain consciousness, the damage will be severe. In this eventuality, I doubt very much that the little boy you take home will be the same as the little boy you brought in here.'

There were questions, thousands of questions, that couldn't get past my lips. Of course, I had been expecting this, but you just hold out with blind hope, don't you? Even if your medical knowledge points towards the most likely outcome in the opposite direction.

This was the confirmation of my worst fears. My son will either die when we give consent for the ventilator to be switched off, or ... or God knows what?

When I held him in my arms two years ago, I'd had the premonition that he would never amount to anything. Remember, on the day he was born?

Well, it looks like I was right, wasn't I?

SIXTEEN

DAVE

Fake news is the subject for discussion on BBC Radio 4.

I don't really understand exactly what fake news is, but to me it sounds like quite a good idea because sometimes the news is just boring. 'The nosedive in the value of the pound against all major currencies is being attributed to Prime Minister Boris Johnson's insistence that he will take the UK out of Europe, with or without a deal, by December.' I mean, that's a pretty good example of boring news.

So what?

Does it affect me? No.

But fake news can be boring too. For example: 'Hillary Clinton suggested Trump should run for President.'

So what?

Does it affect me? No. From what I know about Trump, I don't particularly like him, but as my opinion is based on what I hear on the news, I could very well be wrong ... he could be an amazing world leader and people who say that he's a ginger twat are just jealous. I don't think Gary O'Donoghue likes him very much either, and he probably knows as much about him as anybody.

JFH said that the truth must never be allowed to get in the way of a good story, and although I'm not sure that he actually meant this, I happen to agree because knowing what really happened doesn't make people's lives any better. Unless of course the genuine news *does* affect them – like, if they were in a plane crash, for example, and the news said that they weren't.

So here's a bit of fake news I would like to broadcast, although I have no idea how to do this, which is a pity because I think it's quite a good example of what I *could* write if I ever got to be a journalist:

A quadriplegic eighteen-year-old youth who also suf-fers from locked-in syndrome has been charged with the murder of his parents and twin brothers. The accused, who cannot be named for legal reasons, told BBC reporter John F Humphrys, using a letter selection code communicated through movement of his right eye, that making him do a parachute jump had been the last straw. 'Just because I'm totally f***ed,' he told Humphrys, 'it shouldn't take away my human rights. And I don't know if it's a human right or not, but there should be a law against throwing people out of planes at ten thousand feet when they don't want to be thrown out of a plane at all.'

The family were returning from making the parachute jump at an airfield close to Durham when the accused is thought to have used telepathy to hypnotise his parents. Roger Hempsall, the father of the accused, was driving the car, a wheelchair-adapted Fiat, when it left the carriage-way on the A1(M) before hitting a tree, killing everyone other than the accused, whose wheelchair was securely an-chored in the rear compartment and who was removed un-injured from the wreckage by emergency services who at-tended the incident.

I mean ... that's a good story, isn't it? People would want to read that.

But they'd probably work out that it was fake news for a number of reasons. First, I'm not sure about the let-ter selection code bit, but I don't see why it wouldn't be possible and I intend to work on it. But much as I wish I could do it, I don't think I could use telepathy to make the father crash into a tree. I have tried, but I'm probably not making much progress because if I were, I wouldn't have allowed him to throw me out of a plane in the first place.

Anyway, back to the parachute jump.

The first bit wasn't too bad. We went down the run-way for a bit, but this was much slower than before, alt-hough it was just as noisy because this plane had a differ-ent sort of engine that made a strange throbbing sound so that it felt really close to you, almost like you were sitting on it.

The father and his instructor were making what's called small talk; something about there being a bit of cloud cover about but it shouldn't affect the view too much.

'Can he understand much of what we're saying?' my instructor asked the father, obviously about me. Why do people never ask me? Probably because they assume that I won't be able to answer because I only make my noises, so I suppose they're right.

'Bugger all,' replied the father.

'Well, he's very brave.'

'You're looking a bit peaky, Roger.' I'd forgotten about the father's friend, the one who got him into this in the first place. His name is Dieter and he was in something called the SAS, which means that he jumped out of planes in order to kill people, which I'll have to admit is pretty cool. But he doesn't do it any more. He sells something called advertising space now. 'Sure you're up for this, old boy? Dave's looking more relaxed than you are.'

Dieter was doing a different sort of jump because he's jumped out of planes loads of times. He was doing something called 'canopy piloting', which is where you do tricks quite close to the ground, so I supposed most people would be watching him and not us.

Then we reached what's called our 'ceiling'. This is ten thousand feet above the ground.

'This is what's going to happen,' the father's instructor said. 'We're going to go to the door in a moment.' I could tell where the door was because there was this massive wind coming through it and I've never felt so much wind in my life, even when the ginger twats tried to blow my hair off using two of the mother's hairdryers. 'When the red light comes on, I count to three and we jump.'

The instructors were attached behind the person who hadn't done this before, so I was in front of my instructor and because I can't walk he had to carry me to the door. Even though I'm quite light he made a fuss about this and said 'bugger' a lot and that he should get

59

paid double for doing this. The father and his instructor were going to jump first, so that gave me a good chance of getting this right – my little bit of payback, my special skill ... remember? Of course I'd need quite a bit of luck, but I thought it'd work because I understand a bit about what happens when you drop something from a tall building, and this is pretty much the same thing.

Then everything happened really quickly.

The father and his instructor were at the door, with us behind them, when I heard someone count to three, and then they were gone. I knew this because I felt the wind increase, and for the first time in my life I was glad I couldn't see anything. My instructor didn't bother to count and jumped a few seconds later, and then we were outside the plane, falling through the air, rolling over and over, and all I could feel was this gigantic whooshing of the wind going past us as we fell towards the earth.

Timing was going to be everything. I'd heard that we would only be doing what's called 'freefall' for thirty seconds and then the parachute would (hopefully) open and we'd be upright and on a more gentle descent, as there would then be something to slow down our fall to the ground.

And I needed to do it before that happened, and concentrating on this took my mind off the terror I'd felt, so now I didn't feel too bad. I wouldn't say I was exactly enjoying it, but if I could make my plan work it would a) make me feel a whole lot better about today and life in general, and b) ensure that I would never, ever have to do this again.

SEVENTEEN

GILL

DIARY ENTRY: Thursday, 22 July 2004

I moved back home a couple of weeks ago.

Dr Sullivan said there was really nothing to be gained by continuing to live at the hospital, because Dave's status remains the same and – although she didn't say it – there was nothing to suggest that this is going to change in the near future ... or in the distant future either, for that matter.

Also, I think they want my room back. I don't mind, of course – it's only fair to give it to a family whose child may actually recover or who may die, but who at least is making progress in one direction or the other.

There was no gladdening of my heart at the prospect of moving back into the family home. I suppose I'd become institutionalised and, if I'm to be honest, time away from Roger and all the hassles of home, work and life outside hospital was not unwelcome. My boss has been really good about it and told me to take my time and come back when I'm ready.

Dr Sullivan was also empathetic and told me that I needed to look after myself because I'd lost weight and – although she was too nice to spell it out – she implied that I look dreadful, which I do.

I took a long look at myself in the mirror yesterday.

I would never, even euphemistically, have described myself as beautiful or even glamorous, but I used to be able to turn heads when I made an effort. I probably had more than my fair share of admirers at uni before I met

Roger, and some of this admiration went rewarded. I wasn't totally promiscuous but I enjoyed making men – yes, and sometimes also women – crave my attention, and often that led to more intimate engagements. I think I probably had a carefree confidence, and this was as attractive as my looks ... maybe even more so.

But the woman I looked at in the mirror suggested none of this.

Neglect. If I had to sum up how she looked in one word, that would be it.

My hair hadn't seen a salon for months and was an unkempt mess that looked as if a family of rats could be living in it.

The woman staring back at me looked closer to thirty-eight than twenty-eight ... maybe even forty-eight.

My body evidenced a lack of exercise and proper diet and had acquired a shapelessness bordering upon anorexic-slash-dowdy, exuding a drabness that complimented my negative outlook on life.

And as for what I was wearing ... No thought had gone into this and it showed. Clothes had simply become drapes to cover my body rather than the joyful expression of my personality they had been in my Life Before Dave.

If I had seen this woman approach a public recycling facility with a trolley, I would have assumed that she was there to take things out of it rather than to put things in.

Roger seems to be oblivious to this. I don't know what he's up to, but it seems to occupy a disproportionate amount of his time. I don't think he's having an affair, but something is engaging his attention and seems to control his moods, which are unpredictable at best.

Actually, I'm not sure how bothered I would be if he were having an affair.

But I'm sure he isn't because he pays almost as little heed to his appearance as I do at the moment, and a woman would have to be very desperate indeed to be interested in him. Still, the world's a strange place, isn't it?

He's put on weight – mainly due to his excessive love of beer and hatred of exercise – and has sprouted a ghastly little goatee beard which only serves to highlight the absurdness of his receding ginger hair. Sometimes I really don't know what I saw in him, but he was once a lot of fun to be around and that made him attractive, and not just to me.

When we started dating towards the end of his final year at uni, it even broke a few hearts. Hard to believe that now.

He was doing a master's in education and I was in my second year of teacher training. By then I'd decided that I would complete my BEd then switch to nursing. I'd realised, by the time I'd completed my second teaching practice, that I didn't have the temperament for teaching. Nursing seemed a better option than teaching English to disaffected and uninterested teenagers. It was more mechanical. You followed protocols, and ill patients don't usually answer back or have to hand in homework they can't be bothered to do.

Before I left hospital, Dr Sullivan said that she would ring me immediately if there was any change in Dave's status.

He's been in a coma for almost eleven weeks, and I have to admit that I had almost reached the point of acceptance that we would soon have to make the decision; you know ... the decision whether to switch off life support or not. I know that doctors usually advise stopping life support when there's no hope for recovery – when a person's organs are no longer able to function on their own – and despite a lack of precise information, I think we're getting close to this point. A while ago I checked on the NHS website: '... keeping the treatment going at that point may draw out the process of dying and may also be costly', and avoiding cost – we all know – is a primary function of the NHS. When we will reach this point in Dave's case I just don't know, but I had a feeling it wouldn't be far away.

I felt sorrow, but it was tinged with a hint of relief at the prospect of us both being released from our prison sentences.

But that was before I got the phone call at three o'clock this morning.

Dave had begun to wake up.

EIGHTEEN

DAVE

I didn't realise how successful my plan had been until we were on the way home in the Davemobile.

As we'd landed some distance apart, I wasn't aware of the argument that had gone on between the father and his instructor.

The landing was surprisingly okay.

Once the parachute opened we stopped falling through the sky and, as I'd thought we would, we dropped into an upright position. The first thing I noticed after this was how peaceful it was. We weren't falling any more; I think we were doing something called gliding, and I imagine that the instructor had some sort of control over where we were going, or we could have landed in a river or up a tree, or somewhere like maybe in a lion's cage in a zoo which would definitely not be a good place to land. I don't know if there is a zoo in Durham; they've not mentioned one on BBC Radio 4.

The wind had stopped whooshing past us, and it didn't feel as if we were moving at all. It would have been nice if the instructor could have told me what was going on and maybe described where we were, because I would have found this quite interesting as a) I had done what I'd planned to do, and b) I realised that I wasn't terrified any more.

But the next thing I knew was that the instructor's feet touched the ground and he ran a few steps before stopping and then the parachute fell over us and he grabbed it and pulled it away and it was all over.

Some sort of vehicle had been sent out to pick us up because, otherwise, my instructor would have had to carry me all the way back to the centre and this would have made him say 'bugger' a lot. So we got into something he called a 'buggy' – or maybe he just said 'bugger' again? I'm not sure, but it felt small and was open at the sides, and we were back at the centre before the father and his instructor.

'So how did that go, John?' I recognised the voice of the man who had asked the father about my medical conditions. 'Did you enjoy that, Dave?' he asked me cheerfully.

I tried to tell him that it wasn't quite the fucking nightmare I'd thought it would be, but I don't think he understood me.

John was obviously my instructor. Nice to meet you, John.

'Went pretty much okay, Mike ... no problems,' John replied, laughing. 'Certainly not from our point of view. But I don't think either his father or Darren would agree.'

'Oh, what happened?'

He told him.

'Jesus!'

NINETEEN

GILL

DIARY ENTRY: Thursday, 22 July 2004

Naturally, the first thing I did after I put my phone down was to wake Roger and tell him.

'So how fucked is he … does she know?' This was his first question – his first response to the news that our son wasn't going to die in hospital … that he would come home … that he *may*, possibly, be okay.

'She doesn't know,' I replied. 'But she said that his responses to everything apart from visual cues are significantly better.'

'So that means he's going to be blind?'

'It doesn't mean anything, Roger. Are you getting dressed or what?'

'Getting dressed?' He looked at his phone. 'It's four o'clock in the bloody morning. Why would I be getting dressed?'

'Because you might like to see your son?'

'I'll come in later … as in when it's light, after I've taken the dog out. There's no point in both of us losing a night's sleep. Anyway, he's not going to be a lot different by eleven o'clock than he is now, is he?'

'No … no point at all,' I replied and walked out, slamming the door.

I was slightly surprised not to find Dr Sullivan in the Intensive Care Unit when I got there. Instead there was a senior ICU nurse called Janice, who I'd got to know quite well, and a junior doctor whose name I didn't catch but who looked as if he hadn't started shaving yet.

My heart sank when I saw Dave. He looked exactly the same, only without the ventilator, and its removal only served to make him look smaller.

'He's sleeping now,' said Janice. 'This is normal when a patient comes out of a coma. It's generally a very gradual process and the rebooting of the autonomic nervous system puts a big demand on the body, particularly with someone as young as Dave.' She smiled at me and squeezed my forearm. 'Of course, you know all that.'

But seeing Dave lying there, unresponsive to my voice and my touch, only served to rekindle my nagging certainty: it would be a miracle if the coma had left his brain undamaged.

In my mind, joy at this development fought tooth and nail with fear for the future.

I couldn't pick him up as there were still several tubes attached to him, and my knowledge and experience told me that these would not be removed for some considerable time. There were tubes inserted intravenously to provide fluids, nutrition and medication, a feeding tube placed through his nose, and a catheter – a tube to remove any build-up of blood or fluid from the body, mainly pee.

I don't know what I was expecting really, and I realised that Roger had probably been right. He wouldn't be a whole lot different at eleven o'clock than he was now.

And this premonition, that many, many eleven o'clocks would pass before Dave's body would function at a level beyond this, now had more than a seed of reality where it had been planted.

TWENTY

DAVE

So, I'll finish telling you about the parachute jump.

There was what you might call an 'atmosphere' in the Davemobile.

That meant no one was talking.

But it only lasted a few minutes before the mother broke the silence.

'For God's sake, Roger, don't let it spoil the day. I don't know why you're making such a big deal of it anyway.'

'You don't know?' he repeated. 'Really? You don't *know*?'

I don't think the father has a really bad temper. It's not one of his more recognisable faults; although, I have seen him lose it before, like the one time he tried to feed me, or when he lost a lot of money in the casino. I'll tell you about that in a bit. But generally he just seems to ignore things. I suppose it's how I'd like to be if I wasn't fucked up: not too happy but not too angry either. Anyway, I could tell he was really building up to something that I've heard Boris call 'blowing his top', and although I'm not sure exactly what this means, I had a pretty good idea that it meant something like he was going to explode. I wasn't wrong.

'That little bastard,' he said quite calmly, 'that little retard in the fucking wheelchair—'

'Roger! For goodness sake ... not in front of the children.'

'No ... that little bastard ... you know what he did? He threw up all over us ... the bloody instructor and me.

68

Have you any idea what it's like to be vomited on from five thousand feet?'

'Really, Roger, it was only a bit of sick. He couldn't help it ... you can hardly blame him for that.'

Actually, I could have helped it and I most definitely could be blamed for it.

This is my special skill, you see – I can be sick any time I feel like it. If I'm honest, I don't use this very often, but it does come in useful – as it did today – particularly when there's something I don't want to do or somebody I want to go away, and the only person who's not bothered by it is the mother, probably cos she's a nurse and she says that people throw up all the time when they're in hospital.

So this morning I'd prepared myself for the probability that I might be thrown out of a plane and I ate every bit of Ready Brek the mother shoved into my mouth. She even remarked how hungry I was and made some comment about needing 'fortification' (the mother always uses big words even when small words would do, and I'm not quite sure what fortification is – I thought it was something to do with castles?) for my big day. What I actually needed was ammunition, which is why I seemed hungry. She was basically loading a cannon.

'I mean ... have you any idea what it's like to be spewed on from five thousand feet? Huh? The first lot hit the parachute just as the bloody thing was opening and damned near caused us to get tangled up in it. The instructor thought it was a flock of birds and he only just managed to get us the right way round; otherwise the bloody thing wouldn't have opened properly. We could have both been killed.'

Result – I think – 'back of the net,' as Boris sometimes says, and although I don't really understand this, I think it means that something has gone well and some goal or purpose has been achieved. It may also have something to do with soccer – a game, as I've told you, that I think is played by other people with learning difficulties, but obviously nowhere near as bad as mine.

However, my delight at this news was slightly tinged with a hint of disappointment because I'd come closer than I'd even imagined possible to getting rid of the father. However, then I would have had the instructor's death on my conscience, but I suppose I could live with that. I've heard JFH refer to this as 'collateral damage' when he's talking about hostage rescue situations on BBC Radio 4, and this, you could argue, was a bit like that.

'And then the second load of spew, just a few seconds later, went all over the both of us. It went right into the instructor's face and he damn near lost control of the thing getting it out of his mouth.'

'Well, you got down safely and there was no real harm done—'

'Tell that to the bloody instructor. He went absolutely mental when we landed. I thought he was going to punch me.'

This just gets better and better.

'He said, "If you ever bring that little bastard anywhere near this airfield again, I'll personally see that the next time he goes out of a plane, he does it without a parachute!"'

What is it about me that everyone seems to want to throw me out of planes?

'And of course everyone who was watching found it bloody hilarious. There's Captain fucking Marvel from the SAS looping the bloody loop, and we land plastered in puke. I'll be the laughing stock of the whole school.'

It's a good job that I'm not able to laugh because that would only make it worse. I tried really hard not to make any of my noises but, as this was turning into the best day I could remember since Axel lost a tooth when he put me on the swing and my boot hit his mouth, I couldn't help myself.

'And you can shut up as well. I suppose you're enjoying this. Well, you would be if you actually had a brain.'

Yes, I was enjoying this, and I do have a brain.

'And the bloody local rag were there because of his jump, so I suppose there'll be pictures all over Monday's paper.'

'Well, just think of the money the pair of you raised for the school.'

'Fuck the school.'

Then there was another atmosphere for the rest of the journey and no one spoke until we got home.

I passed the journey trying to use telepathy to hypnotise the father so that he would drive the car into a tree, but I couldn't get it to work.

Still, it had turned out to be a really good day, so I didn't mind too much.

TWENTY-ONE

GILL

DIARY ENTRY: Wednesday, 17 July 2019

'Okay, so I'll look after Dave while you go to see ... "Martin,"' Roger said. I hadn't expected him to concede so easily and wondered what had prompted this about-turn. Not that I cared. 'But I'm not bloody feeding him again. Who's going to do that, then?'

I glanced at my watch. I still had to shower and make myself presentable – no, better than presentable – and for that I knew I'd require at least three-quarters of an hour ... maybe longer. On my run, I'd mulled over what to wear but still couldn't decide between the pink floral Lipsy short-sleeve shift dress from Top Shop and the clingy, backless black number I'd bought in M&S. There was a time, not long ago, when my clothes bore designer labels: Stella McCartney, Vivienne Westwood, Prada, but not any more because the bastard standing opposite me had scythed his way through almost all of the inheritance money.

Maybe, I thought, the floral dress was a little too short, and the backless M&S number – described pretentiously as décolleté, meaning that it had a deeper neckline to reveal more of your neck and breasts – was conceivably a tad formal.

Besides, I wasn't sure if more of my breasts were really worth revealing.

Perhaps the red spot wrap-around button dress I'd bought last week in Next?

Shit. I also had to collect Molly, and that would take a good hour, particularly as I wasn't exactly sure where she lived.

My appointment was at twelve. I would need around two hours for all of this and it was now approaching ten.

Not only that, I wanted to get out of the house without Roger seeing me, or he would ask questions I'd rather not answer. Like why was I dressed like this? And why the make-up? And the perfume? He'd expect me to wear a frumpy, baggy dress, or a pair of slacks, a jumper and court shoes, because this was no different to a shopping trip or a visit to the doctors or Dave's school. So when does relatively smart casual become borderline sexy? Or, if I got it right, deliciously sexy but with a slightly oblique air of subtle innocence?

And then I had an idea ... two birds with one stone.

'You could actually help me, Roger,' I said, trying to fake a smile sufficient to soften my face but not broad enough for him to become suspicious. 'Could you collect Molly for me? You don't need to take the twins with you; they'll be fine here on their own. Just put Dave in the back.'

'Who the heck is Molly?'

'You don't listen to a bloody thing I tell you. She's coming to help with Dave.' God, it really is hopeless. Anything that's not on Planet Roger just totally passes him by. 'She's an OT – Occupational Therapist. She's doing a master's in something or other. It's about communication in brain-damaged paediatric patients, and she asked if she could work with Dave as part of her research project. Lucy, the physio at school, recommended her.'

'Oh ... must have missed that.'

'She *will* feed him,' I replied. 'Besides which, she has an enhanced DBS certificate, so she's been fully checked out. But I'll cancel her if you'd rather feed Dave yourself.'

Roger's silence confirmed that he wouldn't.

'She's very good-looking.' I'd first been attracted to the flyer by her photo: silver-hued grey eyes; rich, dark chocolate-coloured brown hair; high cheekbones; full lips; and flawless, porcelain-like skin. She could be a model or an actress, I'd thought, as my eyes had lingered on the photo perhaps a little too long before reluctantly moving to the text.

'What's good-looking got to do with it? She's here to feed him and do occupational therapy stuff, so what difference would it make if she looked like the back end of a bus?'

'Just thought you'd like to know.'

'As long as she can feed him, she can look like Susan bloody Boyle for all I care.'

'Anyway, will you fetch her, and maybe take her back later? She lives in Ganstead, so it'll take about half an hour each way. She usually drives her dad's car but he needs it today. I said I'd be there at about eleven-thirty. It'll give you some more bonding time with Dave. You like your little trips with him, don't you?' I said with a smile. It was still a source of mystery to me as to why Roger had recently shown an uncharacteristic willingness to take Dave out. A mystery it might be, but a mystery that could be solved on another day. 'And don't forget to put on Radio 4 in the car. You know how much he loves it.'

For a moment I thought he wouldn't go for it. I could almost see the brain cogs ticking over. Decisional balance? Plan scuppered?

Then he replied.

'Sure ... okay, give me the address. Get Dave ready and I'll leave in ten. I need to call at Asda anyway.'

For a second, I thought of asking Roger about his sudden interest in shopping but correctly assumed that there was probably an element of truth buried somewhere therein as well. Another mystery that could be pursued another day.

It got him out of the house; that was the main thing. Job half done.

'And you'll drop her back as well?'

'If I'm appropriately rewarded,' he said, with a lecherous smile.

Not a chance of that, buster. That ship has sailed and the yacht that's replaced it is sleeker, slimmer and much better adorned. Not even a major refit will catapult *you* into that category. So whatever it is you're up to is of little concern or consequence to me. I'm not going to allow idle speculation to spoil my day.

I smiled at him: a smile conceived to fuel his optimism, the thought of my delicious secret pulsing through my veins, pushing guilt aside.

'Of course,' I said, and left the room to shower.

TWENTY-TWO

ROGER

While Roger was planning to pass quite close to the Asda Hessle superstore, he had absolutely no intention of entering it.

At least, not right now.

Maybe he'd call in later, he thought, when he dropped Molly home, to buy some cheap plonk and perhaps a bunch of flowers for Gill, depending on the outcome of activities where he *was* going. The wind would be in his sails after this morning's magnanimity, and he smiled at the prospect of converting this approach work into a rare sexual encounter. Flowers should just about nail it, and this thought took his mind away from the financial precipice he now faced.

He was quite confident that his morning would be productive and – oddly enough – this was because Dave was with him.

Roger wasn't superstitious, but since he'd started bringing Dave along to the Grosvenor Casino, he had struck a rich vein of luck, and that – surely – could not be attributed entirely to coincidence? Of course, he hadn't won all the time, but he'd certainly won a heck of a lot more than he'd lost, which was a major reversal of fortune. He knew this was beginning to attract the management's attention and that it was probably time he took his money elsewhere, but that wasn't how it worked. Same casino, same games, same slots, same Dave equates to same results.

And like so many things in Roger's life, this sequence had begun entirely by accident.

As it was virtually impossible to find a parking space in Dock Street, he'd started to take Dave with him because there were two disabled parking spaces almost right outside the Grosvenor.

And as he couldn't very well leave him in the car, he was obliged to bring him inside.

To begin with, the management of the Grosvenor were less than ecstatic about the presence of a severely disabled young man who made strange noises in their establishment. The manager had asked Roger for Dave's ID but, upon learning that Dave was legally entitled to be on the premises, had concluded that there was very little he could legitimately do to remove him. The gambling industry was going through a bleak enough period, and with tougher standards on advertising recently announced, the last thing anyone wanted was to make the headlines for disability discrimination.

At first the staff, and sometimes even other punters, found Dave's noises, which coincided with the ka-ching of coins as the slot machine gushed out its bounty, to be a source of mild amusement.

But before long, as is often the case when the wheel of fortune favours but one person, annoyance and then resentment replaced this sentiment, and the Golden Cripple became the Mooing Pariah.

The management ruled that allowing Dave's wheelchair anywhere near the blackjack table was a breach of house rules, as Dave could well be communicating information to Roger in a method of cheating referred to as 'spooking'. The fact that Dave was blind – which Roger had told the manager – did nothing to allay his concerns as it seemed to be too much of a coincidence that every time Dave made one of his noises, Roger cleaned up.

On this particular morning, Roger began his campaign in the usual fashion. He had a routine, and that routine resulted in working one machine, then another, and so on, until he had filled the bags contained in his pockets and also considered that he had sated his addiction – for an addiction it undoubtedly was – without drawing

77

excessive attention to himself. Of course, with Dave chortling and mooing every time a machine spat out its abundance, this was virtually impossible, but Roger had the good sense to stop when he was ahead – generally well ahead.

But this morning it was more than an addiction. Roger needed to win and he needed to win big. He had to do better than finish well ahead. Last night he'd checked the joint bank account and had been horrified to find that all that stood between him and bankruptcy was a meagre thirty thousand; in fact, less than thirty thousand.

Two years ago he wouldn't have thought twice about walking into an Aston Martin dealership and chucking thirty thousand at a salesman on a whim, just to upgrade to the latest model.

How had it all gone so wrong so quickly?

Of course, Roger knew the answer: doomed business ventures down whose paths he'd trod when all the signposts were pointing him in the opposite direction. Roger could predict market trends and hostile business activity as effectively as dinosaurs could predict ice ages. Gill had done little to hide her contempt for his entrepreneurship, telling him the only thing he had in common with Donald Trump was the colour of what was left of his hair.

First, there was the wine bar that he'd had to sell for a huge loss when a Wetherspoons opened opposite it. That was just unlucky, he'd told himself, while everyone else – including his accountant – had told him that if he'd bothered to do even the most basic due diligence, he would have seen this coming.

Then there was the travel agency he'd bought at the precise moment that everyone switched to booking everything online.

And finally, there was the Video-Enhanced Grave Marker – better known as Video Tombstones – business fiasco. What might have induced the silicon and Botox generation in Beverly Hills to part with ten thousand dollars in order to have their loved ones' finest moments preserved on their gravestones, and to (hopefully) capture utterances of the departed from beyond the grave, held little appeal for those on this side of the Atlantic.

Hull wasn't ready for it. And while Roger had arrived at this particular marketplace before it peaked – if indeed it would peak at all – this proved to be the final entrepreneurial disaster before he returned to the relatively safe haven of teaching.

And then, of course, there was the gambling. He couldn't even bring himself to think about how much money he'd squandered before he discovered Dave's Midas touch.

And now all that was left was thirty thousand? That would keep a roof over their heads and food on the table for five months ... six, at the most.

And even if the Dave compensation money was coming their (Dave's) way, it was unlikely to come through soon enough. And this wasn't the sort of security you could use to walk into your bank and ask for a loan just to tide you over.

No, he needed a big win – maybe one last big win – and then he'd step away from the casino, at least until the Dave money arrived. A win, he'd calculated, somewhere in the region of twenty grand; that should be enough. Of course, he wasn't going to get this kind of money on the machines. So his plan was to clean up at the slots, put these winnings on a horse called Kaila's Daughter in the 2.20 at Haydock that he'd had a hot tip for, then come back to the Grosvenor later – after he'd dropped this Molly home – and stake what he'd won on the blackjack table. Stick to these rules, and with Dave beside him at the slots and in the bookies', all he needed was a bit of luck and self-discipline at the table.

But today there was no abundance to be had.

The wheels spun but came to rest on barren ground.

With each machine failing to spew forth a river of coins, Roger became more and more agitated. He bore the look and the scent of a loser. With sweat on his brow and trembling hands, he grew ever more desperate before first kicking a slot machine and then turning his anger on Dave with a volley of accusatory expletives, at which point the management intervened, ordering him to leave and informing him that if he showed his face in the Grosvenor again, the police would be summoned.

Roger, for the first time in his life, had seriously lost it. He had lost before, but this was different. Gill knew that money had become tight but had almost certainly no idea as to how bad things were. The hole he found himself in was one, he realised, for which common sense suggested that termination of digging was required.

But, as every gambler knows, Roger understood that the only option was to keep going; all or nothing would be the order of the day.

TWENTY-THREE

GILL

DIARY ENTRY: Wednesday, 7 December 2016

I've neglected my diary.

It's years since I wrote anything, and I suppose the only reason I'm writing now is because Martin says it may help to rationalise things, I think he said, and that it might also be cathartic. And because so much has happened since I last kept a diary, I suppose this is going to be more of a journal. He suggested that I write a blog, but that would mean making my thoughts, emotions and actions public. I told him that this would restrict my openness and therefore defeat its purpose, and he reluctantly agreed. Martin is my therapist, by the way, or shrink, as Roger calls him.

I started seeing Martin when I couldn't cope with the anxiety attacks any longer. It began with sleepless nights, then I started doing things I couldn't even remember doing, like taking the twins and disappearing for two days. He diagnosed me with Persistent Depressive Disorder and told me that I'd been suffering from this for a long time, maybe as long as two years, without being aware of it. That explained a lot, and he said that medication was likely to be counterproductive so it would be better – at least in the first instance – to try psychotherapy.

We started with one session a week but soon built up to two, with the occasional emergency meeting at short notice if things got really bad. I must always call him if I need to talk, he told me; lining his pockets, Roger called it. When I told Martin this – because I have to tell him absolutely everything in order, he said, for him to understand the pressures I'm facing – he replied that Roger was part of the problem, not part of the solution. Nothing new there.

I suppose it was around this time that I began to realise that I was no longer in love with Roger. Martin said Roger's attitude was quite common; 'For God's sake, pull yourself together, woman' was about the level of his understanding and empathy. I was the one with mental health problems, but he did nothing to lift the weight that threatened to pull me right down into the abyss that I was skating along the edge of. His help with Dave and the twins was negligible, and sometimes I wondered whether he might simply be planning to push me so close to this abyss that its darkness would become a comforting lure.

Martin said he thought this was unlikely. But that mild paranoia – beginning by questioning and even suspecting everyone who was not entirely supportive to your predicament – was not uncommon with my illness.

Well, that's a start; I mean, with my diary.

Trouble is, I don't really believe that it's helped me to rationalise anything.

TWENTY-FOUR

DAVE

So, yeah, I was going to tell you about the father losing his temper when he lost most of his money at the casino.

It was what I've heard called a bittersweet experience because some of it was good but most of it was really bad – at least, the way it ended.

And I had nothing to do with it. Even if I'd wanted to, I couldn't have made the machines that clanked out coins for the father stop doing it because, as I've already told you, I'm useless at telepathy.

And I wouldn't have wanted to do it anyway because this was the only time – apart from the time he came into my room and told me I was worth something after all – that the father was nice to me.

It started about six months ago, I think. It must have been around Christmas; I always know when it's Christmas because the parents and the twins argue more than normal, and there are strange smells and different music in the house, and people seem to drink more alcohol and put hats on my head. This happens at school as well, although there's not usually as much arguing.

Anyway, one day the father asked the mother if he could take me out for a drive. She was quite surprised when he said he'd like to spend more time with me, and so was I until I found out why.

Although the father thinks that I can't understand anything, that doesn't stop him talking about stuff, so when the car stopped, he made this laughing noise he makes when he's done something he thinks is clever, and he said, 'Here we go, Dave, I knew you'd come in useful some day,' and then muttered something I didn't catch about parking.

It took him ages to get my wheelchair out of the car because he'd never done it before and the straps kept getting caught up. By that time, I was freezing and he was in a really bad mood, especially when he banged his head on the door at the back of the car.

So then we went into this room where there were really cool noises, and I got excited and started trying to talk to him, and after that someone who worked there came up to the father and told him I'd have to leave, but the father told him that I was over eighteen. This meant that I could stay, and I tried to tell the father that this was good because I loved the noises and it was warm.

Anyway, we were allowed to stay, and after a while I worked out that we were in something called a casino and these things the father was putting coins into were called slot machines. I know this is called gambling and it's also what's called addictive – like alcohol and drugs – and so it's not a good thing, but I was enjoying myself for once. I know about gambling and addiction because there was a play on BBC Radio 4 about someone who went to casinos all the time and gambled all his money away, and this meant that he ended up losing his job and his friends and became homeless.

I was really worried that the father might lose all his money, not because I care that much about him but because I don't want to be homeless. I don't think it's much fun sleeping on a street if you're not handicapped, but I really wouldn't want to sleep on a street in my wheelchair.

I suppose if that did happen, we would always have Scooter, and this would be good because I've heard that homeless people who have a dog stand a better chance of being given money and that means they can buy more drugs or alcohol and maybe some dog food too.

Anyway, the father didn't lose ... or at least, not very often, and this meant that we kept going back to the casino. At first it was once a week, and then we went twice or sometimes even three times.

Maybe you're wondering how I felt about this because I've already told you that I would really like to kill the father? Well, I felt good about it, and for the first time in my life, I felt happy, which was a strange feeling.

At last the father had taken an interest in me, and it made me feel as if I mattered. He talked to me – okay, this was only because he had no one else to talk to, but he called me his lucky mascot and this made me feel as if for the first time ever I had done something important. It would have been nice if he'd given me a drink of water occasionally because it was really warm in the casino and I was concentrating so hard on the noises the machines made and the money pouring out of them and that made me really thirsty.

But you can't have everything, can you?

It was a really great time in my life, and for once I woke up and looked forward to something. The father used to tell me that this was our little secret ... yeah, like I was going to tell anybody? I think the people who worked there liked me too.

And then it all went wrong.

Everything changed this morning when the father's luck ran out.

This morning the machines stopped spewing out coins, and he went quiet and stopped saying stuff like, 'Come on, you little beauty,' or calling me 'Golden Balls' – I didn't like that so much, but at least it meant that he was in a good mood.

Then, after he went quiet, he started shouting at this machine, and when the machine didn't take any notice, he started shouting at me. He told me that he had lost a fortune and that it was all my fault because I could probably communicate with the machines, and that's when he really lost his temper and we got thrown out.

He started driving home, and then he remembered he had to pick up this Molly person and that made him start swearing at me again because he said this was all my fault as well. Then he stopped the car and started smashing his fists, then his head – or that's what it sounded like – against the steering wheel, and I was really worried that he would open the back of the car and start hitting

85

me, and that made me even more scared than the threat of being thrown out of a plane.

But he didn't hit me. I'm not sure if it would have been much worse if he had because I don't really feel pain anyway. I just felt empty and really unhappy because I had stopped hating him for a while and had even begun to like him a bit. Or at least I liked the time I spent with him.

But now I feel just like I used to feel, and all I want to do is to kill him.

TWENTY-FIVE

GILL

DIARY ENTRY: Wednesday, 7 December 2016

I've just sat down to eat lunch and reread the diary entry
I wrote this morning.

There's something really important I've left out.

The twins. God ... I've not mentioned the twins, have
I?

Time has flown by. Today is their tenth birthday, and
Roger's taken them out to the Hull Christmas market and
then to Hamleys, and probably after that to McDonald's.
He has, to be fair, become slightly more involved as a father as they've grown up, but I can't help feeling that this
is a ploy to avoid having anything to do with Dave. And I
also can't help thinking that somehow he blames *me* for
Dave's disability. Trouble is, I'm not sure that he isn't
right. Oh, and he probably spends time with the twins to
avoid spending time with me as well. There ... paranoia
and cynicism: the twin towers of my mental fragility.
Sometimes I'd just like to blow them away and end it all,
to dive into that abyss – but then who would look after
Dave?

Anyway, the twins ...

When they were born a decade ago today, I felt optimistic; I was really looking forward to a normal relationship with – I know this sounds terrible – but 'normal' babies who would grow into 'normal' kids and we would be
able to do 'normal' things with them.

I suppose when I look back on it, this was the main
reason I got pregnant. For a long time after Dave was

born, I didn't want any more children. Dave wore me out, both physically and emotionally, so where would I find the mental and physical capacity to devote to another child? But when I found out that I was pregnant with twins, I saw this very much as a positive. A 'normal' child who has a seriously disabled sibling has to face the burden of being ... I don't know ... maybe marginalised, on their own? But twins, I believed, would support, occupy and entertain each other.

How wrong I was.

Why I agreed to Roger's insistence on christening them Axel and Boris, I really have no idea. Roger was – and is – persuasive ... manipulative even, and his suggestion was to give them what he called 'macho' names that would make them robust in the school playground ... names that would guard them against bullying. Kids can be cruel, Roger said, and he persuaded me that once the other kids discovered that their brother was what he called a 'Timmy', they would make life hell for them.

I suppose he was right.

But despite having Dave as a brother and also having ginger hair – which these days almost guarantees being bullied – the twins have never been picked on. Ever. They never came home bruised or in tears with a playground horror story to tell. Not once.

And this was mainly because *they've* been too busy bullying other kids ... and that includes Dave, who they resent and despise. I've lost count of the number of phone calls or emails from the head, summoning us to discuss their antisocial, aggressive behaviour and bad language. I've also lost count of the number of times I've had to prevent them from physically tormenting Dave.

And how do I feel about this?

I sometimes simply wish that I could wind the clock back, be sterilised so that none of this had ever happened, and just live somewhere wild and remote on my own – I don't know ... maybe even Scotland? Just Scooter and me; nobody has any time for him either.

But I can't, so I just have to make the best of it. And if none of this had happened, I wouldn't have met Martin, and I wouldn't have met the one person who draws me back from the abyss and makes me feel that life is worth living.

***

So, back to my illness.

It soon began to affect my job. I became unreliable and failed to turn up for shifts or called in sick at the last minute. Before long I was taken aside by my line manager and somebody from HR. They were sympathetic at first, but that veneer didn't last long, and I was offered the choice of either receiving treatment or – well, they didn't say it, but there was little doubt that I either get my shit together or get another job. This was when I met Martin.

Martin understands me. He's the first person in a very long time who doesn't treat me as an attention-seeking moron; empathy, not criticism ... what a welcome change. At our first session, he told me to think of him as a soothing sea breeze cooling my skin on a hot day. Or something like that; I can't remember exactly, but his voice was almost soporific, and whatever it was he said achieved that effect. It was utterly hypnotic and it calmed me. It helped me to be told that what I was suffering from was not uncommon and that he would help me come through this; not only that, but on the other side, I would emerge a stronger and more self-confident person. This was important because I always used to be self-confident, but somehow that evaporated a long time ago.

I made the mistake of telling Roger about this, and he told me that I could download that sort of stuff to relax me – what he referred to as 'white noise' – for free from the internet. Would save us a load of money, he'd said, and that just made me feel even guiltier, but I suppose that was his intention.

Anyway, as I said, it all started about two years ago, around the time Roger's parents died.

I really liked John and Eileen, Roger's parents. They were kind to me and they really cared about Dave. John used to play with him for hours, and I remember him once telling me that he really believed that Dave could understand him.

89

Roger said that he probably had a Ouija board in his closet at home because he'd get more sense from the dead than he would from Dave.

They were what you might call elderly parents. John was forty-five and Eileen was forty when Roger was born, and Roger was their only child. Tried it once and didn't like it, Roger used to joke.

Eileen was one of those people who worried about everything. She was deeply religious, and her faith was touching, although, to be honest, it could be slightly smothering and even irritating on occasions, because she couldn't understand why we didn't share her piety. She worried about Dave and she worried about John, who suffered from diabetes. But she held the firm belief that someday Dave would make a miraculous recovery and lead a normal life; that either medical advances or, more likely, an intervention by the Almighty would cure him.

She also held the belief that something really bad was going to happen to her and John.

And how right she was.

I remember the morning they were killed so clearly. The police contacted Roger and he came home and told me. He was so calm; I remember thinking, how can you take this so matter-of-factly? He kept on saying that they wouldn't have known a thing about it and said he had to focus on the funeral arrangements and that grief would come later.

Call me cynical, but I remember thinking that his mind was more on the money than anything else. And yes, I'll admit that thought did cross my mind as well because our financial situation – as it is now – was pretty dire at the time.

I know I shouldn't write this, in case Roger ever finds and reads my diary – in fact, I shouldn't even think it – but somewhere at the back of my mind lurks the thought that he had something to do with it.

He'd gone out early that morning. He said he had a meeting with someone who was flying in from the States about one of his new business ventures. I remember that he went into quite a lot of detail, which was unusual for him. He never used to bother involving me with his get-rich-quick schemes because he knew what I felt about them. I just wished that he'd stayed in teaching; at least there was regular money coming in. So I didn't really listen because I didn't much care. Maybe I should have, but in truth, I wasn't interested because they all ended the same way.

Anyway, he would have had time to call at his parents' house, tamper with John's medication and do something with the security cameras before Eileen returned from prayer group meeting. Okay, this may be overthinking things, but the police wouldn't have been able to read anything into the fact that his fingerprints would have been all over the house. It had been the family home since he was a kid, and we used to go round there regularly, so my fingerprints would have been everywhere as well.

Anyway, the police never went to the house because John and Eileen were killed in a road accident, which the coroner ruled was due to a heart attack caused by an 'inadvertently taken overdose of Sitagliptin' – the drug he took to control his diabetes.

But John had always been meticulous; that was what had helped to make him such a successful businessman. He had a fantastic memory and his mind was still as sharp as a razor.

I don't believe that John would have taken an overdose. It certainly wasn't suicide; this possibility wasn't even considered at the coroner's hearing.

So if John didn't administer the Sitagliptin, who did?

When I look back at it now, this is where it all started … the paranoia, the anxiety, the depression. It all came from this pall of suspicion, this nagging fear that simply would not go away, that the person I lived with, the person I was married to, the father of my children … could be a murderer.

TWENTY-SIX

MOLLY JOHNSON

MSc RESEARCH PROJECT NOTES

RESEARCH PROPOSAL SUBMITTED: Practical Aspects of
Communication in Brain-Damaged Paediatric Patients
RESEARCH SUBJECT: DAVE HEMPSALL (referred to as
Subject X in thesis)
CLINICAL STATUS: refer to confidential medical records
made available by the mother (Gill Hempsall) for the sole
purpose of my research, on condition that the research
subject remains anonymous

NOTE 1: Wednesday, 17 July 2019

Note to self, really.

As I'm doing a research-based master's, I've been advised to start writing my thesis while I'm still conducting
my research.

My supervisor (Dr Josh Simmons, aged around thirty-
five and totally gorg – further note to self: delete this, lol)
also suggested that I keep a detailed log, not just summa-
rising data collated from visits with my subject, but also
of peripheral factors (social setting, family atmosphere,
interfamily relationships, and any other relationships
that might coexist) as this might prove invaluable in con-
textualising my research. He said that although most of it
may ultimately prove to be irrelevant, detailed record-
keeping could help validate my hypothesis, and some of
the minutiae I record may help to underpin my findings.

So, here's my first note: this family is, like, seriously fucking weird.

The father, Roger, arrived to collect me this morning with a right cob on. I was expecting the mother, Gill, to pick me up, and he announced his arrival by sitting in his car outside my house blasting his horn. When I looked through the window to see what the racket was, I noticed someone in a wheelchair in the back of the car and put two and two together.

'You Molly?' he asked, and when I said I was, he told me to get in and hurry up about it cos he'd better things to do than hang around this shithole waiting for his wheels to get nicked. For the record, Ganstead is not a shithole and, as far as I know, no one has ever returned to their car to find it left up on bricks.

So I got in and he drove off, and there was this, like, awkward silence, so I asked him if this was Dave behind us.

'Of course it's Dave,' he replied. 'How many bloody handicapped children do you think I have?'

I couldn't think of a suitable reply, so I said nothing but felt really uncomfortable; then he told me not to expect any conversation from him because his brain was totally fucked. Those were his exact words. No 'Hello, Dave, this is Molly. She's come to help to look after you'. Nothing.

I actually thought about telling him to stop the car and let me out because hostility is the last thing I need right now, but I've left my research really late, and there wouldn't be time to organise another subject.

'I don't know what you imagine you're going to get from researching him, unless the subject of your dissertation is the connection between brain damage and shitting in the bath.'

He laughed at this.

His attitude shocked me. I'd not been expecting this. I had this preconception that all parents with handicapped children were ... I hate to use the word, but 'nice' seems to be a good fit. All the other parents I'd met at the school were supportive of anybody who showed an interest in their child, but my first impressions of Roger

93

were that he was a negative, nasty control freak. I've often received a little more attention from a father than was appropriate; one made a pass at me. But this was worse. I was seriously scared of this man. There was something a bit unbalanced about him.

Anyway, I tried to change the subject and asked him where Mrs Hempsall was.

'Gill? She's gone to see her shrink ... practically lives there. She won't be back until late, so you'll need to deal with Dave because I've got other things to do.'

And that was the end of the conversation.

When we got to the house – a massive, grim-looking place in need of modernisation – I was shown into Dave's bedroom and told to 'do my stuff'. Then, to my surprise, he seemed to mellow slightly, and he showed me into the kitchen and asked if I'd like a coffee.

'I'm sorry we didn't get off to the best of starts,' he said. 'I had some ... well, some bad news this morning. Just before I picked you up, actually.'

I told him it didn't matter and tried to smile at him, which he returned with a sort of weird grimace, almost a leer, and I wondered for a moment if he was about to hit on me.

Thankfully he didn't, but I'd seen enough to conclude that he was someone who has severe mood swings; perhaps *he's* bipolar? Maybe he's the one who should be seeing a shrink – Mrs Hempsall sounded quite normal on the phone.

'Oh, by the way,' he said, 'if you see two little ginger twats hanging around, don't, for Pete's sake, let them anywhere near Dave ... they may offer to take him for a walk or something. They're his brothers – twins, in fact – and all they want to do is to make his life as unpleasant as possible. You probably won't see them, though; they're generally too busy terrorising the neighbours to hang around here much.'

After he showed me where to find Dave's lunch and his nappies, I was left alone with Dave, who was making strange noises as if he was desperately trying to tell me something.

TWENTY-SEVEN

DAVE

I've just met Molly.

If there's one thing I could change about my fucked-up state, it would be to have eyes that work. Although I suppose this would mean that I couldn't be one of the *two* blind journalists who work for the BBC. But as that's never going to happen, I'd rather have eyes that work.

And today is a particularly good example of why I would like to have this.

It's because I overheard earlier that she is really good-looking, and as I don't know exactly what good-looking means, I would like to be able to judge this for myself. I'm guessing here, but I *think* it must be the opposite of bad-looking, which also means ugly. Someone on BBC Radio 4 said that ugly people are not always physically ugly ... like, they've only got one eye or something, or are really fat, or maybe have ginger hair, but their ... what's called 'disposition' can make them ugly. So they can have nice hair and eyes, a short nose, normal-sized ears that don't stick out too much, all of their teeth at the right angles and a mouth that looks okay, but if they don't ever smile and they look miserable all the time, then that makes them less attractive ... maybe even ugly. I think the father must be ugly because I've heard the mother say to a friend on the phone that he's fat, has ginger hair and has become a complete bastard – although I got the impression from other comments that the wind's blown a lot of his hair off by now, so she didn't need to worry too much about him being attractive to other women. In fact, I've heard her say that sometimes she wishes that he was.

And anyway, he always sounds miserable unless he's either winning money or being nasty to people, so he probably looks miserable too. But, as I said, I'm guessing here, and I really, really wish that my eyes worked.

People sometimes go on about beauty, and how looks are dead important, on BBC Radio 4. But there's a programme called *Woman's Hour* – which I really like, by the way – and the presenter, who's called Jenni Murray, is always telling me about how looks are *not* important and how we live in a society that places too much value on how we look. I know people can have something called 'plastic surgery' to get bigger lips and stuff. Actually, I'd quite like to have bigger lips, because I could blow more bubbles with my food and probably make different noises too.

Anyway, back to Molly.

I knew she'd come into my room because two of my senses really do work. I'm talking about my hearing, which I've told you about already, but I also have a fantastic sense of smell. That's not always a good thing either – for reasons I think you can imagine – but on this occasion it was.

She smells terrific.

The mother used to wear nice smells, but she's sort of given up on that unless she's going out, like this morning. I think that – because of stuff the father sometimes says when they're arguing – she used to be really good-looking too, until, the father says, she 'let herself go'. I'm not quite sure what this means, but I don't think it's a good thing because it makes her really mad and she says stuff like 'You can talk ... you fat, balding, ginger wanker'. I've talked about wankers before, but in this instance I don't think she means to tell him how cool he is. The mother's got a really bad temper, and I could tell from the tone of her voice that she wasn't saying good stuff about the father.

Okay ... Molly.

I'm what I think is called 'digressing' because I'm really excited about meeting Molly, and I think this is going to turn a really terrible day into a good one.

At least, I hope so.

TWENTY-EIGHT

MOLLY JOHNSON

MSc RESEARCH PROJECT NOTES
NOTE 2: Wednesday, 17 July 2019

Dave was banging his fists on the arms of his wheelchair in an animated way when I walked in.

He seemed excited, had a big smile on his face and was making noises. Gill had told me about Dave's noises, referring to them as 'his mooing noises'. My initial prognosis is that these represent some form of speech sound disorder. Gill had told me not to read anything into them because they usually meant that he was about to have an epileptic seizure. I'm not so sure I would share that view.

Also, as my research project is on practical aspects of communication, I'd going to disregard this and – until I'm proved wrong – consider these noises and actions as practical aspects of communication, although I'll have to work out what he's trying to communicate.

I'm aware, of course, from the medical notes, that Dave is considered to have no control over movements of his limbs. When he bangs his fists on the wheelchair, this is believed to be an involuntary reaction caused by autonomic neuropathy, which occurs when the nerves that control involuntary bodily functions are damaged. So, for example, if an involuntary muscle seizure results in him placing an arm against a hot radiator, his brain isn't capable of transmitting the signal to retract it because the pain mechanism, which would trigger this reaction in a normally functioning person, doesn't work for

Dave. So in other words, it would appear that he feels no pain.

[Note to self: I know I'll need to google the technical stuff and use the correct clinical terminology to write this up, but these are just my observations, and these notes (well, an edited version) will probably need to be included as an appendix.]

Dave is really small for a guy of his age. According to the notes, he's supposed to be one hundred and sixty-two centimetres, but he doesn't look it; he just looks tiny and a little crumpled in a wheelchair.

I'll also retract this from my notes, but I can't help but notice that he's really good-looking, and although he's small, he doesn't look handicapped at all. He has curly black shoulder-length hair, deep hazel brown eyes, an engaging smile and perfect white teeth. If things had been different, he'd have a queue of girls beating a path to his door.

I introduced myself.

'Hi, handsome, I'm Molly,' I said. 'I've come to entertain you.'

Although there was no discernible response, he continued to bang on his wheelchair and make his noises. Are they meant for me, or as a response to something that's going on in his head that no one else is privy to?

'I'm also here to study you. I'm doing a research project at uni for my master's on practical aspects of communication with guys like you, and I really hope you can help me. How does that sound?'

I'd also decided that until it had been proved to the contrary – which, of course, it could be by lunchtime – I would assume that Dave was capable of understanding everything that was going on around him, and that included linguistic communication. Keep all options open until they're closed, I'd been told.

Dave made some more noises, continued to bang his wheelchair, and then he stopped smiling and went quiet as if he was concentrating really hard on something.

It wasn't long before I realised what it was he was concentrating on.

There was a foul smell in the room. Time for my first poo-clearing action.

'Don't worry, Dave, I'll get you cleaned up in a tick,' I said. 'Then you and I can have a really good chat and get to know each other.'

TWENTY-NINE

DAVE

Shit.

I mean, literally, shit.

The one thing I really wanted not to do was to have a poo the moment she walked in, and that's just what I ended up doing. I think it must have been her smell that did it; I just got too excited.

But she took it really well. I mean, most people say 'for fuck's sake' or something like that when I have a poo, as if I'd actually intended to do it just to annoy them. If you happened to be somebody who cleans toilets for a job, then you'd never stop saying 'for fuck's sake' every time someone came in.

By the way, Sarah – that's my ghostwriter, remember? – says that I shouldn't write so much about poo. But if I'm honest, it's a big part of my life. Anyway, I'll try not to.

So she lifted me on to what the mother calls the changing table and took off my joggers and my shorts and then my nappy. None of the 'carers' that come to help bath me ever lift me cos I think their backs must be weak or something (remember I only weigh six and three-quarter stone) and they use this thing called a hoist which means that I get really cold when I'm taken out of the bath.

Anyway, things were about to get much worse, and when they did, I started to think that maybe today wasn't going to get any better and was just going to end up the way it started, as in being a really terrible day.

What happened was that I got an erection.

Yes, read that again. An. Erection.

This is the only part of my body that I actually feel when it moves, and I have to admit that it does feel really nice and probably puts a smile on my face. Of course, I don't have any control over *when* I get an erection; it just happens ... usually when I'm in the bath and the water's nice and warm.

I know a bit about erections, because one of Jenni Murray's guests once talked about erections on *Woman's Hour* on BBC Radio 4. You need to have an erection in order to do sex to a woman, and your penis – which I know is also called a cock or a dick, and probably other things as well – gets more blood sent down to it when it – this woman said – 'experiences sexual excitement'. The way she said it made me think that this is a really bad thing, so I always feel guilty when I get an erection. I don't know what sexual excitement is because that's never happened to me, and, as I've already said, when I get excited I usually have a poo, not an erection.

But this morning I had both, and that's why I felt sure that today was going to be a terrible day.

But she didn't seem to mind at all.

In fact, she just laughed and she seemed to do it in a way so that I didn't feel guilty, and this made me feel how much I liked her already and that today might be a really good day after all.

THIRTY

MOLLY JOHNSON

MSc RESEARCH PROJECT NOTES
NOTE 3: Tuesday, 23 July 2019

It's almost a week since I started to work with Dave.

This is how I proceeded to work with him.

As an OT working with a patient with minor disability, I would normally begin by conducting an in-home assessment to create a safe living environment. I can see there already is one here. Well ... safeish, anyway – I'm not sure about Roger, and Dave's siblings. My goal would then be to help the patient with everyday tasks such as getting dressed, moving around the house, cooking, eating, gardening, doing school work, using a computer, and even driving.

With a severely disabled patient – such as Dave clearly is – my goals are not so clear. 'Normally' isn't going to happen here.

To go by the book, I would observe patients doing tasks, ask the patient questions, and review the patient's medical history. Dave is incapable of performing even the most basic of tasks, so we can forget all of the above-mentioned.

Next, I would use these observations, answers and medical history to evaluate the patient's condition and needs. I've read through Dave's extensive medical notes and they are pretty bleak. However, due to a long-established, thorough and effective physical and occupational therapy regime, largely delivered through his school, patterns of progressive physical deterioration normally prevalent in quadriplegic brain-damaged patients are absent. Put in simple English, there is no evidence, either from my brief and superficial physical appraisal, or from official and comprehensive biannual medical assessments, that Dave's physical condition is getting worse. His programme is therefore working.

So that's the first positive.

On the negative side, Dave is severely brain-damaged, and it would appear that irreversible damage has been caused. However, it's worth mentioning that the North-Eastern Health Authority had recently admitted medical negligence in the form of a failure to provide a duty of care, causing Dave to stop breathing. This ruling has no bearing on Dave's physical condition, but at least it explains how it happened.

The other positive is that the court – or more likely an agreement reached between the lawyers – is likely to decide that Dave's vegetative state is permanent, and therefore the damages he will receive will not only compensate him for what the NEHA took away from him (actually, his life) but also ensure that he will receive the best possible care and therapy for the rest of his life.

But as I'm not here in the official capacity of an OT, my observations are purely to benchmark Dave's physical condition and to situate my postgrad research.

My research is concerned only with practical aspects of communication, and from my discussions with Dave's mother (okay, that was just over the phone) and his teacher, classroom assistant and the carers at the respite centre he stays at when the family can get a place, Dave is incapable of even basic communication.

[Note to self: this cannot be right. If it is, then what am I doing here? Because I'm not going to get sufficient data for my project – fuck it, I'm not going to get *any* data for my project. I need to look harder, much harder.]

Okay, deep breath … let's not be neggers here; let's start with what we've got.

Dave's just had a poo. The next time he has one, I'll know what's coming by his silence and how he concentrates on it. That's communication, isn't it?

Does it have to be verbal? No.

Does it have to be intentional? Probably not, although he may have been trying to warn me that he was about to have a shit, for all I know. So the next time he does this, I'll give him some privacy and spray a bit of air freshener around in anticipation.

'Okay,' I said, 'I'm going to nip out to make a coffee, Dave. I'll give you some water when I come back.'

No response. I squeezed his forearm.

'I'll be back in a minute.' This will be my way of telling him that I'm either leaving or have entered the room. I don't know what his hearing is like, so this is belt and braces; although, from his notes, his hearing is supposed to be pretty good. It's just that the perceived wisdom is that he can't understand anything he hears.

I went to the kitchen and made a coffee.

There was a strange sort of snoring noise coming from under the kitchen table. For a second I thought it might be Roger, but when I looked below, I saw a large jet-black dog sending me mixed messages by wagging its tail and growling at the same time.

I like dogs, so I cautiously offered him the back of my hand, which he licked. I went to stroke his head, but he started growling again, so I thought better of it, picked up my coffee and took it back to Dave's room. As I entered the room, I noticed the dog had followed me, and before I could close the door on him he'd sidled past me with more agility than his frame would suggest and had parked himself beside Dave's wheelchair, head tilted to one side, one ear cocked, the other down in typical mongrel style. If I had to take a stab at his ancestry, I'd say collie (mutts usually are)-slash-Alsatian with a dollop of setter thrown in. Actually, although he smelt a bit, he's a nice-looking dog and, to judge by his proximity to Dave ... maybe I'm reading too much into this, but they look as if maybe they share a sort of bond. Maybe it's his smell, lol! Dave definitely knew he was there because he started banging his fists again, and I've worked out that this is how he shows excitement when someone comes into his room. First it was me, and then it was the dog. So ...

wristbanging is a form of expression, but can it be classed as communication? I'll need to ask Dr Josh that.

I sat down in an uncomfortable armchair opposite Dave, sipped my coffee and studied the pair of them.

Water. I'd said I'd give him some water.

I was about to get up and fetch his plastic beaker when something really weird happened.

At first I thought I'd imagined it. But then it happened again.

And this was when I knew I didn't need to worry about lack of data for my thesis.

This was such a breakthrough moment that I hadn't even realised I'd dropped my coffee until the hot liquid started to burn through my jeans.

I knew exactly how I was going to communicate with Dave.

Unless I'd got this wrong, Dave could understand absolutely everything.

And if I'd got this right, why the fuck was I the first person to pick up on the fact that he has locked-in syndrome?

THIRTY-ONE

DAVE

Molly's let Scooter into my room.

I can smell him.

I like Scooter, but he's not allowed into my room because he tries to eat everything and once he ate one of my nappies before the mother could get rid of it. She got really mad with him – I've told you that she has a bad temper – but in this case, I didn't blame her because right after he'd eaten it, he licked me on the mouth, which was actually pretty gross. It tasted even worse than Ready Brek. But I've forgiven him now, and I'll tell you why in a minute.

I once heard a play on BBC Radio 4 about someone who was left on a desert island and he wrote a message, put it into a bottle and threw it out to sea.

Some time later – it didn't say how long – someone in a ship found it and came to rescue him.

It was obviously a made-up story because a) where would the person on the island have found paper (it would need to be dry) and a pen? When I'm at school, my teacher often can't find paper and a pen if she needs to write a note to send home with me, so I don't think this would be something that you would find on a desert island. But I could very well be wrong because I've never been to a desert island. There's a programme on BBC Radio 4 called *Desert Island Discs* and I've never heard of anyone having a pen and paper there. All they have are some records, the entire works of William Shakespeare –

who wrote plays, and most of them are quite boring – and a copy of the Bible.

Also, b) how did the person on the ship find the bottle? I know that ships are huge things, so there would be very little chance that anyone on the ship would notice a bottle floating on the water. There are other things wrong with the story, but sometimes if you take everything out of a story that you don't believe then it's not worth listening to.

So what has this got to do with me?

This is what it's got to do with me: I decided to send Molly a message in a bottle.

Not, of course, an actual message in a bottle but what I think is called a metaphorical one.

Today got off to a terrible start, although I believe, like the father, my luck has changed; but, unlike the father, mine has changed in a good way.

My first piece of luck was that Molly came here to study how I communicate. Everyone else in the world – well, everyone I've met anyway – thinks that I can't communicate and that's because my brain is fucked. But, as you know by now, it isn't. And I *can* communicate; it's just that no one can understand what I'm saying. I once heard someone on BBC Radio 4 talking about communication and I remember that he said communication was the 'exchanging of information by speaking, writing, or using some other medium.' Okay, you could argue that when I make my noises, there's not much of an exchange of information happening. To be honest, maybe there's none at all. But that doesn't stop me from trying. Maybe it's because I'm using what he called 'some other medium'?

But you don't give up, do you, just because no one understands you? If that were the case, Donald Trump would have stopped talking on the radio ages ago.

And this man went on to say that 'television is an effective means of communication', and I happen to know – well, okay, I got this from the father so it may not be right – that most people who watch a documentary or an arts or scientific programme on television are too stupid to understand it. So, if this is the case, then television isn't an effective means of communication at all.

But this man on the BBC Radio 4 programme also talked about something called 'non-verbal communication', and that means you can communicate without using actual words. That's what I've been working on and what I'm going to tell you about in a minute.

And the second piece of luck was that Molly let Scooter into my room.

Scooter is the bottle I'm going to put my message in.

And if Molly is as clever as I think she is – because she's interested enough in communication to do a degree in it, and also because she's shown more of an interest in me than anybody has done for ages so I really like her already – then my bottle will find a way to get to her.

She's going to read the message.

And then she's going to save me.

PART TWO

THE ACCIDENT

THIRTY-TWO

MOLLY JOHNSON

MSc RESEARCH PROJECT NOTES
NOTE 4: Tuesday, 23 July 2019

When I looked back on what happened that day, after Gill had taken me home, I felt exhilarated, but I also felt a huge burden of responsibility. And perhaps some guilt for what I'd done.

To be accurate, it was what I'd *not* done.

The first thing I did was to go up to my room and write up my notes. I'd taken brief notes throughout the day at every opportunity but, because things happened so quickly, I wanted to be sure that I'd got it right. And although my notes are supposed to be objective and focused on my research, I have a feeling that working with Dave is going to lead to more than a decent thesis. Who knows, there may even be a book in it, lol, so I'm going to keep a record of absolutely everything I think may be even remotely relevant to Dave's situation. And, because there's also the possibility that I may need to stand up and defend myself in court, it's important that I document everything; not only events, but also who said what and when.

So what *did* happen?

Okay ... back to Dave's room, where yesterday I'd made my discovery.

It was near lunchtime, and I was about to give Dave a drink when I saw it.

At first I thought I'd imagined it, but when he did it a second time and then a third, I knew that this was no co-incidence. Dave was trying to tell me something.

First, he rolled his head to the left, made a long, steady noise – one I'd not heard him make before – and then his right eye focused directly on the dog and he blinked three times, slowly and deliberately. This was no seizure; he was doing this intentionally. I knew that he was able to turn his head to the direction of sound, so this was nothing new.

Then the dog stood up, walked to the left of his wheelchair and slowly sat down.

And a minute or so later, Dave rotated his head again so that his right ear was close to his right shoulder, then appeared to be looking at the dog, and he blinked slowly and deliberately; again, three times with his right eye. The dog got up, returned to Dave's right, and sat down.

This routine was repeated twice more, and on each occasion the dog responded to Dave's head movement and eye blinking.

This can't be the first time he's done this. How the hell had nobody noticed this before?

Dave looked shattered, as if what he'd just done had taken a huge physical effort. Maybe it had.

I needed a second or two to think how best to follow this up. I needed to respond convincingly to let Dave know I understood what he was telling me.

'I'm going to give you a drink now, Dave. Would you like a drink?' No response; I wasn't expecting one. I gave him a drink and sat down again.

'Dave,' I said, 'I want you to listen to me very care-fully.' My heart was beating fast. If this didn't work, then maybe I *had* read too much into what had just happened.

I spoke really slowly and clearly.

'Can you understand what I'm saying, Dave? If you can, I'd like you to blink your right eye twice, please.' I was so excited that I almost told him to blink three times if he couldn't understand me, but that would have been stupid.

For a few seconds, nothing happened.

And then he blinked, slowly and purposely, just as he'd done for the dog.

And after he'd blinked for a second time, there was this huge smile on his face, a smile that I felt certain was no fit, no seizure, no random episode going on inside a brain that didn't work.

No, this was a smile because he was pleased with himself.

THIRTY-THREE

DAVE

She got it!

Molly got my message in the bottle – halle-fucking-lujah!

It's only taken, like, eighteen years for someone to work out that there's nothing actually wrong with my brain?

As you may well understand, I don't think very much of the people whose job it was to make me better, or the people whose job it is to care for me since the people whose job it was to make me better fucked me up in the first place.

The people whose job it is to care for me – let's call them 'damage managers' and not 'carers' because their job isn't to care about how I got to be damaged; their job is to push food into me, wipe my arse, bath me, drink coffee and talk about sex with other 'damage managers' after they've stuck me in front of a video on comparative religion. Or something.

I know I sound bitter, and I shouldn't sound bitter because someone has finally understood that I am not a vegetable, and this is going to change my life.

I should be happy ... and I *am* happy, but remember I talked about bittersweet? This is also a good example of something that's bittersweet. This is what I think is called a cliché, but I'm never going to get all those years back, am I?

Anyway, I don't know how I knew, but I just felt certain that Molly coming here would be the most fantastic thing that's ever happened to me.

But I should point out that not much has happened to me that I would call fantastic.

THIRTY-FOUR

ROGER

Roger's morning had been spent in a desperate search for liquidity.

A path which had finally led him to the one place he knew he should never visit, Gill's jewellery box.

Having exhausted all other avenues, by one o'clock he had amassed the sum of nine hundred and thirty-seven pounds and twenty-five pence. And this was about two grand short of the three thousand he intended to stick on Kaila's Daughter's nose in the 2.20 at Haydock.

Someone, whom you might describe as 'the horse's mouth' – a person whose infrequent tips had always been on the money in the past – had told him that Kaila's Daughter should really be the odds-on favourite. No doubt about it. But because, he'd said, of some dubious jiggery-pokery instigated by his trainer, which Roger didn't understand nor frankly give a flying fuck about so long as it won, it was likely to go under starter's orders at around ten to one.

With a stake of three big ones, Roger stood to trouser around thirty-k, and this would give him the breathing space he required, hopefully, until the Dave money rolled in.

Of course, the simple thing would have been to 'borrow' the money from the joint account. After all, he was intending to return it – with considerable interest – in around three hours' time. But on the off chance that Gill decided to check their balance, he would be rumbled. A

118

plausible explanation would be required and he couldn't think of one.

But to 'borrow' Gill's Van Cleef & Arpels Sweet Alhambra ruby and diamond-encrusted effeuillage ring – a ring she had inherited from her mother, and a ring that Roger had hocked at the pawnbroker's once before – and to replace it after Kaila's Daughter had strutted her stuff, would once again be a crime undetected. No harm done.

So, following a drive into Hull to visit the premises of Pledge Pawnbrokers, Jewellers & Body Piercing, Roger walked across the road to the bookies' and stuck three grand on Kaila's Daughter. This left him with around a grand burning a hole in his pocket, but providence had earlier intervened, and thus, he had been precluded from any further losses at the casino.

He drove home, poked his head around Dave's door – mainly just to ensure that Molly was still with him – then found the twins and made lunch. In all honesty, he felt a little apprehensive, but as there were only six horses in the race and he'd been assured that one would be withdrawn prior to the off, and four of the remaining five were rank no-hopers whose greatest achievement in any race thus far had been to finish, Roger extracted the burnt cheese on toast from the grill and tried to relax. What was the worst that could go wrong? That didn't even bear thinking about.

'That looks gross,' said Boris. 'Pass the taste, will you?'

'Please?' replied Roger. 'If by "taste" you're referring to the Lea & Perrins, you can reach it yourself.'

Boris grabbed the sauce bottle, poured a lake of the black liquid over the incinerated cheese and forked a mouthful.

'Ugh … It's. Still. Fucking. Gross.'

'What have I told you about using that kind of language, Boris?' Roger asked calmly. Maybe playground robustness had been achieved, but he dearly wished he could flick a switch and turn the twins into normal human beings when they were at home.

'That's rich coming from you, Rog,' Boris replied.

Molly entered the kitchen pushing Dave in his wheel-chair, interrupting Roger's negative thoughts about his progeny, and started to prepare his lunch.

'Guys, this is Molly. Molly, this is Axel ... and this is Boris,' Roger gestured at each as he introduced them.

'Hi, Molly,' said Axel, 'want some burnt cheese on toast? Dave could cook better than Roger.'

'And we all know how fucked he is.'

'Boris. Do *not* use bad language. Especially in front of our guest.'

'Guest? I thought she was just here to wipe his arse.' Molly looked as if she might reply, but before she could, he continued. 'You've got nice tits, by the way.'

'That's it, Boris, that is it! I've had just about enough of your disrespect and insolence. Go to your room. Now!'

There was silence around the kitchen island where Roger and the twins sat. Tumbleweed or even a herd of wildebeest could have swept through the room, majesti-cally or otherwise, and no one would have budged or even noticed.

Hillcrest's kitchen, with its antique oil-burning Aga and units so old as to look fashionably distressed, was the one room in the house that could justifiably be de-scribed as homely. Today, as was not uncommon on an occasional glorious summer's day, bright sunlight sof-tened the room through ceiling-to-unit sash windows that framed a view of the garden, the path leading down to the tennis court, and the unspoilt countryside that lay beyond the curtilage of the property.

No one moved. No one spoke. An air of tension per-meated the room as Boris stared at Roger, holding his gaze, challenging him. Time passed ... twenty, thirty sec-onds, then he averted his eyes, smiled and turned to-wards Molly.

'I'm sorry, Molly. That was rude. I really don't know what came over me.'

Molly returned his smile, a little uncertainly.

'It's all right, Boris. I've had worse comments hurled at me.' She looked at Roger questioningly. He shrugged. The moment passed.

'Who fancies a game of tennis this afternoon?' asked Roger.

'The post that holds the net's busted,' said Boris.

'And how did that happen?'

'Dunno ... must have just fell out.'

'Must have just *fallen* out, Boris.' Roger sensed that Boris knew rather more about the demise of the post than he was prepared to disclose, but he also knew that pursuing this information would be a waste of time.

'Yeah, whatever. Anyway, we need something to fix the net to. I know! We can tie it to Dave's wheelchair. It's got a brake on it so it won't go nowhere. Sorted!'

Axel got up and tipped his lunch into the bin, clicked the kettle on and fetched a Pot Noodle from a cupboard. 'Anyone else want one?'

'Yeah, me, bruv,' Boris said. 'Sounds like a solution. What d'you think, Rog?' Roger's thoughts were solely focused on the 2.20 at Haydock.

'Hmmm? Yeah, okay, maybe not a bad idea ... as you said, sounds like a solution. Dave could do with some fresh air anyway, couldn't he, Molly?'

THIRTY-FIVE

ROGER

Roger had once been a competent tennis player.

Perhaps more than competent; he had represented the university tennis team, and this despite the fact that most of the students who played sport at Borough Road were studying for a certificate in physical education and, therefore – to Roger's mind at least – were like performing dogs: short on brain but high in physical prowess, acumen and the ability to catch, fetch and juggle balls.

Even back then, Roger had been one of a dying breed whose quintessentially middle-class English values dictated that he wore white to play. If the first rule for Wimbledon tennis players was that their outfit must be 'suitable tennis attire that is almost entirely white', the same should apply to anyone else who took to a court ... or such was Roger's view.

So after lunch, Roger trundled upstairs to change.

It had been a while since he'd played tennis, and the sole reason for his sudden urge to take to the court was that it seemed as good an occupation as any to take his mind off his impending situation.

It had also been a while since Roger had participated in any sort of physical activity, and to his horror he found that both his Fred Perry shirt and his Fila Bjorn Borg shorts no longer fitted. The shorts, which he had purchased in the early nineties, were of the variety that was fastened by a metal clasp and a zip. He found the hook would no longer dock with the bar ... not even close; therefore, he had no option other than to wear a belt, and

thankfully he'd had the foresight to buy a pair of shorts –
all the rage in the nineties, he remembered – which had
belt loops.

His next challenge was to find his tennis racket.

The garage seemed like a good place to start – this
was where Gill stored anything she considered no longer
to be of use or value.

Roger disliked visiting the garage because it reminded him of happier times when it housed exotic machinery and not junk. Well, it won't be for long, he
thought, almost salivating at the thought of how much
money Mr Charles Cuerliez would sign the (Dave's)
cheque for.

The garage was now home to an assortment of discarded children's toys, broken garden machinery, a collection of rarely used garden furniture, and a box of an-
tique-looking sports equipment on top of which sat
Roger's trusty Dunlop Power Master.

Roger took the racket from its cover and performed
a few swatting D'Artagnan-style swishes. Satisfied that
he still 'had it', he rolled his shoulders, jogged on the spot
momentarily and then set off in the direction of the tennis court.

THIRTY-SIX

MOLLY JOHNSON

MSc RESEARCH PROJECT NOTES
NOTE 5: Wednesday, 24 July 2019

Because of what happened today, I think it's important that I keep a record of this.

I was in the kitchen eating a sandwich when the house phone rang.

I thought about answering it but decided I didn't like this family anywhere near enough to take a message for them.

In fact, if it hadn't been for my breakthrough moment before lunch, I'd have called a taxi and be gone by now, data or no data.

I couldn't believe Roger had actually agreed to allow the tennis net to be tied to Dave's wheelchair. I mean, what would happen, I'd asked him, if someone hits the ball really hard into the net? Wouldn't it pull his wheelchair over?

'He'll be fine,' he'd replied. 'We'll stick a couple of breezeblocks either side of it to anchor him.'

Terrific.

Roger went to change, and as he wouldn't let the twins anywhere near Dave on their own – note to self: they really are two totally overindulged, odious, foulmouthed little whingers – I'd been instructed to wheel him down to the tennis court and wait for Roger to arrive.

A few moments later, Roger appeared wearing what looked like vintage tennis clothes that were way too small for him, and this ridiculous white headband. I seriously thought he was, like, going to a fancy-dress party. It was all I could do not to laugh, especially when the twins started to take the piss. Twats or not, it was quite funny.

'Fuck me,' said Boris. 'Look who it is, Axel. Isn't that a fat Roger Federer in drag?'

'Nah, it's that guy from the eighties ... what was he called? Bjorn Pork.'

'That's not funny, you two,' Roger replied, 'and what did I say about swearing, Boris, hmmm? Anyway, we'll see if you still think it's funny when I've given the pair of you a damned good thrashing.'

'Try that, Rog, and we'll be straight on the phone to Childline.'

Roger grabbed the end of the net cord, looped it behind Dave's back through the arms on his chair, tied it in a knot and placed a large breezeblock on either side of each wheel. He then shook the chair and turned to me.

'There ... that's pretty secure.' He tugged the net, and to my surprise, the wheelchair didn't move. Nor did Dave. 'Happy now?' No need for you to stay now, he's not going anywhere.'

I shrugged and walked back up to the house.

'Come and get him in an hour, will you?' Roger shouted after me.

I'd just made a coffee to replace the one I'd thrown over myself earlier when the phone rang again. Again, I ignored it.

I heard the sound of someone running up the path, and Boris burst into the kitchen, out of breath.

'Didn't you hear the fucking phone ring, Molly?'

'I'm not here to answer the fucking phone, Boris.' I replied. There – have some of your own medicine, you little shit. He didn't flinch.

'You'd better come down to the tennis court. And Roger says to tell you to bring a first aid kit. There's been an accident.'

'Dave?'

'Yeah, his wheelchair got pulled over and he's banged his head. There's blood everywhere. And I think he's out cold.'

Of course he hadn't a clue where the first aid kit was, but I guessed lucky, grabbed it from the second cupboard I opened, picked up my phone and ran towards the door, Boris behind me.

'What happened?'

'We'd just finished a game, and Roger made this phone call. I don't think it was good news cos he totally lost it and threw his phone down, then smashed a ball as hard as he could. I don't think he meant to hit Dave, but he did, and it knocked his Timmy-wagon over. He banged his head on this concrete block, and I think Roger's phone's fucked. Axel rang you on his phone, but you didn't answer, so I had to get you.'

By this time we'd reached the court, and I could see Dave lying beside his upturned wheelchair. Boris was right; he was out cold and there was a lake of blood on the breezeblock he must have collided with, and blood still pouring from a nasty-looking gash near his temple.

'How about someone helps him up?' I asked.

'How about someone calls, like, an ambulance?' Axel said, and actually looked quite worried.

'Axel, help me lift him into his wheelchair, will you?' He did, and I examined the wound. 'This needs urgent attention, Roger. Axel's right: call an ambulance.'

'No ... he'll be fine,' he replied and fiddled with his phone. 'Just take him back to the house and clean it up, will you? It was your fault anyway.'

'*My* fault?'

'Yes, your fault. You're in charge of him today,' he said, looking at me in what I would call an intimidating manner. 'And if you'd bothered to check the straps on his chair, you'd have noticed they were too loose. That's why he fell out.'

'No, Roger,' I told him, 'he fell out because *you* hit him on the head with a tennis ball, hard enough to knock his wheelchair over.' I felt my resentment rise; I was not having this. 'And can I remind you that it was your idea to tie the net to the wheelchair, despite my concern? You're supposed to be his parent, so you're in charge. Don't blame me for something you're clearly responsible for.' I was really angry now. I got out a dressing, pressed it to the wound and started to stem the flow of blood. Dave showed no signs of regaining consciousness.

'I'm going to ring Gill,' I said and scrolled through my recent calls looking for her number.

'No, you're not. You're going to take him up to the house, dress that wound and give him a drink. Like I said, he'll be fine in a few minutes.'

'He needs to go to hospital, Dad,' Axel said, a little uncertainly. 'Please let her ring Mum. She'll know what to do.'

I found the number and pressed the call button.

'Give me that fucking phone.' Roger lunged at me, but I easily sidestepped him.

'So look who's using bad language now, Rog?' said Boris, with a sardonic laugh.

Gill answered on the third ring. I told her, omitting most of the reasons for the accident and her husband's irrational reaction.

She took it quite calmly.

'Okay, tell Roger to get him into the car and take him to Hull Royal Infirmary. I'll call Dr Sullivan, tell her what happened and ask her to have someone standing by who knows Dave. On second thoughts, put Roger on. I'll tell him myself.'

I passed my phone reluctantly to Roger. He listened for a few moments that seemed to last for ages, grunted, then passed the phone back to me.

'Hey! I almost forgot,' said Boris. 'Did anyone hear him say "fuck" when the ball hit him? I'm flippin' sure he said "fuck". Either that, or his wheelchair said "fuck", but something definitely said "fuck" because I definitely fuckin' heard it.'

'Don't be ridiculous, Boris, and stop swearing, will you? There's as much chance of Dave saying anything, let alone "fuck", as there is of that tennis ball reciting the entire works of William Shakespeare.'

I could see the fight had been drained from Roger, and a shroud of resignation had replaced his anger and aggression towards me. Maybe Gill had some hold over him, and I was pleased with myself for calling her. It had at least moved things on a bit. There was absolutely no doubt that Dave needed urgent medical attention.

'Molly,' he said, turning on the charm as if his eccentric behaviour of the last five minutes hadn't happened, 'could you help us get him to the hospital, please?'

'Of course,' I replied, with a forced smile. But why not try to lighten the mood? 'You might want to go and change quickly?' I suggested. 'We wouldn't want anyone to mistake you for Bjorn Pork again, would we?'

PART THREE

AFTER
THE ACCIDENT

THIRTY-SEVEN

GILL

DIARY ENTRY: Wednesday, 24 July 2019

I'd just taken a first sip of Chablis when my phone rang.

I'd managed to get Roger to collect Molly again this morning. And not only that, he'd even offered to take charge of Dave, provided that Molly looked after him. He's definitely up to something. Who cares, if it meant I could escape for the day?

It was Molly.

What the hell can she want?

I scrolled through the list of possibilities in my mind: A) something's happened to Dave. Could Roger not deal with this? No, probably not. B) Something's happened to one – or both – of the twins that Roger doesn't know about. C) Maybe the twins have killed Roger? No ... that would be too good to be true. D) More likely there's been a complaint from one of the neighbours about the twins and Roger's gone walkabout.

'I have to answer this.' I smiled at Ali. 'I'll be as quick as I can.'

'Take your time, darling. I've got a couple of calls I need to make myself.'

Ali is Martin's practice partner. I fell in love with her the moment I saw her, and we've been having an affair for over three months now. I know Roger possibly thinks I'm having an affair with Martin, which is amusing in a way because – despite how I've benefitted from seeing him – Martin is almost as unattractive and as unkempt as Roger.

He'll absolutely flip when I tell him I'm leaving him, of course, but the fact that my lover's a woman and not another man will probably cushion the blow a little. Not that he'll be that bothered. All he seems to be interested in is money, and when Dave's compensation finally comes through, that will cushion the blow even more. But I'm not going to leave him yet. I need to find a permanent home for Dave and make sure he's settled and has everything he needs, and once that happens it'll be the end of my responsibility.

Time for me.

It'll take two, maybe three years to reach this point, and by then the twins will be around sixteen. I'll probably wait until after they've sat their GCSEs, but who knows? Of course, this is a long way away, and anything could happen before then. I'm not acting like a love-struck teenager; I know I have responsibilities, because, as I've said, I bear a burden of guilt for what happened to Dave. Maybe I've been encouraged to bear it, but that doesn't make it any easier.

I've talked to Ali about this, and she's fine with it.

'There's no hurry, darling,' she'd said. 'We have forever, so what's important is leaving when you feel the time is right.'

We don't have forever, of course. Who does?

Ali is the most remarkable person I've ever met. She's not what you might call classically beautiful, at least not in a conventional way, but she has this amazing aura ... a confidence she derives from her self-belief, inner strength and all the qualities that have driven her to succeed in everything she's done.

She's tall – much taller than me – slim, with an athletically toned body, and everything about her physical presence bears evidence of thoughtful but not excessive or overindulgent maintenance. Her eyes are a glimmering emerald shade of green; full and sensual lips frame a slightly small mouth beneath a short nose, curved gently in profile. She wears her brown, slightly wavy hair short but it's not blokeish – I know it's silly to say it, but there's nothing about her that suggests she's gay. She's not girly in any significant way either, but I've noted how men

132

look at her with unmistakable desire. She looks different, and that difference marks her out as a very attractive woman. I know looks shouldn't be that important, but they are, aren't they? And her looks, coupled with her aura, were why I fell in love with her.

In addition to being a top psychotherapist who has published several well-received clinical books, she also played cricket for England, runs marathons and rides horses – and not as a happy hacker – in her spare time.

At first I worried that having a relationship with her would cause some sort of ethical issue that could compromise her career because I was her practice partner's patient, but she reassured me that we were doing nothing wrong.

No one knows, in any case, and that's the way I intend it to stay – until I leave Roger, of course, and then I won't care who knows.

Anyway, I stood by the entrance to The George, lit a cigarette and called Molly.

I listened to what she had to say with a sense of foreboding and anger. If Dave was unconscious, how the *fuck* could Roger be so ... I don't know, so callous as to suggest he'll just come round, have a drink of water and be okay?

I told Molly to put him on the phone.

'First of all, why is Molly taking responsibility for our ... for your son?'

He told me that his phone seemed to have stopped working, so he asked her to call me on hers. And that was complete nonsense, he said ... what she said about him saying that Dave would come round and be fine. Of course, he was going to get him checked out.

I just felt the anger boil up inside me.

God, how I'm beginning to detest this man.

'Listen to me, Roger. I'm going to call Dr Sullivan.' Of course, he didn't have a clue who Dr Sullivan was. I told him. 'And I'm going to ask her to try to have a paediatric neurologist standing by at Hull Royal Infirmary and ask her to be there too. Just drive him to the hospital and I'll handle the rest. Do you think you're capable of that, or is it too much to ask?'

He said he could handle it.

Saving Dave

'And one more thing, Roger. If anything happens to Dave, I'm going to stand up in court, at the hearing where the compensation figure will be decided, and cite your neglect as a reason why you shouldn't receive a penny.'

I rang off, gave my apologies to Ali, got into the car and sat for a moment crying tears of pure anger and frustration.

Then I started the engine and drove towards the hospital.

Richard Grainger

THIRTY-EIGHT

MOLLY JOHNSON

MSc RESEARCH PROJECT NOTES
NOTE 6: Wednesday, 24 July 2019

[Okay, I'm putting this in my notes because, although it has nothing directly to do with my project, what happened next was seriously fucking strange, and this whole situation is starting to freak me out a little. Maybe I should just rethink my project? But knowing what I know already, it's just too good to chuck away.]

We were sitting outside the Neurology department on the fourth floor.

The room was too warm; it was a hot day and the Hull Royal Infirmary's budget didn't stretch to air conditioning.

Gill said something I didn't quite catch ... something about me being to blame?

She spoke quietly, although there was hardly anyone in the waiting room, so I asked her to repeat.

'If you'd just fucking well looked after him, this would never have happened ... just done what you were asked to do.'

That I heard.

First Roger, whose accusation I'd not taken seriously because this was clearly his fault and he'd only had a go at me because something else was eating him, but now Gill? This was the last thing I'd expected.

'I'm sorry, what ... what are you trying to say, Gill?'

135

'I'm not trying to say anything, Molly. You're a fucking OT, for God's sake. Do you think it's okay to allow your patients to be tied up to tennis net cords?'

I couldn't believe this. She'd seemed so nice, so calm, so understanding, when she'd arrived. There was nothing to suggest I was going to be subjected to this tirade of accusation. This must have come from Roger – he probably suggested it was all my idea.

'Is this how you treat all your patients, Molly? You were asked to look after Dave for the day – for one day ... not to skulk back up to the house after leaving him in what any right-minded person – let alone a qualified OT – would clearly see was a precarious and vulnerable situation. I mean, are you stupid, or what?'

She had a point. But I wasn't going to just sit here and take this.

'Look, Gill, I'm really sorry about what's happened. But I told Roger that I didn't think it was a good idea, and he's Dave's father. My job isn't to intervene between a parent and their child—'

'Oh, it isn't, is it? So I suppose if he'd got a machete out and started chopping off Dave's limbs, you wouldn't have interfered either?'

Actually, I didn't know what I would have done in that situation ... probably run a mile, but I suppose she was right. We react in different ways, don't we, depending on our prejudices. [Note to self: delete this later. But I admit that I would have probably approached the situation differently if I'd been visiting a chav family in Myton and not a middle-class, professional family with a big house in a posh village. Although I doubt if they'd have been playing tennis in Myton.]

'We'll see what your superiors think about this when I make a formal complaint. Because you can bet your arse – whatever Dave's outcome – I'm going to make sure you never work in occupational therapy again.'

Silence.

Through the haze of emotion and confusion in my brain, I heard someone call Gill's name ... softly at first, then more urgently.

'Mrs Hempsall ... Mrs Gill Hempsall, can you come through, please? Mr Patel would like to speak to you.'

I felt a firm hand grip my thigh, and then the hand was beneath my chin, gently lifting it, and I turned my head to find myself looking into Gill's eyes. She was smiling. There was no anger in her eyes. Either it was gone or—

'You nodded off, didn't you, Molly? Don't blame you, it's hot in here and you must have had a really traumatic day.' I tried to return her smile, but all I felt was this enormous sense of relief. 'Come on, let's go and hear what he has to say.'

She squeezed my hand gently.

'Don't worry, this wasn't your fault. If anyone's to blame, it's that moron of a husband of mine. He's never had any time for Dave.'

But the thing is ... and the reason that I've written this is because I *am* starting to question if I'm the one to blame.

THIRTY-NINE

GILL

DIARY ENTRY: Wednesday, 24 July 2019

I checked my phone when I arrived at the hospital and found a text from Dr Sullivan telling me to go straight up to the Neurology department on the fourth floor.

She was there to meet me and told me that Dave's wound had been treated and that he was waiting for a CT scan to see if there was a need for surgical intervention.

My blood froze at the mention of surgical intervention, but then the thought struck me – ridiculous as it may seem – surely if they did find that he'd suffered a traumatic brain injury or TBI, it couldn't make things any worse, could it?

I told Roger to go home, because it was clear he didn't want to be here and he was about as much use as ... I don't know ... let's just say as much use as Roger ever was. He might as well go back and police the twins. God knows what havoc they'll have wreaked in his absence.

That left Molly and me sitting in the waiting room. After a few pleasantries, we fell into an awkward silence and she dozed off. It was hot and clammy, but nervous anticipation kept me awake.

She's an incredibly beautiful young woman, Molly ... even more striking than her photo on the board at Dave's school had suggested. And as she slept, her head drifted on to my shoulder. I left it there.

I suppose we were lucky because Mr Patel holds a specialist MDT complex spinal clinic twice a month, and today happened to coincide with one of these. I'd not worked with Mr Patel, but I'd heard of him; he was considered to be the top neurologist in the North East. So if shit had to happen, at least it had happened in the right place.

We were ushered into his consulting room. He looked up from his notes and smiled at me.

'Mrs Hempsall—'

'Gill.'

'Gill.' He laced his fingers together and leant forward. I recognised this as an 'I'm giving you my full attention, so this is fucking serious' mode of non-verbal communication; I'd witnessed it scores of times.

'Dave has suffered a severe traumatic brain injury.'

My worst fears confirmed. If he'd been a vegetable before today, what was he going to be like now? A super vegetable? Stupid thoughts ran through my brain, so stupid that I almost laughed.

'We've conducted a CT scan, and it has revealed that the incident has resulted in a haematoma ... an epidural haematoma, which, along with the cerebral oedema, must be removed as quickly as possible.' He paused, presumably for me to comment, to ask questions. I had none, except how the fuck can I be going through this again? This was a question he couldn't answer. 'Are you aware as to what an epidural haematoma is?' I nodded. He ignored this and told me anyway. 'An epidural haematoma is when bleeding occurs between the tough outer membrane covering the brain – the dura mater, it's called – and the skull. Often there is a loss of consciousness following a head injury, as was the case with Dave, and I believe he briefly regained consciousness and then lost it again. This is concurrent with the symptoms of an epidural haematoma and confirms what the scan has told us.'

After a lengthy silence, I asked, 'What happens now?'

'The haematoma requires an emergency surgical evacuation, Gill. If it is performed as soon as possible, there is a significant chance there will be no permanent brain damage.'

Again, I almost laughed.

139

'No permanent brain damage to be added to the permanent brain damage Dave already suffers from?'

He didn't reply to this. Why would he? But there was something else. I could tell. I just knew there was worse to come.

'I'm afraid that there is a further complication.'

'Jesus.' I fucking hate it when I'm right.

'The CT scan also revealed a meningioma, which appears to be in a phase of aggressive increase in the middle cranial fossa.'

'That's a tumour, isn't it?'

'That is correct. However, these tumours are often slow-growing, and as many as ninety per cent are benign. However, in my opinion, there are indications of recent proliferation on the cranial base. Under normal circumstances, I would recommend removing the haematoma and scheduling further surgery to remove the tumour, perhaps in a few weeks' time. However, because of the aggressive rate of the proliferation, to delay the removal of the tumour – which is a relatively straightforward procedure – I believe would significantly increase the chances of the meningioma becoming malignant.'

It never rains but it fucking pours.

We sat in silence. Words were queuing to burst out of my mouth, but I just couldn't get them past my lips.

Patel broke the oppressive silence.

'I can perform the surgery immediately, Gill. I have a team standing by. There is still time to … no, of course you are right. I can't undo the damage that has already been caused, but I *can* reduce the possibility of any further damage that may be caused by intracranial complications and, of course, the tumour. In some ways, you may look upon Dave's accident as divine intervention … if you believe in such a thing. Without the accident, we would not have discovered the tumour.'

My lips quivered. I wasn't sure which would come first: words, or tears of frustration and anger.

Somehow I managed to speak.

"No, I do not believe in divine intervention. So,' I asked again, 'what happens next?'

'I just need you to sign a consent form.'

'And what if I don't sign it?' I felt my eyes fill with tears and noticed Molly looking at me, an expression of puzzlement on her pretty face. There was silence in the room as my words lingered like a murderer's sudden and unexpected confession. I glanced at the pictures on Mr Patel's desk, pictures of a wife and three young, smiling children in a well-tended garden on a sunny day. Pictures of a life of normality that had been denied me.

'If you do not give your consent, Gill, Dave will die. Without surgery, death will follow, and quite quickly due to the enlargement of the haematoma causing a brain herniation. As for the tumour, my opinion is that it has been there for a significant length of time, but – pardon me for repeating myself – in my opinion, it also should be removed. Now.' He shuffled forward, placed his elbows on the desk and steepled his hands. 'If you do not sign, I will have no alternative other than to seek your husband's approval.'

My mind was in a whir.

One moment I'd been sipping Chablis, enjoying sweet intoxication at the prospect of the freedom of a rare afternoon with Ali. We would have an intimate, leisurely lunch, finish the bottle, then go back to her apartment and make love.

But the next, here I was. Another hospital … another Dave-related interruption to my life. Another life-fucking-threatening crisis. For a moment, I felt an illogical but blinding anger at Dave, at Roger, and even at Mr Patel whose job it was to fix, no … whose job it was to save Dave.

I didn't want Dave saving. I just wanted him out of my life.

But I signed anyway.

141

FORTY

DAVE

I woke up with a really dry mouth.

This usually happens when I've had to go into hospital for something, like the time I had to have my tonsils out. These are things that were in my throat. Then after that, I had to have something called my appendix out, and this is – or was – somewhere near my stomach. I'm not sure why I had to have these things taken out; maybe they just grew too much and my body didn't have room for them any more. I say that because I've heard people say that my body is quite small for a young adult, which is what I am now.

Nobody bothered to tell me why I was going into hospital, what my tonsils or my appendix were and why they couldn't be left inside me, and nobody has bothered to tell me why I'm in hospital now.

I know I'm in hospital cos I recognise the smells and the noises and I feel really dopey, which means that I've been to sleep for a while, because I'd been given an anaesthetic? It's quite nice, actually. The person who gave me the anaesthetic asked me to count backwards from ten, which I tried to do, but I can't remember much after eight, and it probably wasn't all that important anyway.

I've been in hospital loads of times – mostly if I've not been given enough to drink and I get ill. I don't mind being in hospital – in fact, I quite like it cos people are generally nice to me – to begin with anyway.

But it would be nice if someone had told me why I had to go into hospital.

Maybe there's another part of my body that needed to be taken out because my body doesn't have room for it. I hope it's not my penis, cos – as I've told you – I quite like it when I get an erection. It would probably be a shame not to have one, but maybe it's just too big and there isn't enough room for it?

There's not much I can do to work out why I'm in a hospital, but I'm going to think back through what I can remember and maybe I'll find something to remind me.

Molly, for example, I can remember.

Molly is the only person clever enough to work out that I have this locked-in thing. I remember this morning ... or at least I think it was this morning, Molly worked out that I can move my head from side to side and, more importantly, that I can blink. And she was clever enough to work out that I can communicate by doing this because I used Scooter to demonstrate. You've no idea how hard it is for me to move my head, but I needed to do this cos I found out later that Scooter always follows my right eye, so if I move my head to the left, he moves to the left. I don't think Scooter's particularly intelligent; it probably just has something to do with smell or maybe him wanting to lick my mouth, which he likes to do, or something else ... I don't know.

Anyway, now that Molly knows I can control the movement of my right eye, this means that I can actually communicate with someone for the first time in my life, and I can't begin to tell you just how exciting this is.

The only trouble is that there aren't many people I want to communicate with other than Molly, but at least it's a start, and who knows where it could lead?

There's someone in the room.

The effect of the anaesthetic is beginning to wear off a bit, and I can tell there's someone moving towards me; I hear footsteps, then the smell hits me and I know it's Molly. I don't know if she's the only person in the room, but I think she is.

'How're you feeling, Dave? You've had a nasty accident.'

That's sort of good news because it's unlikely that my penis would have been removed if I'd just had an

143

accident. Of course, I have no recollection of any sort of accident, but it would be nice if it had been a car accident and the parents and the ginger twats had been killed.

'You were hit on the head by a tennis ball.'

Was that it?

It's not the good news I was hoping for, and my heart sinks – I've heard it called – although it probably doesn't move at all. It doesn't sound as if my family have been killed.

'Your wheelchair was knocked over and you hurt your head really badly on the concrete block that was put there to protect you. You've had to have an emergency operation to have a lump of blood and something else removed from your skull. But it went really well, and the surgeon said you're going to be fine. In fact, you should be able to go home after a few days. They just need to keep you in for observation ... just to be sure you're okay.'

I hear her pull up a chair and sit down by my bed. She smells really nice, and I haven't felt this good for years. The anaesthetic probably helps because I still feel nice and woozy. In fact, I don't think I've ever felt this good, because nobody ever sat by my bed when I'd been in hospital before.

And this is somebody ... an actual person that I can communicate with.

'Can you hear me, Dave?'

I want to tell her that I can, but it's too much of an effort to open my eye. My eyes just feel so ... heavy?

'Did you understand what I said, Dave? If you can open your eyes, try to blink twice ... you know, as you did before. D'you remember? You did it before lunch. Two blinks for yes ... if you can understand me. Please?'

She's really close to me now, and I can tell she's excited cos I can hear her breathing become more shallow and rapid. It's like how the father breathes after he's had a lot to drink and the mother tells him to lift me on to the changing table, but in a much better way. I think she's excited, maybe cos she could communicate with me and now she doesn't know if the accident and the operation have might have changed this.

And the thought that all this hope might be taken away hits me too, and I'm more scared than I was when I was forced to jump out of a plane. To have nothing, then to have something that you know is going to change your life in a really good way, then to have it taken away from you, is far worse than never having anything at all.

I know, no matter how much effort it takes, I have to open my eyes and blink twice.

Or my message in the bottle will float on an ocean of emptiness where no one will ever find it.

FORTY-ONE

ROGER

Roger drove in the direction of home, his mind in a whirl, beads of sweat forming and cooling on his brow.

He pulled a grubby handkerchief from his pocket and mopped his forehead. Shouldn't have taken off the sweatband, he thought. No ... shouldn't have listened to that bloody tipster. Why the hell had he been such a fool?

Kaila's Daughter had finished in first place; that was the good news. But according to the rules of horse racing – about which Roger knew little – it was necessary to cross the finishing line with a jockey on board, and the poor sap who began the race in Kaila's Daughter's saddle was ejected from it when he started celebrating half a furlong from home.

Two grand down the drain.

Two fucking grand short of replacing Gill's ring.

A day that started out with more than the remotest possibility of a rare sexual engagement with his wife was rapidly becoming one that he hoped would end without him having to have a knife removed from between his shoulder blades.

So Roger chose the only course of action he considered logical; he drove into Hull and went straight to the bookies – not to collect his winnings, as had been his expectation, but to place the remaining grand on the other hot tip he'd been given – Harry Trotter, who was running in the 4.45 Premier Handicap at Fairyhouse. As odds-on favourite at three to one, Roger knew that this was purely an exercise in damage limitation, but at least if Harry

Trotter could manage to cross the finishing line ahead of the field, with his jockey still on board, Gill's ring would be back where it lay this morning.

And that would be one less problem for him to worry about.

FORTY-TWO

DAVE

I have to open my eyes.

I have to open my eyes.

I *really* have to open my eyes.

But all I want to do is count backwards and go to sleep again.

Ten ... nine ... eight ...

If I don't open my eyes and blink, I feel sure that Molly will go and I'll be left on my desert island alone ... without records, without Shakespeare, without the Bible and, more to the point, without someone who understands that I have a fully functioning brain and want to use it.

I remember that Molly's here to find out stuff about communication for her degree, and unless I can show her that I *can* still communicate, she'll give up on me, just like everyone else has done.

And I can't blame her for that.

No ... that's not true – everybody else just assumes that my brain is mush and they don't even bother trying to communicate with me. I blame the parents for this, particularly the father. When he's asked if I can understand stuff, he always replies with stupid comments like 'he can understand about as much as that table over there.' Remember I told you what he said to the instructor when we did the parachute jump? People believe this and so they don't tell me stuff except if they're being what's called politically correct. But then they only say stuff to me so other people – maybe like the head teacher at school – think that they're really patient and that

148

they're good with people who're fucked like me. I've given up trying to show them that I understand.

But I can't give up trying to show Molly that I understand her, no matter how tired I am.

Seven ... six ... five ...

I have to force my eyes open.

Four ... three ... two ...

'Dave, can you hear me? I'm still here, but I'm going to have to go in a minute.'

I'm just so sleepy ... so sleepy.

FORTY-THREE

ROGER

Roger cranked a can of Coke from the vending machine.

He hadn't drunk anything since lunch and was parched. The Premier Handicap would be off in just over five minutes, so he might as well stay here, catch his breath, collect his winnings, then retrieve Gill's ring before Pledge Pawnbrokers, Jewellers & Body Piercing shut up shop for the day.

Bookies' shops hadn't changed much over the years, he thought. There was a pervasive and unmistakable stench of desperation, and although smoking had been banned for years now, the place reeked of stale tobacco coupled with the lingering pall of body odour, contributing to a distinctive aura of seediness. People who spent a significant proportion of their leisure time in bookies' shops, Roger considered, were people for whom life could have gone significantly better.

Which, of course, he reluctantly acknowledged, was precisely why he was here right now.

Bookies' shops, like snooker halls, were the stomping grounds of ne'er do wells, lazy and irresponsible work-dodgers who were but one step away from an underclass who lived precariously close to the wrong side of the law.

Roger would acknowledge that he was nothing if not a snob, and he placated his middle-class values by the reassurance that he was here out of necessity rather than by lifestyle choice.

Needs must when your luck changes, leaving you in the proverbial.

The clerk – the same girl with whom he had placed his ill-fated bet on Kaila's Daughter this morning – recognised him but took his stake without comment. It can't be every day someone comes in and places a three-grand bet on a horse that wins by a country mile but jettisons its jockey before crossing the line, and Roger knew the smile she bestowed on him as she handed him the betting slip was a mocking one.

He would be collecting around thirty k right now instead of parting with another grand had that idiot of a jockey done his job properly instead of showboating before he crossed the line.

As if to underline this, one of the TV screens was replaying the race while an animated Cornelius Lysaght described the event with an undisguised air of hilarity.

Roger picked up a discarded copy of *Racing Post* and found the form guide for the Fairyhouse meet. Harry Trotter hadn't exactly covered himself in glory, a solitary win from an outing at Tipperary five years ago being the highlight of his unremarkable seven-year career. So why on earth was he odds-on favourite? The other nags must be as utterly hopeless as Kaila's Daughter's stablemates at Haydock ... maybe even worse.

One of the screens was showing the Fairyhouse meet, and Roger pulled up a stool and sat down. He had no idea where Fairyhouse was, but it could be on Mars for all he cared as long as Harry Trotter won. There were six entrants in the 4.45 Premier Handicap, a race over seven furlongs.

Roger tossed his crumpled Coke can nonchalantly into the bin and turned his full attention to the TV screen.

They were under starter's orders.

And then they were off.

FORTY-FOUR

DAVE

Two... one ...

'Dave ... can you hear me?'

I can, but I just can't open my eyes and blink to tell her.

'I've got to go, Dave.'

Wait a minute ...

There ... there ... I've done it! You wouldn't believe how much effort this took but it was worth it, because something just happened that I never, ever expected would happen!

In fact, the effort was worth far more than everything else I've ever put any effort into, because this was an actual life-changing moment.

I've heard people talk on BBC Radio 4 about lifechanging moments and sometimes I think they're overrated. It's a bit like someone saying 'that dessert was to die for', which is just silly because a dessert isn't worth dying for and if they mean it could kill you, I think you'd have to eat a massive amount of it before it became lifethreatening.

But my moment really was life-changing because, when I finally managed to open my eyes, I could see.

Yes, read that again: I. Could. See.

At first all I could see was light, and as all I've ever seen is darkness, I can't tell you how good this felt. Of course, it could just be the effects of the anaesthetic, but suddenly I didn't feel sleepy any more, so I don't think it is.

And then I saw shapes. One was leaning over me and looked like it was standing up, so I guessed it must be Molly. There were other shapes too. None of them were moving, but I could make them out because there was something solid about them and the darkness of a shape was very different to the light around it.

And then the most amazing thing happened.

I saw Molly.

At first she was just made up of blurred colour and movement and then she came into what I've heard called focus? The whole room actually came into focus. My whole world came into focus.

You probably wouldn't know this if you've never been blind: colour is just the most amazing thing in the world, and seeing colour and then seeing shapes come into focus ... this was *easily* the best moment of my life.

It's really hard to explain, but if you've never been able to see anything, and suddenly you *can* see, colour is what strikes you first. Colour is everything. It's shapes and light and darkness that make up the meaning of the world but it's colour that makes it come alive.

The world around me started to make some sense at last.

After eighteen years, two months, three days and some hours (I'm not sure how many hours because I still don't know how long I'd been in hospital for), I can begin to make some sense of the world I live in.

And I can communicate—

'Dave, are you okay?'

Yeah, I'm way better than okay; I'm fantastic.

Remember I said that there's not been much that's happened to me that I would call fantastic?

Well, there has now.

It was then it struck me that I'd not blinked yet, so I calmed down a bit, blinked twice, and Molly sat back down beside me.

FORTY-FIVE

ROGER

Roger fired the car towards Rising Bucklebury in a manner, had the police intervened, that would justifiably been described as 'driving without due care and attention'. He was, in fact, driving without any care and attention.

And it wasn't that he was in any hurry to get home.

It was simply that his mood was a bleak reflection of how his day had gone from bad to worse with the failure of Harry Trotter to move at a greater pace than his surname would suggest, and thus he finished sixth in a six-horse race.

That was it with horses, Roger thought. Stick to what you know, in future.

A sense of impending doom almost overwhelmed him as he reached the top of the drive and parked on the gravelled crescent adjacent to the front door.

Without intending to, he sat in the car barely aware of his surroundings, stuck in a quagmire of negative thoughts. He hadn't yet summoned the courage to count how much he'd lost at the casino this morning. Then there was the three grand he'd lost on Kaila's Daughter, followed by another grand that had gone west on that other bloody horse. And to top it all, Gill's ring was still the lawful property of Pledge Pawnbrokers, Jewellers & Body Piercing and was likely to remain so unless he could find a way to repay the loan on the ring before the two-month credit period expired.

Roger's attention was drawn to something unusual at the front of the house.

At first he wasn't sure why his gaze was focused on his front door; all he was aware of was that there was something that wasn't right about it.

And then it struck him.

The front door was open; not wide open, but open enough to suggest that someone had either entered or exited through it in a hurry.

And this was strange because the front door, which in the tradition of rectories and other substantial residences built around the turn of the century led into a small vestibule, which in turn led into the main hall, was a door that was never used. And this was because the inner door – the lower part of which was wood-panelled, while the upper part contained small, ornate stained-glass panes – was impossible to open. The key was in the outside of the door, but it couldn't be accessed because the key to the outer door had been lost not long after the Hempsalls had moved in, and therefore it was impossible to open this door other than from the inside.

A locksmith could, of course, have rectified the problem in a matter of minutes, but in typical Roger style, nothing had been done to generate such a renovation, so the only entrance to the house was through the scullery door leading to the kitchen.

But now the outer door lay open, as did the inner glass-panelled door, and it didn't take Roger long to work out that the stained-glass pane adjacent to the lock had been smashed and that the key which had sat redundantly in the lock for almost a decade was no longer there.

At first Roger concluded that someone had broken in.

But unless it had been someone who had discovered the key to the outer door – someone who was either blind or too stupid to notice the key to the inner door sitting in the lock – it could only mean one thing.

Someone had broken out.

And for whatever reason this had happened, it gave Roger the grain of an idea.

155

FORTY-SIX

MOLLY JOHNSON

MSc RESEARCH PROJECT NOTES
NOTE 7: Wednesday, 24 July 2019

Gill left me alone with Dave.

She said she needed to catch Dr Sullivan before she left, but I think she just wanted a fag. I don't blame her after what she's been through, although I really don't understand her attitude to Dave.

Okay, I don't know much about her – I'd only spoken to her on the phone until today – but what she said about not signing the consent form really shocked me. She meant it – it wasn't even said in a jokey way. It came across as a comment made by someone who was bitter, filled with anger, and I could tell Mr Patel was stunned by it too. I felt quite embarrassed because, illogical as it sounds, I felt being with Gill in the room meant that in some way I supported her comment. That couldn't have been further from the truth.

I feel a bit concerned about Dave's future because I'm not sure that he is in a safe place. It's hardly what can be described as a loving environment, and I need to speak to someone [maybe Dave's social worker?] and flag up my concerns.

Okay, this is way beyond the remit of my research project, but – like it or not – I've become involved with this family, and both parents have displayed behaviours I would consider likely to have a negative influence on

Dave's future well-being and, by implication, this impacts on his ability to communicate.

Back to communication.

I was really worried that the surgery would have somehow reversed the capacity to communicate that Dave had demonstrated, particularly with the additional complication of the tumour. Somehow this portal may have been closed – who knows what side effects can occur when someone experiences retro-sigmoid craniotomy?

At first I thought it had ... but it hasn't.

It took a long time to get there – I suspect because of the anaesthetic – and I was just about to give up and leave when he blinked twice; just what I'd asked him to do.

And that was only the start of it.

I don't know how, but I could tell that something else ... something really fundamental, had changed.

So I asked Dave a couple of questions. I asked him if he wanted a drink: two blinks for yes, three for no, and he blinked twice. I gave him a drink, and he drank the entire beaker.

Then I asked him if he was hungry. Same drill. He blinked three times.

But something was different to this morning, and it took me a few moments to work out why.

Not only was he blinking with both eyes, but also I had this really strong feeling that he was actually *looking* at me because his eyes were moving everywhere with the pace of a camera held by a professional photographer, as if he was trying to capture everything and capture it really quickly before it disappeared.

And that's when I knew it. I somehow knew that he could see.

FORTY-SEVEN

ROGER

It took Roger less than five minutes to check the house.

As he'd expected, it was empty and nothing appeared to be missing.

That ruled out a burglary ... at least for now, he thought.

He then went to the study, put the disc into the DVD player and reviewed the video footage from the security cameras. Hillcrest was protected by a system that could in no way be described as state of the art but had been installed – when the house and garages contained items that were worth stealing – for the simple reason that even a cheap installation involving cameras and alarms significantly reduced the cost of home insurance.

The disc showed what Roger had expected: nothing ... until he fast-forwarded it to the point where the camera in the vestibule showed an orange ball fly through the stained-glass windowpane, followed by Boris's hand turning the key and both twins entering the vestibule amid unrestrained joy, then exiting through the front door, which could now be opened by turning the interior knob. Boris picked up the offending ball on the way, and they left the house, leaving both doors ajar.

Perfect, Roger thought, just perfect, and pretty much what he'd been expecting.

Fate had dealt him an unequivocally shitty hand so far today, but – as every gambler knows – it only takes a moment for your luck to change, and here it was. The gods had thrown him a bone, an opportunity a lesser man

– a risk-averse man who lacked courage – would pass up, to even the score. Maybe, he thought, the remote possibility of sex with Gill might have crept back onto the cards. This thought lasted only as long as it took for him to remember the last conversation he'd had with her: the one concerning his handling of the Dave incident. Add to this the fact that the house had been 'burgled' and that all of Gill's few prized possessions, including her Van Cleef & Arpels Sweet Alhambra ruby and diamond-encrusted effeuillage ring, had been stolen. No, he reflected with a grim pragmatism, even the remotest possibility of sex would be very far removed from the cards.

But now he had work to do.

Roger removed the disc from the security system, inserted a blank one, clicked the system back on and placed the disc showing the 'young offenders' in a concealed top drawer of his antique mahogany partner desk. This had been his father's desk; he'd loved and coveted it for years, and when his parents died, it was passed on to him. It was the one item of inherited worth he hadn't managed to squander yet.

He clicked the mechanism of the drawer to lock it, withdrew a pair of latex gloves from a box in an adjacent cupboard, and went to work.

He already knew from this morning's search that there was no money in the house, but a burglar wouldn't, so his first objective was to make it look as if someone in a hurry had ransacked the house looking for items of obvious value.

Half an hour later, he stood in the kitchen and surveyed his handiwork. The room, in keeping with every other room in Hillcrest, was now a mess. Drawers had been flung to the floor, crockery broken, cutlery strewn everywhere, and the two piles of untended letters and papers, the larger of which was his and the smaller, Gill's, had been rifled through and now lay in a heap on the floor.

He had placed anything he could find of value into a large, leather-handled eighties Adidas sports bag. This amounted to the contents of Gill's jewellery box, some antique silver cufflinks he hated, his laptop, iPads from each of the twins' rooms and their JBL speakers, several porcelain statuettes he detested, and an assortment of silverware, trays and cutlery that had come from his parents' house. He considered that these were the items to which a burglar's eye would be drawn.

And as the burglar – whose persona Roger had mentally constructed in an attempt to make the intrusion appear opportunistic rather than premeditated – was a petty criminal whose only interest was in objects which were readily convertible into cash, he reluctantly ignored the artwork, most of which reflected Gill's taste and which he would gladly have seen the back of.

In total, Roger thought, the value of this 'burglary' should be in the region of fifteen to sixteen thousand pounds.

That should do.

The value of the contents of Gill's jewellery box alone – and he knew this because they'd had, at his insistence, a valuation conducted for purposes of insurance – was around twelve grand. And this, of course, included Gill's Van Cleef & Arpels Sweet Alhambra ruby and diamond-encrusted effeuillage ring.

It struck Roger that he hadn't accumulated much of value over the years, even with the benefit of his inheritance. If anyone had benefitted from this, he reflected, it was the casinos, the car dealers and the businesses that he had fuelled with proverbial sackloads of money, only to watch it all go up in smoke.

Roger stood at the sink absently gazing at the glorious pastoral view, removed the latex gloves, and was about to add them to the Adidas bag when he heard a noise behind him.

He turned to see Boris and Axel.

'Where the hell have you two been?'

'Just went to the village. No harm in that, is there?' Boris replied, surveying the debris. 'What the fuck's been going on here? And why are you wearing rubber gloves, Rog?'

'It appears there's been a break-in. I don't suppose either of you know why the hall and front doors are open?'

Boris shrugged.

'No idea. So … what's with the gloves, then?'

'The gloves,' replied Roger, searching for a plausible explanation, 'are so that I don't contaminate what the police – when they get here – will undoubtedly call a "crime scene". So don't touch anything, either of you.'

'But we live here, Rog … and so do you. Our prints will be everywhere. So what's the point of wearing gloves?'

Roger had no answer to this; Boris was right, although the real reason he was wearing gloves was that – despite living here – finding his prints all over Gill's jewellery box might cause the police to question what they were doing there.

'Unless you're the burglar?'

Roger felt his brow bead up again. A good time to change the subject, he thought.

'I know what happened to the hall door, by the way, so don't lie to me. I've reviewed the video footage, and it shows a ball going through the glass and then both of you going out by the front door, leaving it open. That's how the burglar got in.'

No one spoke, and for a brief moment, Roger felt he had the upper hand.

'I'd keep that to yourself if I was you,' said Boris, 'because I don't know that much about insurance, but I'm not sure they're going to pay up if somebody, like, left the doors open? I might be wrong, but I think you're supposed to lock up your house when you leave it.'

'Yes, but it was you who left the doors open.'

'You're not getting the point here, Rog. It doesn't matter *who* left the doors open. And standing here in the kitchen with this mess, wearing a pair of rubber gloves … well, to be honest, it looks a bit suspicious to me.' Boris turned to his brother. 'What d'you think, Axe? It almost looks like it could have been … like, staged?'

'Sure, bruv,' replied Axel. 'Probably best if the insurance don't know how the doors got to be open, I'd say.'

Silence once again reigned.

'You're trying to blackmail me, you little bastards, aren't you?'

161

'Steady on, Rog. Blackmail's a bit strong. All we're saying is that it would be better if you could ... what's the word, Axe?'

'Corroborate?'

'Yeah, corroborate – nice one, bruv ... if that's the word – your story. Just so nobody questions it should someone "accidentally" happen to come out with something else.'

'Right,' replied Roger, with bravery which was little more than bluster. 'And who are the authorities going to believe? Me? Or you two?'

'Wouldn't want to put that one to the test, Rog.'

There was silence in the kitchen, and it occurred to Roger that if tumbleweed, or even the proverbial herd of wildebeest, had swept through amid the debris, majestically or otherwise, for the second time today, no one would have noticed.

'How much?'

Boris looked at Axel and raised his eyebrows, sucked his teeth and blew out his cheeks before replying.

'I reckon two grand should make sure that we're all ... what's the head call it ... singing from the same hymn sheet?'

'For fuck's sake, you cannot be serious!'

'Deadly serious, Rog. And that's two grand each, by the way; and what was that you said about swearing? Oh, and one other thing, part of the deal is that we won't be going on that Sedburgh cricket thing either. So you can take our names off the list tomorrow morning. And we'll have our iPads back.'

FORTY-EIGHT

DAVE

It's going to take a really long time to get used to this –
being able to see.

I mean ... it's just amazing.

There are billions of people in this world who wake
up every morning and go to bed each night without once
thinking about how lucky they are to be able to see. It's
called taking something for granted, and I will never,
ever take this for granted because I may not have it forever. Something good has finally happened inside my
head and my big worry now is that it may not last.

But while it does last, I'm going to make the most of
it.

The room I'm in is quite nice. There's just me, and opposite my bed there's a window, and through it I can see
fields and trees – I know quite a bit about nature because
I listen to *Open Country* on BBC Radio 4. It's a programme
about the people and the wildlife that live in this country
and sometimes there are cows mooing in the background, and if the father hears this, he asks the mother if
that's me. Anyway, apart from that, I really like it.

There was a television attached to the wall, and on
the screen there's a man talking and he's smartly dressed
and has a brightly-coloured thing tied around his neck,
but I can't hear what he's saying because the sound is really low and even I can't make it out. It might be the news
because he looks serious. You might be wondering how I
know that he looks serious, but I know what a smile is
and he's definitely not smiling. There are some words

floating past in a coloured strip along the bottom of the screen, but I don't know what they mean because, of course, I can't read. And this makes me realise – if my sight is here to stay – how much I'm going to have to learn, and learn quickly if I want to become a journalist, because I wouldn't imagine that you could be a journalist if you can't read, even if you work for what's called a tabloid newspaper like *The Sun*.

There's not much else in the room apart from Molly.

She is really beautiful, and looking at her gives me this funny feeling I've never had before. I would say that she's the most beautiful woman I've ever seen, but as I've not seen any other women to compare her to yet, this could be what's called an overstatement.

But I don't think so.

If there's anyone more beautiful than Molly, I would be really surprised.

But there's just so much to look at right now and my eyes are drawn back to the television, and when I concentrate very hard – which is difficult with Molly sitting by my bed – I can just about make out what the man is saying.

He says: 'Now we're going over to Orla Guerin, our international correspondent in Istanbul. Orla, what can you tell us about the ...' but I'm not really interested in what he's saying because when this correspondent called Orla Guerin appears on the screen, I realise that not all women are as good-looking as Molly. In fact – and I don't mean this is a nasty way because I've heard of her before and she's probably almost as good a journalist as Gary O'Donoghue – or maybe even JFH – but I would describe the way she looks as scary rather than beautiful. But maybe she is attractive to some people and anyway – as I've already said – good looks aren't everything, are they?

But Molly *is* really beautiful and just having her sitting close to me makes me feel happy. She has bright, smiling eyes; straight long dark hair; a nose that doesn't take up too much space; and lips that I think are probably natural – because she seems like a natural person – and she also has really nice skin. She's wearing jeans and a tight black top that has two pictures on it: one with a

164

smiling face surrounded by fire and the other with a long face inside a pair of curved lines, and this face isn't smiling. I don't know what her top means but I think it's probably for decoration rather than to tell people something about herself, although I could well be wrong.

And I can't help noticing that she has really nice breasts.

I hate to say it but Boris was right, although I got the impression from what the father said that you shouldn't comment on a woman's breasts, at least not in front of her. Anyway, Molly has the sort of breasts that I could easily imagine my head resting on and just going to sleep. I expect that's what breasts are probably for.

I think she's about to say something, but before she can, the door opens and two people come in. One is a woman who isn't very beautiful but is smartly dressed and looks as if she might have been beautiful once, or maybe could be again if she made what the father calls 'an effort'. There's something about her that makes me sure that she's the mother. I can't quite work out what it is at first, but then I remember that it's her smell, which is different to Molly's, and I remember this smell from this morning, although it's not as strong now as it was before.

The other person is a man. He has very little hair, very dark skin, and is quite fat. He's wearing a white coat and glasses, and I'm pretty sure that he's not the father because a) he hasn't said anything horrible to me yet, and b) he doesn't look how the mother described the father, although he hasn't got much hair.

'So tell me, young lady, how is the patient?' he asks Molly in a concerned sort of way. That confirms he's not the father.

'He's good,' she replies. 'In fact, he's better than good. I think ... I think something really amazing has happened to him. I know this sounds crazy, but I'm pretty sure that he's able to see now.'

FORTY-NINE

ROGER

Roger was about to call the police when something made him hesitate.

Once this call had been made, a Rubicon had been crossed.

Being blackmailed by his own sons was the least of his worries. Four grand was a lot to part with, and the little bastards had demanded half of it up front – the rest when the insurance money came through – so that made raiding the joint bank account inevitable now. He would have to come up with something plausible to placate Gill, which, he realised, was what he should have done in the first place. But amid the carnage that their lives had become, this transgression, he imagined, might just lie undetected for some time.

And knowing his sons, particularly Boris, he suspected that this wouldn't be the last he'd hear of it. By acquiescing to blackmail, he had now become the go-to cash cow, and he anticipated that Boris would threaten disclosure to the authorities whenever the money ran out. But that was a worry for another day.

There was something else niggling at him ... something that prevented him from making the call to report the break-in.

He was about to lift the receiver of the landline when he realised Boris was standing behind him.

'I wouldn't do that just yet if I was you.'

'I beg your pardon?'

'Well ... I don't think you've thought this through, Rog, have you? And as you're paying us four grand, I suppose it's only fair that we should help you. After all, if the feds or the insurers become suspicious, that's not going to be good news for us either.'

'And, may I ask, what do you suggest?'

'Well, for one thing, there's no sign of a break-in. The front door may have been open, but they're going to want to see *how* it got to be open. There's no sign of what the cops call "forced entry". And for another, if I was you, I'd do something about the security cameras.'

'As in?'

'As in it looks dead suspicious just taking one disc out and putting another one in, which is what I assume you've done, particularly as it happened at the time of the "break-in". If I was you, I'd smash the cameras. I might be wrong, but I'm pretty sure that's what a proper burglar would do. He certainly wouldn't change the disks, would he? If anything, I'd remove the disc cos the feds will ask for it, and if "your burglar" had removed it, then there wouldn't be any footage for them to review, would there?'

Never had Roger felt quite so deflated and humiliated. To add to everything that had gone wrong so far today, his twelve-year-old son was now lecturing him on the art of making a faked burglary look genuine. Perhaps, he thought, this particular skill set would be of value when teaching SMSC (Spiritual, Moral, Social & Cultural Education – including careers) to the semi-literate primates at Wiley Hall Academy.

'No ... no, I don't suppose he would. I've already removed one disc and put another one in,' he replied, lamely.

'Well, if I was you, I'd take that one out as well, then get rid of them both. And another thing; you're going to need an alibi. Maybe it's not occurred to you, Rog, but the first question the police are going to ask is, where were you?'

'Hmmm ...' It hadn't occurred to Roger. But two things *had* occurred to him: the first was that he would make a lousy burglar, and the second, which was of greater importance, was that he knew he was going to have to rely on his offspring for an alibi, and this would inevitably mean further extortion at some point in the future.

He was right.

'Fortunately, me and Axel can provide you with an alibi, and it's not even going to cost you … well, not that much, anyway.'

'And just what would that be?'

'That would be that you'd taken us to McDonald's, which is what you're going to do on the way to the bank to pick up our two grand.'

'Dear Lord—'

'Nah, I wouldn't rely on him, Rog. You go and deal with the security cameras and smash the front door around a bit, then remove the other disc, and we'll be waiting in the car. All this helping you has made me hungry. I could murder a Happy Meal. Think I'll go for the McNuggets. What about you? And then you can ring the feds when we get back.'

Unable to think of a reply, Roger slunk off to the garage to look for a suitable tool to jemmy open the front door and something appropriate to shatter the security cameras, thinking that life couldn't really get much worse.

And in this thought, he was only partly correct.

FIFTY

DAVE

I'm not sure how I feel about sharing my good news.

At least, not just yet.

On the one hand, it's fantastic to be able to see. I can't remember if I ever had sight – if I had, it would have been before the operation that led to me being totally fucked up – but I think I must have done. On the other hand, I'm not sure that I want anyone to know that I can see until I've figured out how it's going to change things. I know that sounds a bit ... maybe devious, but here's why:

I still want to kill my family, remember?

Particularly after what's happened today. And I would have a much better chance of getting away with it – I know it's what's called an alibi – if everyone thinks I'm still blind. Actually, I don't really want to kill the mother because I just feel sorry for her, but arranging for them all to be in the same place and then to have some sort of 'accident' would definitely be the best solution. But I've not got a clue how I'm going to manage this. Maybe when I've learned to communicate better, Molly will agree to help me, but I doubt this because Molly seems too nice a person to agree to murder someone ... well, to murder four people. That's what's called mass murder, and Molly doesn't strike me as someone who could become a mass murderer, no matter how much she dislikes the father and the ginger twats.

But I wish I could somehow have told Molly not to say anything about my sight.

I needn't have worried.

The dark-skinned man in the white coat laughed.

'I really don't think that there's a snowball's chance in hell of that, Molly.'

I think by this he means that it isn't very likely, because snow is cold – I know this because the ginger twats once buried my wheelchair and me in snow. Then they put stones in front of my eyes, a carrot in my mouth and called me a 'snow Timmy' and it was, like ... really, really cold. And I don't think that a place called hell actually exists – other than my home – but if it does, isn't it supposed to be really, really hot?

So I don't think that the man in the white coat – who I think must be a doctor – believes that I can see.

'Golly no, there would be very little chance of that,' he said, 'very little chance indeed. The removal of the tumour would certainly eliminate the possibility that it was pinching the optic chiasma. But I think it most unlikely that this in itself would restore his sight. However, I wouldn't completely rule it out.'

'So can you tell if it was benign or not? As you removed it?'

'It's impossible to tell just by visual examination. We shall see when the pathology report arrives, but in my opinion, the tumour is most likely to be benign. As I said earlier, only around ten per cent of meningiomas become malignant.'

Fucking hell! What's this about a tumour? And on my brain? That's the first I've heard of this. And he says there's a one in ten chance that it's malignant, which I happen to know means that it will kill me. I'd love to be able to tell him that ... hello ... I *am* in the room, and I *do* actually have a name ... and it's *me* he should be passing on this information to, but of course I'm used to being treated like a piece of breathing furniture.

'So you said.' The mother didn't sound that interested. I think I have probably messed up her day, particularly as I happen to know what she was up to. So discovering a tumour on my brain is not going to do much to improve that, is it? 'What exactly leads you to suspect it was benign?'

170

'Because the symptoms of a malignant tumour would surely have been easy for you to recognise. Your son would have suffered from severe headaches, which would have become more and more frequent over time. He would also have suffered from unexplained nausea or vomiting. I am quite sure you would have noticed evidence of this, had it been the case.'

Personally, I'm not so sure about that.

The only thing the mother notices when she's 'administering' – as she likes to call it – to me these days, is her phone. Maybe this is something nurses are taught at nurse school, but she can actually change my nappy with one hand and text with the other, or carry on a conversation with her phone pressed to her head while she's bathing me. This is called multitasking and I suppose nurses have to be good at it, but I would imagine most nurses pay more attention to their patients than she does. I suppose I should be glad she doesn't have to bath me very often.

'No,' she replied, 'I've not witnessed any of these symptoms. He does vomit occasionally—'

Which is a) when I *want* to, or b) to stop her forcing Ready Brek into my mouth.

'—but it's not a regular occurrence and I'm quite sure I would have noticed if he was having regular headaches.'

Again, I'm not so sure. But then I'm not involved in this conversation.

Then there's this silence for a bit, and I can't help thinking how typical of my life this is. First, I get my sight back, then I find out that my brain had a tumour and I could be dead soon. I mean, why does it always rain on me?

'So what makes you think he can see, Molly?'

This is not a good thing.

But then I had an idea.

I can see Molly looking at me, and I think she's having something called a dilemma, so then I try to help her … well, to help myself, if I'm being honest.

So then I tried really hard to scream the word 'no', but it probably just sounded like what the father would say was one of my mooing noises, but at least it got Molly's attention and she was looking at me.

Then I blinked three times.

For ages no one moved or even said anything. Then Molly shook her head slowly and in a ... I think, sad sort of way.

'Perhaps I imagined it,' she said, 'but I thought I felt his eyes following me, almost as if he was watching me when I moved. But now I come to think of it ...' She laughed nervously. If I am ever able to give Molly a bit of advice, it would be not to become an actress. 'It was probably, like ... I don't know ... nothing?'

'He was probably just having a fit,' the mother said. 'Normal for Dave.'

'That would be the probable explanation,' said the man in the white coat.

'However, we will conduct a further CT scan in a day or so. That should inform us as to whether there is evidence of increased or reduced brain atrophy. However, the latter is extremely unlikely. But it will also reveal any changes to the blood vessels, and other problems such as hydrocephalus and additional subdural haematomas.'

I'm lost in the medical science now, and I think everyone else is too – even the mother, who's a nurse.

I was right.

'But what's that got to do with his sight?' the mother asked, in a slightly panicky way. I can't remember her showing this much interest in me for, well, forever. 'Will it definitely confirm that he can or cannot see?'

Then there's another long silence before the man in the white coat answers.

'No, Gill, it would not answer that question. From both my extensive experience – and in my professional opinion – as I've already said, it would be most unlikely that the removal of the tumour, benign or otherwise, would restore his sight. However, the tumour was self-contained and was perfectly formed in the shape of a small nut, and it was in close proximity to the optic nerve head; therefore, I would have to conclude that this eventuality could not be entirely impossible.'

'So ... now you're saying that he *could* have got his sight back?'

'I'm not saying anything categorical, Gill. I'm only stating that we cannot entirely rule this eventuality out, and the only way you will know if he can see is from his responses, and for that, we would revert to the Glasgow Scale.'

This is good news. And it's making a good day an even better one.

I happen to know what the Glasgow Scale is, and I also know how easy it's going to be to fake it.

And that, at least, buys me a bit of time.

All I have to worry about now is the one in ten chance that I'm going to die.

And I happen to know that these odds – this is something I *did* learn from the father – are a lot worse than being chucked out of a plane and finding that the parachute doesn't open.

FIFTY-ONE

GILL

DIARY ENTRY: Wednesday, 24 July 2019

Today should be a Monday, because shit always happens on a Monday.

Not every Monday, of course, but when shit happens, it happens to me on a Monday.

But now it's happening on a Wednesday.

And this, the shittiest of shitty days I can remember since Dave stopped breathing, isn't even over yet.

I went to the study, locked the door and eventually managed to calm down enough to start writing about what happened. This is one of Martin's coping strategies. It goes something like this: I find a quiet area which I associate with relaxation – or at the very least, an absence of stress and conflict – calm myself by practising a breathing routine, then record everything that happened to trigger this episode of acute anxiety – or meltdown, as Roger calls it – particularly my thoughts that surround it. The only trouble with the study is that it's a room more associated with Roger than with me. His stuff is everywhere, even after I'd tidied it up – I'll come to that in a minute. And then there's this bloody desk, which I really hate. It's so ... so very Roger.

However, this is the only room that is possible to lock, and in what's becoming our dirty little war, it seems to be a nominated shared space, a sort of no man's land.

So, my diary ... I have to write about what happened as if it happened to someone else in order to distance myself from it, and I also have to write as if somebody, at some point in the future, will read this and empathise with what I experienced, and with how I felt. Martin calls this 'shared empathy'; Roger calls it bullshit, but it seems to work.

What I'm going through right now is what Martin refers to as 'catastrophising'. This is, he says, a cognitive distortion that prompts people like me to jump to the worst possible conclusion after a minor setback. When a situation is upsetting but not necessarily disastrous, I tend to regard it as a catastrophe. And I need to deal with this before this acute anxiety morphs into chronic stress and reboots my depression or leads to a build-up of my anger. Martin encourages me to practise mindfulness, observing a thought from a distance, without judgement, as it comes and goes. This is why he insists that I keep this diary.

There, I rationalised something and it's made me feel slightly better.

But I want a drink.

Probably a very large vodka and tonic, but I have the sense and willpower to understand that this would only make things worse. I'll have a drink later, when I've done what I have to do.

Anyway, if anybody *is* reading this, you can judge for yourself whether this is simply me jumping to the worst possible conclusion after a minor setback, or not.

Dave will be in hospital for several days, possibly a week or longer. It very much depends on his post-operative recovery and the outcome of the CT scan. I'm still not sure what the point is of this. Even if it does show further brain atrophy, he can't be any more disabled than he already is. And if – God knows how – there's been a reduction in brain atrophy, what difference will that result in? I mean, unless a total miracle has somehow occurred with the removal of the tumour, he's hardly going to be singing, dancing, and applying for a place at Cambridge, is he?

But I do think that Molly observed something and, for some reason, she's being coy about it.

I like Molly, from what little I know of her. I have a good feeling about her.

She's extremely intelligent, and already she seems to relate to Dave far better than anyone else has done. Yes, even me. She's only known him for one week, but she seems to have formed a bond with him, and I can sense – call it female intuition – that this is a two-way thing. Okay, I've neglected Dave; I'll admit that. Dealing with Dave on a day-to-day basis with no support from Roger, with no end in sight, has just become too much. Maybe there is an end in sight, but it's still a very long way away, and what happened today may even have jeopardised it.

Administering to Dave isn't what I was put on this planet for, and meeting Ali has only served to underline how desperate I've become to have my own life; a normal life, and one that doesn't revolve entirely around Dave.

I drove Molly home from the hospital, and we had the chance to chat.

I asked if she was married or in a relationship, and I soon realised from her silence that I'd touched a nerve.

'I was with someone for three years,' she said at length. 'I left him six months ago when he tried to kill me.'

Oh fuck. Stupid question.

'Oh my God, I'm so sorry, Molly.' How to make a bad day worse. 'I'm so sorry for asking. I ... I didn't realise.'

She smiled at me.

'How could you? Actually, I don't mind talking about it,' she said, 'if you want to.'

'Of course.' I managed to stop myself from saying something cheesy like, I don't know ... women like us who are physically or mentally abused by men should support each other. 'What happened?'

'Oh, we'd been together for about nine months when it began. He started to push me around, verbally first, then physically. I thought I was in love with Charlie; I really thought he was the one. He was good-looking, athletic and confident, a semi-professional footballer who still believed he'd get a breakthrough to the big-time. I think as time went on, though, he realised that this wasn't going to happen – especially when he started getting dropped – and that seemed to change him ... his confidence, I mean. But I just didn't see this coming. It started with him accusing me of always looking at other blokes,

176

which I wasn't, well, not intentionally anyway. And if I ever talked to another man when we were out, he really would lay into me when we got home. First, it was just verbal, then he started to slap me and call me a slut, and then he punched me really hard. He was jealous, really jealous. The day he punched me, he'd gone into my phone and found a text from Darren, my ex. It'd been there for ages and I don't know why I'd not deleted it. Charlie and I were living together by then, and when I started to cry – just after he'd punched me – he started screaming at me to shut the hell up and started pulling my hair. Then the neighbours knocked on the door to see what was going on and he told them that I just had really bad stomach pains – which was true – and that everything was okay.'

'Oh my God,' I repeated, 'poor, poor you.'

'So this went on for the next two years and I just tolerated it. I even managed to convince myself that maybe I was to blame in some way?'

'You're a very attractive young woman, Molly. I would imagine you'd receive a lot of male attention. But how could you think you were in any way to blame?'

'Maybe I was … maybe I wasn't.' She smiled. 'It didn't happen all the time. Most of the time he was kind to me … really thoughtful. He was always buying me flowers and perfume and talking about our future together. Then, one day, just before Christmas last year, I had a call from this guy at work called Billy. He told me there was a Christmas dinner arranged for our department and he'd seen I was the only person not to sign up for it. He wondered if I'd not seen it, and whether I wanted to go. I hadn't signed up for it because partners weren't included, and I knew Charlie would go mental. Charlie was in the next room and heard the entire conversation. He accused me of having an affair with Billy, and that's when he took a knife to me.'

She showed me her right arm. There were three scars on the inside of her forearm.

'Fucking hell, Molly. What a bastard!'

'Oh, these will disappear in time. But it's going to be a hell of a long time before the scars in my head vanish and I can trust another bloke. And the irony of it all was that Billy was gay. But I was lucky. Charlie'd had a lot to drink and I managed to duck past him and get out of the house, and the neighbour who'd intervened before took me in and called the police. In the end, I just moved out and didn't press charges, but I got a restraining order on him, and I've not seen nor heard anything from the bastard for months now.'

'Christ ... I don't know what to say.' I didn't. Roger and I may have our problems, and I know I have to tolerate him until I can finally walk out of the door, but physical or even verbal abuse isn't something I fear in our relationship, no matter how shitty it is.

We sat in silence for a while, the rush hour traffic slowing our progress.

'It's left here,' she said, directing me into the threshold of a run-down housing estate. She read my thoughts.

'It's not a great area, I know. Dad and I moved here when Mum died three months ago. He couldn't stand looking at the same wallpaper without her in front of it any more, and this was all we could afford.' She laughed. 'It's not been a great year for me. Just drop me here, thanks.'

I parked. She got out, but lingered as if she wanted to say something more. I dropped the window.

'Would it be okay if I visit Dave tomorrow, Gill? I've not got anything on, and if you have stuff to do, I don't mind spending the day with him. I can get a bus there.'

My thoughts instantly strayed to Ali and the warm feeling of the possibility of rearranging what we'd planned for today. And Roger would believe that I was at the hospital. He wouldn't show any interest as long as he wasn't asked to do anything. My heart beat faster. Perfect.

'Of course you can. That would be fantastic. I have a couple of appointments tomorrow,' I lied, 'and I'd rather not cancel them. I'll pop in and see how Dave is first thing, though.'

I watched until she reached her entrance and saw her wave at me before closing the door.

***

And then I got home and my shitty day got even shittier.

The first thing I noticed as I pulled up was a police car and van parked outside the front door.

Inside there was chaos.

Roger was giving a statement to a uniformed police-man and several others were, I presume, dusting the kitchen and the rooms beyond it for fingerprints.

The twins were nowhere to be seen, and the house was a total mess. I was told in no uncertain terms not to go beyond the hall because this was a scene-of-crime area and they hadn't finished with it yet.

Before I could ask what had happened, the bizarre thought that Roger might have murdered the twins flashed through my mind, and I hate to say it, but really I didn't know how I'd feel about it. Family ... gone.

Where the hell were they? And there was something about Roger's manner that wasn't quite right, and I couldn't help but think that whatever had happened had something to do with him, and that thought brought back my suspicions about what had happened to his parents.

Roger finished talking to the policeman and turned to me.

'There's been a break-in, Gill. I'm afraid they took all your jewellery.'

Fuck.

'My mum's ring?'

'Yeah, I'm afraid they took that as well. Everything.'

This really summed up my shitty day. I loved that ring. I'm not a materialistic person, but it was the one thing I would have gone back into a burning building for. I felt the anger build and tried to calm myself.

Roger shrugged. 'Sorry.'

'Why? Why should you be sorry? Did you let them in? What were you doing when this happened? For fuck's sake, Roger, I'm out for a few hours and I come back to *this*? What the fuck were you doing?'

'Please, Mrs Hempsall.' The policeman turned to-wards me, gesturing with his hands that I should calm down. 'We're the ones who're paid to ask the questions.'

I ignored his attempt at humour.

'And where are the twins, Roger?'

179

'Outside playing. Don't get your knickers in a twist, Gill. It's all covered by the insurance anyway.'

'Insurance ... Jesus!' I screamed. 'And I suppose the insurance is going to clean up the fucking mess after this lot have finished wading through it?' I was livid now. None of Martin's coping strategies were going to put Humpty Dumpty back together again. 'And what about my mum's ring? No amount of fucking insurance can bring that back.'

I walked out of the kitchen towards the study.

What I really wanted to do was to escape from this house, escape from this fucking family, but I knew I had to calm down ... to rationalise, to get a grip on reality rather than do something I would regret.

'I'm sorry, Mrs Hempsall. I just need to ask you a couple of questions. It won't take—'

'And you can fuck off as well. Make a fucking appointment or have me arrested,' I yelled, then slammed the study door, locked it, sat down at that ... that idiot of a husband's desk and burst into tears.

So, you can make your own mind up – worst possible conclusion or a minor setback?

FIFTY-TWO

DAVE

I didn't sleep much.

I was too excited. And I was worried that if I went to sleep, when I woke up my sight would be gone again, and I don't know what I'd do if that happened.

Well, I'd do nothing, because although I'd probably want to kill myself, I couldn't even do that.

It's funny, but no matter how bad my life has been, I've never actually wanted to kill myself. I suppose you might think from this that I'm an optimist, but I don't think I am. I think that all my life I've just sort of thought, well ... things can't really get much worse, can they? But now they can, and this is because if I lost my sight then I would never be able to kill my family, nor become a journalist.

I felt really calm when everyone left.

I found listening to the mother and that Indian doctor quite stressful.

Anyway, although I'm used to people talking about me as if I'm not there, this was different. They were talking about a tumour, and I happen to know that tumours kill people in what I think is a worse way than being thrown out of a plane without a parachute. So I'm probably going to stress about it until the pathology comes back and says that it is benign, which means I don't have to worry.

Then when I was alone, I pushed it to the back of my mind and concentrated on looking at things. I don't want to bang on about it, but sight is just amazing when you haven't been able to see anything.

The television took most of my attention. I don't know if the nurses meant to leave it on or they may just have forgotten to turn it off, but I was really glad they did.

There was a quiz show called *The Chase*. I'd heard about this before on BBC Radio 4 and I know roughly how it works.

A woman called Lorraine, who was one of the con-testants, had to answer questions to stand a chance of winning a share of forty-two thousand pounds. She had to choose one answer from three and hope it was right, and also hope that this man, called The Sinnerman, got it wrong. The Sinnerman, who's also called The Chaser, is a man who has dark skin and wears a white jacket

The quizmaster is someone called Bradley Walsh. He tries to be funny without smiling and has a strange ac-cent … I think it's called an estuary accent, which the fa-ther says means that he's working class. But the father says that northern accents are working class too. I don't think there's anything wrong with being working class, but the father seems to think there is.

'Okay, Lorraine,' said Bradley Walsh, 'the chase is on. Good luck. Here comes your first question: *Rosencrantz and Guildenstern Are Dead, Jumpers* and *The Invention of Love* are all plays by which Czech-born British play-wright?

'Is it: a) Tom Stoppard, b) Harold Pinter, or c) John Osborne?'

Bradley Walsh then said: 'I don't know nothing about any of these, cos it ain't got football in the title.' I don't know what football could have to do with this question, but the father says that working-class people always try to get football into every conversation.

After he read the question out, it appeared in a box at the bottom of the screen with the three possible answers, so the people who were watching could choose. I can't read them yet, of course, but I don't need to because – as I've told you – I've got a really good memory.

I know this. The answer is Tom Stoppard.

Lorraine got it right.

The Sinnerman got it right.

I got it right.

The Sinnerman then said that Harold Pinter wrote plays called *The Birthday* and *The Dumb Waiter*. I knew this, and I know that he also wrote *The Homecoming* and *Old Times* and that he won the Tony Award for the first one and was a nominee, but didn't win, for the second one.

Then The Sinnerman told us that John Osborne wrote *Look Back in Anger* and *The Entertainer.* I'm not sure why The Sinnerman needed to do this, but I think he may just be trying to establish some sort of psychological advantage by showing just how much he knows. I knew this too, by the way, but I don't want to show off.

Bradley Walsh just looked bored and said, 'Thank you. Right, here's your next question: which hospital beginning with the letter M is Britain's leading hospital specialising in eye injuries?

'Is it: a) Maidstone and Tunbridge Wells, b) Moorfield, or c) Manchester?'

I know this one too. It's Moorfield, in Bath, which is a private hospital and this means that poor people can't use it ... well, unless they have insurance, which is unlikely.

Lorraine got it right.

The Sinnerman got it right.

I got it right.

'Yeah, nice one, Lorraine.' This time The Sinnerman didn't add anything about other hospitals to show off.

'Next question: which bridge – one of the oldest roadway bridges in the United States – was completed in 1883 and spans the East River?

'Is it: a) Brooklyn Bridge, b) Queensboro Bridge, or c) Manhattan Bridge?'

Okay, I'll admit that I'm not one hundred per cent sure of this one. I'm pretty sure that it's Brooklyn Bridge because I happen to know that it's a hybrid cable-stayed bridge that connects Manhattan and Brooklyn. It has a main span of 486.3 metres and a height of 40.5 metres. It's one of the oldest roadway bridges in the United States and was the world's first steel-wire suspension bridge,

183

as well as the first fixed crossing across the East River. I learned all this from a programme on BBC Radio 4 called *Bridges Over Troubled Waters*. But I can't remember if 1883 was the year it was completed. I know it's not Queensboro Bridge because I know that this was built in 1909, and I don't think it was Manhattan Bridge either because I'm sure that was completed the same year that the *Titanic* sank – that's 1912, by the way. Yeah, so I'm pretty sure that it's Brooklyn Bridge.

Lorraine got it right.

I got it right.

The Sinnerman chose Manhattan Bridge and got it wrong.

Ha!

'A step closer to home , Lorraine,' Bradley Walsh said. The Sinnerman didn't look happy. He didn't say anything about bridges either. 'Look at that, Lorraine' — the camera zoomed in on some numbers — 'It looks like we've got forty-two grand in our cash builder.'

I don't know what a cash builder is but I'm starting to get quite excited. Not for Lorraine, but for myself.

I could do this.

'Next question coming right up, Lorraine. How're you feeling?'

Lorraine just smiled. 'A bit nervous, Bradley.'

'Here we go then: what is the normal lifespan of an Asian elephant?

'Is it: a) fifty years, b) fifty-five to seventy years, or c) seventy-five to ninety years?'

Hmmm ... I know that Asian elephants are smaller than African elephants and also have smaller ears, which they have to keep moving to cool themselves down. And they need to eat about a hundred and fifty kilos of food a day. This is mainly grass, but they also like to eat bark, roots, leaves and stems, and they like things like bananas, rice and sugarcane cos they're sweet, and this sometimes annoys the humans. Which, I suppose, is one reason why they're an endangered species. The females are more social than the males, and the oldest female, who is called a matriarch, leads the herd. The males just go and do stuff on their own. I suppose this is a bit like my own family, although the mother's started to go and do stuff on her own as well.

But this information doesn't help with their lifespan. I heard that they live about as long as a human, so I'm going to say, b) fifty-five to seventy years.

Lorraine got it right.

I got it right.

The Sinnerman got it right and said, 'And did you know that Asian elephants are the continent's largest terrestrial mammals? They can reach six-point-four metres in length and three metres at the shoulder, and weigh as much as five tonnes.'

Yes, I did know that. Sorry, I don't want to show off.

'Okay, Lorraine, well done. Is The Chaser getting rattled?'

'No no no no no no no,' replied The Sinnerman. Which I think meant yes.

'Here's your next question: with which country might you associate the musical instrument the bodhrán?

'Is it: a) Ireland, b) Norway, or c) Germany?'

Easy peasey.

It's Ireland, although I know the bodhrán is used throughout the Celtic music world. Maybe that's why he said 'might you associate'. But that rules out Norway and Germany because they're not Celtic. And JFH once said that the only people who are likely to listen to German music are the Germans themselves, and I think he probably had a point. Anyway, Germans are more famous for instruments like the accordion or the zither, and I know the bodhrán is a sort of drum but you can also use it to follow the tune being played.

'The correct answer is ... Ireland.'

Lorraine got it right.

I got it right.

The Sinnerman got it wrong. He put Norway. 'Yeah, I was getting my bukkehorns, langeleiks and my bodhráns in a muddle.'

No, you just got the answer wrong.

Ha again!

Bradley didn't sound that convinced either.

'Yeah ... here we go, Lorraine. One more, and you're home and dry.' I'm not sure what he means by this because even if she wins, she'll still be here, and I don't think that contestants get water thrown over them for getting something wrong. 'You've got three chances of getting this.'

He turned to Lorraine's teammates and said, 'She's playing well, isn't she?' They looked happy. 'That's an understatement,' he added, and the audience laughed at this, although I didn't see why it was funny. She *was* doing well.

'Here's your question: which of the following is the most southerly racecourse in the UK?

'Is it: a) Kempton, b) Towcester, or c) Exeter?'

Okay ... I'm not sure about Towcester, but I know that Kempton Park is near London and I know that Exeter is further south. The father always listens to the racing tips on BBC Radio 4 and sometimes Towcester is mentioned. Nope, I'll admit, I'm not at all that sure about this one. But I'm going to rule out Towcester because the other two are definitely in the south and they're bound to have one that isn't – unless it's a trick question, which, of course, it very well could be.

Lorraine chose Exeter.

I chose Exeter.

The Sinnerman chose Exeter.

'You've put Exeter, Lorraine?'

'Yeah.'

'You sure Towcester ain't near Goodwood? Because that's more southerly than Kempton or Exeter.'

'Yes. Quite sure, Bradley.'

So am I, because if it was, it wouldn't be called Goodwood; it would be called Towcester. I know because that's how naming racecourses works.

'For forty-two grand, the correct answer is ... Exeter.'

The audience went wild and the money flashed up on the panel where the other contestants were standing. Music started to play and then the adverts came on.

I felt exhausted but really excited, because today had been the best day of my life and I could have won a share of forty-two grand if I'd been on that programme.

I'd just have to figure out a way to do this.

And with that thought, I fell asleep and dreamt about The Sinnerman. This was actually slightly scary because he didn't like it that I got a question right and he got it wrong, and in my dream he turned into an Asian elephant and chased me through what was probably a jungle, until someone shot him.

I also dreamt about Molly, which was much better.

FIFTY-THREE

ROGER

Roger sat at the kitchen island drinking wine.

Overall, he thought, that had gone quite well, other than Gill's overreaction.

She'd stomped off to the study, locked herself in and left him to tidy up.

To his surprise, this hadn't taken nearly as long as he'd thought. Perhaps, he assumed, if you're the person who creates the havoc, you have a sort of emotional detachment from it and you just get it done. There's no 'How the hell could the bastard have done this?' angst because you're the bastard who did it.

The police left about an hour ago and appeared to be convinced that the break-in was genuine. They still wanted to question Gill, but Roger had persuaded them that because of Gill's psychological fragility, and Dave's accident, this would be better done at another time. There was nothing she could say to challenge his version of events anyway, and there were only three people who knew the burglary had been faked. Two of them were upstairs right now, probably counting the wad of cash that was the physical manifestation of their bought duplicity.

But one thing did worry Roger, and he would need to do something about it first thing tomorrow morning. And right now he had absolutely no idea how he was going to do this, because it would require another three grand, and the only way he could get his hands on that kind of money would be to raid the joint bank account again. And as he knew Gill frequently checked the balance before withdrawing cash, he was sure to be found out. He hadn't even come up with a plausible story for the two grand he'd had to shell out to the twins.

Before the police left, Roger had done some fishing, and he didn't like what had ended up in his net.

'I don't suppose there's much chance of you recovering the stolen items, is there?' he'd asked Detective Constable Bragg, the officer in charge.

'Oh, I wouldn't be so sure, sir,' he'd replied. 'This break-in looks quite amateurish to me, so I shouldn't be surprised if the villain was equally casual about the disposal of your property.'

'Meaning what, officer?'

'Meaning, sir, that he may or may not have what we refer to as a "fence" – someone who specialises in converting desirable stolen objects such as your wife's jewellery, particularly that ring, into cash, for a price.'

'So what would he do with the stuff, then?' Roger felt his forehead start to bead up and realised that he had to be careful not to draw suspicion his way. 'I mean, he wouldn't just stick it on eBay, would he?'

DC Bragg laughed.

'We always assume it's a "he", don't we, sir?'

'I'm not assuming anything. I'm just curious to know what your lines of enquiry will be and if we have any chance of getting our possessions back. You saw how much that ring means to my wife, didn't you?'

'Yes, of course, sir. I have every sympathy for Mrs Hempsall. I know exactly how she must be feeling. Her reaction is something we come across time and again, and it would have been insensitive for me to demand that she made a statement this evening, particularly after the day she's had, what with your son and all. All in good time.' He smiled. 'To answer your question, sir, believe it or not, our first line of enquiry is to check out the local pawn shops. You'd be surprised how many villains we apprehend because they're too stupid to realise that a pawnbroker keeps a record of every customer and issues a receipt for every item that's been hocked. Most of these shops are legitimate businesses nowadays, and they even have their own professional body. It's called the

National Pawnbrokers Association. So anyone foolish enough to hock nicked gear to one of them is asking for trouble.'

Roger felt his forehead begin to drip, turned towards the sink, pulled out his handkerchief and mopped his brow.

'Warm evening, sir, isn't it? So that's where we'll be starting our search for your property tomorrow morning. You'd be surprised how many times we strike gold ... pardon the pun.'

Left to the solitude of his thoughts, his worries and his third large glass of Pinot Grigio, Roger realised that at one minute past nine tomorrow he would be standing on the threshold of Pledge Pawnbrokers, Jewellers & Body Piercing. Somehow, between now and then he would have to come up with a plan to redeem the loan on Gill's Van Cleef & Arpels Sweet Alhambra ruby and diamond-encrusted effeuillage ring.

And he would also have to pray that DC Bragg and his merry men didn't choose the same threshold to commence their line of enquiry.

FIFTY-FOUR

GILL

DIARY ENTRY: Wednesday, 24 July 2019

I was still at my laptop an hour later.

I'd written loads – I just let it all pour out. To my surprise I felt better, well enough to leave the study and rejoin my dysfunctional family.

But there was something nagging at my consciousness, and the more I tried to grasp it, the more it slipped away.

My subliminal mind was telling me to let it go, that it was a needless worry ... a worry with no solid basis.

But then I had it, right in front of me, laid out like a painting I detested but was unable to drag my eyes away from.

Molly – what if she was right? What if she had seen something? What if Dave could not only see but had a fully functioning brain?

I knew that I should feel delighted, that I should take this glimmer of hope and pursue it with the sort of intensity a normal mother would. But I wasn't a normal mother, was I? I was a mother whose desire to sever the ropes that bound her to her disabled son – to her family – was stronger than her desire to help him. I wasn't a mother at all. I was a woman who had the honesty to put herself first and, in order to do this, would be willing to sacrifice her son's future for her own happiness and freedom.

I tried to bury this thought as I left the study, but I couldn't dig a deep enough grave to restrain it.

***

There was no sign of the twins, which was normal. When they aren't tormenting Dave, destroying what's left of the garden or annoying the neighbours, they spend most of the time in their rooms.

Which is fine by me. What they get up to is of little concern right now – out of sight, out of mind.

Roger was sitting on a stool in the kitchen, drinking wine. At least he'd tidied up before he hit the booze.

He looked distraught, and for a brief moment I felt guilty about having a go at him over the break-in. I mean, it wasn't his fault; there was no way he could have prevented it.

But my compassion evaporated the second I thought of everything he'd done – or not done – to cast us into the dire financial situation we now faced. The fact that the inheritance came from his parents was an irrelevance. Families work together to support each other, yet one way or another, all he'd done was to squander the money on his own interests. I hadn't dared check the bank account for a couple of weeks, but I'd made it clear to him that what little there was left was for the benefit of the family, and not just himself. He'd seemed to take that on board. I suppose I could go online and check the balance right now, but I'll leave it until tomorrow when I'll need to withdraw some cash. I don't like paying by card when I'm out with Ali. Devious, aren't I? No, just cautious.

'Want some wine?' he asked. I wanted a stiff vodka and tonic, but that would just give him something else to have a go at me about. Roger drinks like a fish, but beer and wine don't count, according to him, and people who drink spirits are the ones with a real drinking problem.

I poured a large glass and sat at the island.

'Have we got anything to eat tonight or shall I whistle up a takeaway?'

'Do you know what a fridge looks like, Roger? Oh, of course you do. That's where you keep your beer and wine, isn't it?'

'I was only asking.'

'Pity you didn't see fit to ask about your son.'

192

'Actually, I've been a bit preoccupied with things. So how is he?'

I took a large mouthful of wine.

'He had an emergency surgical evacuation to remove a haematoma, which seems to have relieved the pressure caused by the oedema. Mr Patel – that's the consultant neurologist, by the way – said he needs to stay in for a few days. I'm going to be there all day tomorrow, so you'll need to supervise the twins.'

Roger took this without either comment or dispute, much to my surprise.

'But Molly's offered to help, so after tomorrow she's going to do most of the sitting with him.'

'That's good of her.'

The absence of a sarcastic remark made me suspicious, but I had to remind myself that we both had our own agendas. I still had no idea what Roger's was, but, as I said, I had no doubt he was up to something he'd rather I didn't find out about.

But the mention of Molly raised that ghost of a worry once again.

We sat in silence. I wasn't surprised by Roger's lack of interest in Dave's medical condition. I tossed a mental coin. It came down heads. I decided to share.

'Oh, something a bit, I don't know ... a bit odd happened.'

'Don't tell me ... Dave started solving quadratic equations and talking in Mandarin?'

I ignored this.

'Molly said she'd felt sure that something had happened to his eyes and that he was able to see. This was after the operation. It was quite strange, actually. At first she sounded really convinced about it. She said she could track his eyes following her. But then, after I'd pressed her for more information, she said she'd probably imagined it, and totally played it down.'

'What? She thought he was able to see? You mean that his eyes were working?'

'Did you work that out all by yourself, Roger?'

That was a waste of breath. Roger has never really got sarcasm.

'Not that you're interested,' I continued, 'but Mr Patel discovered a tumour that was attached to the optical nerve head, and he removed it when he evacuated the oedema.'

This got Roger's attention.

'A tumour? Fucking hell ... that could kill him, couldn't it? He'd better not bloody die before they agree the settlement figure.'

'That's all you think of, isn't it? How much money you can get from this whole thing. That money's supposed to be compensation for Dave having a wrecked life, not for you to fill the garage with fast cars. Anyway, Patel said the tumour was almost certainly benign but they'd get it checked out.'

'Yes, well, part of the settlement figure *is* for us, due to the fact that we've had our lives wrecked because of Dave, let me remind you. And, as we'll be administering the trust fund, if Dave wants a Ferrari in the garage, I can't see any good reason to deny him one. Can you?'

Silence.

There's no point in me jumping onto my morally elevated high horse. I want some of that money too, so that I can get as far away from Roger and this family as I can and start my new life with Ali.

So I said nothing.

'So what happens if Molly was right? What if Dave *has* miraculously got his sight back? Will that affect the settlement figure?'

There was another heavy silence while we both processed this. With all that had happened today, this thought hadn't occurred to me. Roger had a point. It could very well change everything. Well, not everything, but the defendants' legal team wouldn't pass up the opportunity to have the case reassessed, and, if nothing else, this could delay agreeing the settlement, possibly even by years.

Roger voiced what we both were thinking.

'Anyway, how will they know if he can see? I mean, even if he can, his brain's still fucked, isn't it?'

'They're going to carry out something called the Glasgow Coma Scale. You might remember it?'

'Yeah, I remember, the one Dave scored three on. But he's not in a coma – not that you'd notice – so how is this relevant now?'

'It's relevant because, I would imagine, they'll use the same protocols to assess him. An ophthalmologist will shine intense pinpricks of light into his eyes and check under magnification for any reaction in the pupil or iris.'

'Fuck.'

Roger poured himself more wine, and as an after-thought, tipped the rest of the bottle into my glass.

'Is there any way we can refuse this? I mean, we have to give consent for everything in connection with Dave, don't we? So why should this be any different? What if they find he can see, and maybe even that his brain isn't totally fucked? That would completely screw up the com-pensation, wouldn't it?'

'They did a CT scan before his operation, and they'll do another one tomorrow or the day after. Patel says this'll give evidence of increased or reduced brain atro-phy—'

'Can't we just discharge him from hospital? Say that we're going to arrange for private medical cover at home?'

'Oh really? That wouldn't look suspicious, would it. Can you imagine what the defendants' legal team would make of that? No ... we let him have the CT scan. I very much doubt it'll show anything different. It's Molly we need to worry about. I'm not totally convinced that she didn't see something. I need to get to the bottom of this ... and, if necessary, I know how to make sure that she won't interfere.'

There, the ghost was out and I felt a little better. At least I knew what I needed to do now.

FIFTY-FIVE

MOLLY JOHNSON

MSc RESEARCH PROJECT NOTES
NOTE 8: Thursday, 25 July 2019

I can't believe what happened this morning.

I didn't get to the hospital until almost eleven because I'd decided I needed to talk to Josh, and that meant a trip into the university. I emailed him first to check he'd be there. (I'm trying really hard to get his number, lol, but he's too professional to give it out … yet! Note to self – remove this!) I was lucky to catch him, and we went for a coffee and chatted through the ethics of what I've already done, as in lying about not being convinced that Dave can see, and the non-disclosure of what I believe is his locked-in syndrome.

Josh's advice was that this was a really murky area, and one he had little experience of. His view was that Dave was my subject; therefore, the practitioner–patient rule applies and I have a duty of care towards him, but not towards his parents. If I was absolutely convinced that Dave had wilfully instructed me not to disclose information about his sight, then it was my duty to respect his request.

However, it wasn't as simple as that; nothing ever is. I felt I had to tell Josh about the medical negligence case. He agreed that – as my supervisor – sharing this confidential information was not a breach of confidentiality. But his view was that if I withheld the information concerning my observation as to Dave's status, it *could* be

196

prejudicial to the outcome of the settlement. But he didn't know; he's not a lawyer.

'Maybe it would be simpler if you looked for another subject for your data collection, Molly,' he said.

'Would you if you were presented with this opportunity?'

There was a long silence as he thought about this.

'No,' he replied. 'Just remind me of the precise title of your project?'

"Practical Aspects of Communication in Brain-Damaged Paediatric Patients',' I replied. 'Why do you ask?'

'I ask because you'll never ... no, no one will ever – based on what you've told me – be presented with a better opportunity to carry out cutting-edge research into an area that's never really been properly explored. I mean, it's almost a blank page. There's so little known about locked-in syndrome.'

Again we sat in silence. We were the only ones in the refectory.

'Are you sure of this? I mean, are you absolutely sure that he can communicate?'

'Yes. I am quite sure.'

He laughed softly.

'What's so funny?'

'I'd love to collaborate with you on this, Molly, I really would. It's the sort of project I've dreamt of for years.'

(OMG! I'd love to collaborate with Josh on absolutely anything. God, he is soooooo gorgeous. And he's sensitive and gentle and intelligent, and I know that he would definitely be the one to heal my scars and help me to move on from the past.)

'But I can't, Molly. It would be unethical. It's your project. I'll help you in any way I can, but it's down to you to do the research and collect the data. Get this right and it'll get you more than a distinction; it'll set you up academically for life. You could absolutely base doctoral research on this.'

'And if I get it wrong? What if I'm sued for non-disclosure?'

'I don't know the answer to that. I'll try and get an opinion from the legal department. Trouble is, most of them are on leave, so it may take a while. For now, if I were you, I'd take the view that your honestly held belief is that Dave suffers from locked-in syndrome, and that you are convinced that he has instructed you not to comment on his ability to see. If you can, try to obtain an instruction from him as to whether he wishes you to disclose information about his mental condition, as in the locked-in syndrome, or not.'

I nodded.

'Oh, and one other thing: try to video your interactions with Dave. It may not only be useful for your data set, but – perish the thought – if this ever ends up in court, it might be invaluable.'

I nodded again.

'And one other thing: don't get emotionally involved in this.'

Too late; I already am.

Richard Grainger

FIFTY-SIX

DAVE

Why do they wake you up so early in hospital?

I don't understand this.

It's not as if you have to go to work or even do any-thing, apart from either get better or maybe even die. All you have to do is lie in bed and do nothing.

I think it's for the nurses' convenience. Once they've woken you up, they feed you and they change you, and then they probably just get on with really important stuff like drinking coffee and talking about wankers in their nurses' space.

The nurse who fed me was nice, but she wasn't very good at it.

I'm not sure what she was trying to feed me but it tasted worse than Ready Brek – if you can believe that – and I had trouble swallowing it without throwing up, so she said that I mustn't be hungry and then she gave up; but at least she talked to me. But I *was* hungry and I prob-ably would have eaten it all if she'd given me more time, even though it tasted gross.

I know from BBC Radio 4 that there's a shortage of nurses because they don't get paid very well, and that most of the nurses who still work for the NHS come from Eastern Europe, mainly from Poland. I think this nurse was from Poland because she spoke with a funny accent. She sounded a bit like the voice of the small furry animal wearing glasses I'd seen in this advert on the television last night. I think it's called a meerkat, but I'm pretty sure meerkats can't actually talk, so it was probably just

199

what's called computer-generated. I'd be surprised if meerkats wear glasses either, cos I've never heard of glasses for animals, but I could very well be wrong. You see how much I still have to learn? Anyway, the nurse who was probably from Poland told me that her name was Gosia.

The other reason I couldn't eat very quickly was because I was too busy looking at her. Her hair was tied back so that it looked like a tail coming out of the back of her head. She had pale skin, eyes the same colour as the sky, which was dark and cloudy this morning – I think this is called grey – and her cheekbones were a lot different to Molly's, the mother's or Lorraine's, who was on *The Chase*. I think she is really good-looking, and I remembered someone saying – maybe on *Women's Hour*? – that many Polish women are really beautiful. But if I had to choose between her and Molly, I would choose Molly because I don't think that Molly would give up trying to feed me so easily, and being good at feeding someone like me is more important than being good-looking.

Although Molly *is* really good-looking.

The television wasn't on this morning. I suppose someone must have turned it off after I fell asleep. I don't mind, though; there's plenty to look at and I'm still really excited about being able to see.

My room has two windows. One looks out over fields and trees but the other is on the far side of the room and looks over buildings, and in the distance I can see hills. I hadn't noticed this window last night, because I would have to had turned my head to see it and this normally takes a lot of effort. But this morning I can do this quite easily. And this makes me wonder if something else might have happened when the doctor called Mr Patel went inside my head?

I'm not going to get too excited, though, because so much has happened since yesterday that I can still hardly believe it.

This time yesterday no one knew that my brain works perfectly well and it's only this locked-in thing that prevents me from winning *The Chase* and maybe even becoming a journalist like Gary O'Donoghue ...

except I'm able to see now, so I wouldn't be quite like Gary O'Donoghue.

This time yesterday I hadn't seen Molly, and I hadn't been hit on the head with a block and had my head drained. In fact, this time yesterday I couldn't see anything at all, and I never thought that I would.

Maybe you'll understand what I mean when I say that quite a lot has happened and I'm not expecting, or even hoping, that anything else amazing might happen.

Of course, I would love to be able to stand up, walk to the window and look at the view. I would love to get dressed all by myself, have a poo (sorry) into a proper toilet and not into a nappy, walk out of here all by myself, then do something like tamper with the brakes on the father's car so that there would be a terrible accident and my family would die.

But if none of this ever happens, I don't really mind because being able to see is just amazing, and anyway, if I could walk out of here and tamper with the father's brakes, I would just go prison like normal murderers do, and that would be even worse than being trapped inside a body that doesn't work.

I just need to decide what I'm going to do next.

But I think I already know.

FIFTY-SEVEN

MOLLY JOHNSON

MSc RESEARCH PROJECT NOTES
NOTE 9: Thursday, 25 July 2019

I got to the hospital at around eleven and Gill was already there.

She was sitting in the uncomfortable, institutional armchair I sat in yesterday, reading a magazine. I noticed that she'd moved the chair closer to the window, away from Dave's bed.

I said hi to Dave and added that I hoped he was feeling better. I got no response, but I wasn't expecting one.

Gill seemed agitated.

'Is everything okay?' I asked.

'Yeah, just great,' she replied, with a smile that told me that it wasn't. 'I got home last night to find the house a complete tip and police crawling over everything. Apparently there'd been a break-in. All my jewellery, including a ring my mother had given me that I really treasured, had been stolen.'

'Oh, Gill, I'm so sorry.'

It was my turn to empathise now. Time to change the subject.

'How's Dave?' I asked. 'Did he have a good night?'

'He's fine,' she replied, but I sensed that her mind was elsewhere.

I was right.

Richard Grainger

'Molly, you know yesterday, when you said you felt sure that Dave could see, you said that you'd felt his eyes following or tracking you?'

'Yeah, I'm pretty sure that I imagined it. It'd been a long day.'

Gill put down her magazine and looked at me in what I would call a confrontational sort of way.

'I don't believe you, Molly.'

'What?'

'You heard. But let me repeat it. I don't believe you. I think you saw something. I think you observed something different about Dave.'

'I—'

'Let me make this perfectly clear, Molly. You know about the medical negligence case. I know you do because you'll have read Dave's medical notes, or at least some of them, and that was the most recent, so it's at the front of the file. Don't tell me you don't know about it.'

'Yes,' I replied. I didn't like where this was going and I didn't like Gill's attitude. I knew, because of what Roger had said, that she was having counselling, but of course I didn't know why. Maybe she was bipolar? Her behaviour and attitude was more like it was in the weird dream I'd had yesterday than last night, when she drove me home. 'I'm sorry, but I don't see what that's got to do—'

'It's got everything to do with it, Molly. Have you any idea of the amount of money that's involved? And I don't just mean the initial lump sum payout. I'm talking about the annual periodic payments, which will run to almost half a million a year. The North-Eastern Health Authority will do anything to avoid paying up, or at least to have the case reopened, and it could take years. Dave could end up with a pittance.'

I couldn't believe this. It was about to get worse.

'I'll level with you, Molly. I think you saw something and I believe that if you go public on this, it will open a can of worms that we – and Dave – really don't want opening.'

Gill stood up and walked to the window opposite Dave's bed. It was as if Dave wasn't in the room, and I wondered if she would be saying all this if she knew what

203

Saving Dave

I knew. She stared out of the window with her back to me
for a minute as if weighing up her options. Then she
turned and faced me, a grim look of ... I don't know ... anger on her face.

'So here's what I'm going to suggest: you say nothing
about what you saw. If you think Dave somehow, miraculously, is able to see, and that he can make some sort of
sense out of what he sees, you keep it to yourself. The
lump sum is mainly calculated on loss of future earnings,
and should the defendants get even a sniff of an idea that
Dave may at some future point have the remotest chance
of earning a living, the gloves will come off.'

I couldn't believe I was hearing this.

'So I'm going to offer you a deal, Molly. You say nothing about your presumptions, absolutely nothing to anybody, and I'm going to offer you one hundred thousand
in cash, following the settlement.'

We stared at each other and let the silence settle
around us, like particles of dust dancing in a shaft of sunlight, seeking somewhere to land.

'But if you ever breathe a word, I will block your access to Dave. You will have to look elsewhere for your research, because you'll never see him again. And not only
that, Molly; I'll have a little word with Charlie, your abusive ex, and make sure he has your new phone number
and knows where to find you without violating the restraining order.'

Jesus Christ.

So not only am I the victim of attempted blackmail,
I've also been threatened with more violence. How could
she do this after all she'd said last night? This is why I'm
writing all this down in such detail; because this is all going to come out someday, and when it does I want complete clarity as to what was said.

The sensible thing would have been for me to pick up
my stuff, say goodbye to Dave, walk out of the door and
have absolutely nothing further to do with this utterly
odious family.

But I knew I was never going to do this, and it wasn't
just because of what Josh had said about the prospect of
my research opening some pretty iridescent academic

gates for me. And it certainly wasn't because of the money, which I had no intention of accepting.

It was because Gill's little sales pitch-slash-intimidation speech had only served to reinforce my view that Dave was completely alone, and if I walked out of the room, I would be closing the door to his world, now and probably forever.

'I don't want your money, Gill. I'm not interested in it. All I want is for Dave to help me with my research, and in return I'll look after him until I've completed it. I give you my word that I will say nothing.' As the words came out, I knew how fraudulent they were. You can only take altruism so far, and the point of my research was to share it, especially after Josh's enthusiasm.

Gill smiled. Her hostility had evaporated.

'We have an agreement then.'

I managed to force a half-smile.

'We have an agreement.'

FIFTY-EIGHT

ROGER

It took Roger almost twenty minutes to find what he was looking for.

As the study clock ticked ominously, he felt a growing sense of desperation start to choke him. Had Gill been 're-arranging' his files? He was normally quite well organised when it came to archiving important stuff, or stuff that might conceivably acquire an importance, as was the case with what he was looking for.

What he sought should be filed – using his system – under the letter 'D', for two reasons: 'D' for 'Dad' and 'D' for 'Dead', which in effect were one and the same.

He had postponed his search until Gill had left for the hospital. This, he figured, would still give him ample time to do what he needed to do without arousing her suspicions.

Eventually he found what he was looking for under the letter 'P', which was, he realised, where his search should have commenced. 'P' stood for Probate, and inside a thin buff file he found the valuation of everything that his parents, having departed this life, had left behind for him to wallow his way through.

And there, towards the bottom of the fourth sheet of A4, was what he was looking for: the listing, description and value of the antique mahogany partner desk, at which he now sat.

He loved this desk, but needs must, and having agonised about it for most of a sleepless night, he could think of no other way of extricating himself from the cesspool that he was rapidly sinking deeper and deeper into.

'Antique mahogany partner desk,' the listing read, 'valued at six thousand pounds.'

Westmorland Antiques Reclaimed had valued the desk along with the rest of his parents' furniture, and Roger found their formal letter-headed valuation sheet in the same buff file.

He looked at the clock; it read eight thirty-five.

These sort of blue-collar establishments, Roger figured, usually had a loyal, ageing, beige work-coated, tie-wearing retainer – one who either owned or who had spent most of his working life devoted to the same firm, and one who found rummaging amongst antique furniture in the warehouse more appealing than an extra hour in bed – and he would be on the premises from around sun-up. This being the case, someone should answer the phone.

Roger wasn't wrong.

The phone rang three times before it was answered.

'Westmorland Antiques Reclaimed, how can I help you?'

Roger explained precisely how he could be helped and was told if he could bring the desk in, it would be valued straight away. But, he was advised, the valuation to purchase the desk might very well be significantly lower than the probate valuation. Roger realised that he was in no position to dispute this.

He then set about emptying the contents of the desk into a black bin bag, with a complete absence of methodology.

Fifteen minutes later, he pulled the Davemobile into Westmorland Antiques Reclaimed's yard and was helped with the removal of the three principle parts of the desk, plus the drawers, by the beige work-coated, tie-wearing employee who – but for the absence of a moustache – could have walked straight off the set of *Open All Hours.*

Inside the warehouse, a thorough examination followed.

'Are you actually authorised to put a value on this?' Roger asked, a little impetuously. A glance at his watch told him that he now had less than ten minutes to do the deal and hotfoot it to the premises of Pledge Pawnbrokers, Jewellers & Body Piercing to retrieve Gill's Van Cleef & Arpels Sweet Alhambra ruby and diamond-encrusted effeuillage ring, before DC Bragg potentially got his size elevens over the threshold.

'Of course, sir. Allow me to introduce myself.' The Ronnie Barker lookalike pulled a pipe from the pocket of his work coat, tamped it with his thumb, struck a Swan Vesta, and puffed furiously until he was satisfied with the industrial quantity of smoke the thing belched out. 'I'm Zachariah Westmorland, the fifth generation of Westmorlands to own this establishment, and as the sole proprietor, I am the valuer, auctioneer, chief bottle washer and—'

'How much?' asked Roger, bluntly. He had no time for the history of the Westmorland antique dynasty, not even on a normal day.

Westmorland stroked his chin and furrowed his brow.

'Three thousand would be the most I could stretch to.'

'Oh, come on! You valued it at six, and that was after I'd asked you for a low valuation for probate.'

'Let me explain to you, sir, the difference between—'

'Look, I really don't have time for this. I'll sell it to you for five grand, but I'm not taking a penny less.'

Roger mentally checked the figures, perspiration once more beading his brow, while Westmorland tutted, murmured and shook his head in a well-rehearsed and theatrical ritual of decisional balance. He needed four grand to get the ring back. Of course, he had hoped to do significantly better than this so that he could replace the two grand he'd had to withdraw from the bank to bribe the twins.

But he knew he needed to sell it more than Westmorland needed to buy it, and that much was clear to both of them.

'I'll stretch to three and a half, then.'

'Four and a half,' countered Roger. If he didn't reach an acceptable agreement and get out of here within the next few minutes, it wasn't going to matter anyway. The stretch he'd be looking at in clink would be longer than four and a half years.

'Four, and that really is my final offer, sir.'

'Okay ... four it is then, in cash, and right now.' Roger proffered his hand and they shook.

'I'm not sure if I'll have that amount of cash on the premises. I can do a bank transfer?'

'Rubbish. You're a cash business. Cash, and right now, or you can forget it.'

At eight fifty-eight Roger stood on the threshold of Pledge Pawnbrokers, Jewellers & Body Piercing as an anonymous hand turned the closed sign to 'Open' and unlocked the door.

And at one minute past nine, he pulled the Davemobile out of the disabled parking space opposite the pawnbrokers; and as he turned left out of Holderness Road, he caught a glimpse of a Battenburg-marked BMW pulling into the space he had just left.

FIFTY-NINE

DAVE

If I had any doubts about what I'm going to do, I don't now.

A while ago – you may remember – I said that I didn't want to kill the mother because I felt sorry for her.

But after everything I've heard this morning, I don't feel sorry for her any more.

Not only did she try to blackmail Molly, but she also threatened her with someone called Charlie, who she called an 'abusive ex'. I'm not totally sure what this means ... I know what abusive means, and I think that Charlie was Molly's boyfriend and – for some reason that I can't imagine – he beat her up or something. I've heard JFH talk about something called domestic violence on BBC Radio 4, and it's usually when men are violent to women, but sometimes women can be violent to men, and until this morning I wouldn't have minded if the mother had been violent to the father, but I'm not so sure now.

There's a play by Shakespeare about two lovers called Romeo and Juliet and they both end up killing themselves, so if the mother and father killed themselves, even by accident – which is what happens in the play – that would be what Boris calls 'a result'. But I'm pretty sure they don't love each other, so I doubt very much if the father would stab himself to death if he thought that the mother was dead.

He'd probably just open a beer.

What she said to Molly actually scared me a bit, because I've never noticed this side of her before. I thought she just had a really bad temper and exploded when things annoyed her, but she spoke to Molly in a very calm way, like she'd thought about this and maybe even planned it out.

Anyway, I'm really shocked.

Perhaps this might make Molly want to help me to kill my family? I doubt it, though.

I'm quite a good judge of character, and from what little I know about Molly – even with the mother's threats – I just don't think she's a potential mass murderer. But once I get to know her better, I might try to radicalise her. JFH once talked about people who get radicalised, but they're mainly Muslims who are told that they will go to heaven where they will meet loads of virgins and do a lot of sex to them if they blow themselves and other people up, or stab them and then get shot by the police.

I don't think this would appeal much to Molly, so I think I'm going to try to get her to help me in a different way ... a way that doesn't involve her in mass murder.

This may come as a surprise to you, but I'm really very upset that the mother is only interested in me because of the compensation claim. I know that she's having what's called an affair – which means that's she's doing sex with someone else other than the father. I'll tell you how I know about this in a bit.

And I'm not stupid enough to believe that she cares about me more than she cares about her lover, but I really thought that at least she cared more about me than she cared about the money. I thought it was just the father who only cared about the money, but now it's clear to me that it's both of them.

Maybe someday I'll be able to get Molly to buy them both a T-shirt that says, 'I'm only in it for the money', to pay them both back for the parking T-shirt the father bought me and made me wear.

The mother left after she'd been horrible to Molly, who just sank into the chair where the mother had been sitting and started to cry really loudly.

211

And that was when I realised that if I could stand up, walk to the window, get dressed all by myself, then do something like tamper with the brakes on the father's car so that there would be a terrible accident and my family would die ... I realised that if I *could* actually do that, I probably wouldn't want to do it.

What I would want to do – more than anything – would be to hug Molly and tell her that everything will be all right and nothing bad will happen to her because I will always be here to look after her. I know what a hug is because the mother used to pull me close to her and say how nice it was to hug me. But that was years ago.

I know that this will never happen, but I think I *may* have the beginnings of a plan.

SIXTY

MOLLY JOHNSON

MSc RESEARCH PROJECT NOTES
NOTE 10: Friday, 26 July 2019

I wouldn't describe myself as an overly emotive person, and I know very well why Josh had warned me about forming an emotional attachment, but I was totally staggered by Gill's outburst.

It took me ages to pull myself together and begin what I had come here this morning to do.

Dave had been propped up in bed and ... maybe I imagined it, but I'm sure he looked a bit sad. Perhaps I read too much into this, but I felt sure he'd understood everything Gill had just said, and it would have been upsetting for him almost as much as it was for me.

It must be an emotional rollercoaster for him – two days ago, pure joy at getting his sight back, then yesterday having to face the prospect that he could remain locked-in forever. But I'm not going to let that happen. I don't care what I agreed with Gill; I'm here to study Dave's communication, and in my opinion, that relates to maximising his communicative ability ... even if it's only to test my thesis's hypothesis – which, by the way, I've not nailed down yet. I know it shouldn't be, but because Dave's ability is such unchartered territory, I suppose this will be a retrospective thing.

So I'll find a way to let his light shine out into the world. I don't know how I'm going to do this yet, but I'll somehow persuade Gill to let me help him.

***

Anyway, putting my sensible, unemotional head on, I decided there was no time to waste.

Part of Josh's advice had been to try him with an alphabet board. This is pretty much as it sounds: a two-sided letter board, measuring roughly thirty by twenty centimetres. Each row is numbered and contains four letters, with the last one containing two letters and two symbols. As it's American, hashtag is obviously one, lol. In addition to letters, it has a row of numerals along the top, and at the bottom, set in larger spaces, are blocks allowing the user to select shortcuts to communicate additional information: yes, no, space, start over, mistake, guess, or new word.

The idea is that the communicator (Dave) is asked which row the first letter or numeral is in, and then which of the four letters is first, and the interlocutor (that's me) repeats this process until they've written down sufficient letters to form most or all of the word. This is done by the blinking 'yes–no' method we've already established.

I had a quick practice with Josh (maybe this is as close as I'm going to get to him giving me the eye, lol – delete this!) and from this I know how laborious a process it's going to be. I also had a brief look at a couple of YouTube videos, which made me realise that this is a highly skilled operation for a trained speech therapy practitioner and not some duffer like me who's never done it before.

Okay, I thought, let's not be neggars here, and let's just give it a go.

'Dave,' I said, 'we're going to try to communicate using this thing.' I held up the board. I'd already prepared myself mentally for interruptions, particularly those of a parental variety, although I figured that the chances of Roger visiting Dave in hospital were about as high as him ever fitting into those tennis shorts again. But if anyone enters the room, the board will disappear into my bag faster than a packet of fags into a schoolgirl's knickers.

'This is what's called an "alphabet board". I want you to blink twice when I point with this pencil at the first letter of the word you want to spell out. Then we repeat this until I either know or can guess the word. Then, when I think I know the word, I'm going to guess and point at the word "yes". If you're happy I've got it right, you blink twice again, and so on.' OMG, it sounds so complicated. It's going to take forever just to say 'good morning'.

'Do you follow this, Dave?'

Two blinks.

His look of sadness seems to have evaporated. Maybe it's displacement – positive action pushing his negative emotions from earlier to the back of his mind.

'Okay,' I smiled and squeezed his wrist, 'let's get started then.'

I had no idea of how stupid I was going to feel and how disappointed we were both going to be.

It was so obvious afterwards; why the hell hadn't it occurred to me?

SIXTY-ONE

DAVE

I think Molly is a really strong person.

If I'd been her, I'd probably just have gone home and forgotten about me after what the mother had said to her.

If she'd done this, my message in the bottle – remember I mentioned this yesterday? Well, it would have wound up on a shore beside a hundred billion other bottles that no one would ever pull a message from. There's a song about this by a band called The Police. I think it's quite an old song and I don't think that they *are* actually proper policeman, because the father says that the police are just stupid people who have difficulty constructing a sentence without using at least three swear words, and there aren't any swear words in the song. I know that there's also a band called Queen, and I'm pretty sure that the actual queen doesn't play in it, because her job is to be head of state, open parliament, meet Boris Johnson every week and do visits to countries that Britain used to own, so I think it's probably unlikely that she'd have time to be in a band as well, but I could very well be wrong. She certainly doesn't sing, cos that was done by someone called Freddie Mercury, but she might play the guitar or drums, or shake a tambourine or something, I suppose.

I know about how they name racecourses and things like that, but I don't understand much about how bands get their names.

Sorry ... I'm getting a bit off the point.

216

So, Molly came over and sat down beside me and pulled this board thing out of her bag and explained what she wanted me to do.

I looked at the board for quite a long time, and she said nothing and just let me study it.

She'd asked me if I followed what she'd told me to do and I responded that I had, but I realised that what I was looking at made no sense at all.

There was just a load of meaningless shapes on the board ... well, meaningless to me anyway, and my heart sank once again because I realised that I didn't know what these letters and numbers meant. I know that the ancient Egyptians used things called hieroglyphic symbols, and that they explained the objects they wanted to talk about, and also that these symbols stood for particular sounds or groups of sounds. So these would probably do the same thing if I could make some sort of sense from them.

The shapes on Molly's board made as little sense to me as a hieroglyphic symbol probably would to a policeman, unless maybe he was in the Egyptian police and had learned about hieroglyphics.

'Dave,' Molly said, 'think of a word and try to spell it out. Hey ... this will be your first word! How about that?' She laughed, and that made me feel a bit better, because I knew she was expecting this to work, and after what the mother had put her through, I really wanted her to be happy, and I understood that she was taking a big risk by trying to help me.

This may be what's called splitting hairs, but I don't think it *would* be my first word, because I've said millions of words. It's just that no one has been able to understand them. And I can remember about the accident yesterday now, so I must have suffered from short-term memory loss. I have this memory of yelling 'fuck' when the thing hit me on the head and I'm sure that I heard Boris say, 'Did he just say "fuck"?' So if I did, and if Boris understood it, then that was technically my first word.

It doesn't matter anyway, because no matter how much I want to, I have no idea what these shapes on the board mean, so there's about as much chance of me being able to spell a word as there is of me standing up from this bed, hugging Molly and telling her that everything is going to be all right.

I know I'm digressing quite a bit, but this is because I'm actually starting to feel angry. I've only felt anger once before – maybe you remember, when I had to do the parachute jump? But this is a different sort of anger; it's a mixture of disappointment, sadness, stress and frustration.

So what I do when I feel like this is I clench my fists and bang them really hard against something so that I make a lot of noise, and the only thing I could find happened to be the rails on either side of the bed. When this happens, I have no control over it – it just happens. I'd heard one of the doctors who'd examined me years ago call it 'involuntary autonomic reaction'.

After a while ... I don't know, it could have been ages or it might just have been a few seconds, I saw Molly place her hands over mine really gently. She did this in a comforting and not what you might call a restraining way, and it calmed me down so my fists stopped banging. My mind was still really cloudy, and I couldn't think straight – I'd heard someone say that this is what anger does to you and it's sometimes called 'seeing red'. I'm not sure if I 'saw red' because I'm not sure what red looks like yet, but after a while I started to feel better, and that was when I realised that Molly still had her hands on top of mine, and at last I could think properly again. The first thought I had was that I wished that she would stay where she was forever and never leave me. But I also felt the greatest fear I've ever felt – yes, even worse than the parachute jump or being forced to fly. I was terrified that she would get up and go and that I would never see her again because of the letters and numbers on the alphabet board thing that I was too stupid to understand, so I wouldn't be any use to her—

'Dave,' she said softly, interrupting the flood of fear clouding my mind, 'Dave, listen to me.' She let go of my hands and leant forward. She looked so beautiful and she smelt really nice. Her hair was loose and it fell down the sides of her face – quite close to my face – and this made her eyes look even more amazing. 'I'm not going to abandon you. I'm going to help you. I'm not sure how I'm going to do it yet, but I'm going to help you to learn to spell and read somehow. Do you understand?'

I blinked twice, and some of the fear started to drain away.

'I'm really, really sorry. It was totally stupid of me to think that you'd have been able to read and spell by the time of your ... your problem. How many two-year-olds can read?' She laughed nervously, as if what she'd said was funny ... but not very funny. 'It was really thoughtless of me. I'm sorry.' She squeezed my right hand and leant further forward, and for a second I thought she was going to kiss me. Yeah, right, in my dreams! What she did was to lift my head and rearrange the pillow, which was good anyway cos it meant I could see her better.

'I'm going to speak to Josh – that's my supervisor at uni – and see what he recommends. Don't worry, Dave, I'm going to help you talk, and no amount of threats or bribery is going to stop me.'

And then the weirdest thing happened. Her eyes filled with water and a drop ran down her cheek and landed on my face. She dabbed it away with something, then wiped her eyes and smiled.

'Silly me,' she said, and kissed me on the flat bit of my head above my eyes – I'm not sure if that counts as a proper kiss, but I'm going to claim it anyway – and then she got up, turned the television on, told me that she'd see me tomorrow, and left.

So, for the second day in a row, a day that had started out really badly had turned into a fantastic one.

And I'd probably go so far as to say that apart from what the mother had said, it was the second-best day of my life.

And for the first time in my life, I actually wondered if there could be better to come.

SIXTY-TWO

MOLLY JOHNSON

MSc RESEARCH PROJECT NOTES
NOTE 11: Wednesday, 18 September 2019

Dave is back at school.

That's the second piece of good news to record. The first is that Gill received a letter a few days ago informing her that the tumour Mr Patel removed from Dave's head was, as suspected, benign. Phew.

Getting Dave back to school took a lot of negotiation by all the 'stakeholders', as Dave's social worker keeps referring to everyone who's involved with Dave, and that includes me.

The main reason for Dave being back at school is that there's nowhere else for him to go ... at least not until the compensation money comes through. And I've a feeling that when it does – call me cynical – it's going to benefit Dave rather less than it will benefit Roger and Gill.

Dave's social worker is called Wendy. She's not all that old – maybe late thirties but could pass for fifty. OMG, why do people give their children such archaic names? Although it suits her, as she takes frumpiness to a new level. She's actually called a Case Manager, which depersonalises the detached relationship she appears to have with Dave even further.

Anyway, several lengthy meetings were held at Dave's school. These were attended by the principal – a woman in her early fifties named Fran, totally gagging for retirement, who showed scant interest in Dave's

220

situation – Gill, Wendy, myself and Beverley, Dave's teacher from last year, who would officially take responsibility for him if he's to stay on beyond school-leaving age.

Eventually it was agreed that Dave would be readmitted for a further year, provided that I agreed to be responsible for him on a day-to-day basis. I'll be honest, this was a bit more commitment than I was expecting, but I either accepted this role or Dave would spend the next few months lying on a bean bag in his bedroom listening to the radio.

Beverley doesn't care what we do as long as she doesn't have any responsibility for Dave – this generally means paperwork – and Gill never visits the school anyway.

After the total cock-up over the alphabet board, I did some research. I found a couple of websites – Letters and Sounds, and Jolly Learning – that specialised in the acquisition of linguistic skills for young learners. However, I couldn't find anything that fitted exactly what I needed to do; well, let's face it – it's beginning to look as if Dave is the first person to have a get-out-of-jail-free card from locked-in syndrome, so that makes him kind of unique.

I'll go into much more detail for the thesis, but for now I need to note that by adapting the methodology used by those two websites, combined with some of my own ideas – which included flashcards for a variety of uses: alphabet, of course; adjectives (okay, that was a bit advanced and didn't go so brilliantly); objects; action; animals and body parts – I developed a syllabus I thought was appropriate for Dave.

One of the first things I worked on was colour. This wasn't as easy as I'd thought. I have this theory that everyone has their own definition of colour, and Dave was no exception. I used a range of colour wheels for this, but we got a bit bogged down by primary, secondary and tertiary colours.

However, after some really encouraging initial success, I had to have a total rethink of my teaching technique and a re-evaluation of Dave's learning style.

I'd never formally taught anyone before, and I realised my approach was too simplistic. My plan was to make an assessment of what Dave needed to learn and present him with the information in a way that I thought would work. This was based on selecting teaching aids (such as flashcards) and simply telling him what each represented.

But this was flawed for several reasons: first, because there were no assessment protocols for establishing Dave's learning. So I simply assumed that because I had concluded that Dave had a high level of intelligence (again, this was an assumption), Dave would absorb all – or most – of the information I was presenting him with.

This was no more measurable in terms of learning assessment than had I been showing the cards to a dog and telling it what each represented.

I had put the cart in front of the horse.

I'd got carried away by making rapid progress in areas that, on reflection, were not that challenging. For example, he learned numbers from one to one hundred in less than an hour. Wow, I thought, Superteacher take a bow.

I made what I considered (see supplemental notes) good progress on alphabet learning, and was able to test this by calling out a letter and getting Dave to point to it on the alphabet board. After three weeks he had learned vowels and consonants, and I really thought I was about to start to piece it all together. I'll go into the specifics of the precise milestones he reached when I write this up, but for now I just want to flag up his overall progress.

And then I really screwed things up by starting to work on phonology.

Why did I do this?

Okay ... the subject of my thesis is Practical Aspects of Communication in Brain-Damaged Paediatric Patients, and using my scattergun approach I started to study the theoretical framework of language development. And as this was something I knew nothing about, where did I go? Mr Google, of course. And he told me that language development is thought to proceed by ordinary processes of learning in which children acquire the forms, meanings, and uses of words and utterances from the linguistic input. Theoretically, the LAD is an area of the brain that has a set of universal syntactic rules for all languages.

So I dug a bit deeper and began to study both phonological and phonemic awareness. And not only did I study it, but I concluded that this was a vital cog in the wheel of Dave's language learning, and that it needed to be done before further progress could be made.

My big mistake here was to inadvertently replace the keyword in my research, 'practical', with 'theoretical.'

So that was one of the two main mistakes I made.

The other was to make assumptions about Dave's learning preferences.

Okay, I thought, I was pretty safe in discarding kinaesthetic, as the only voluntary movements Dave appears to be capable of are those made by his right eye and rotating his head, which appears to require a huge amount of effort.

So that leaves visual (spacial) and aural (auditory–musical). I made assumptions and failed to recognise that there was a further learning style which was not only relevant to Dave, but without which not only did he fail to absorb information, but he had little or no trust in the information he was being fed.

It took me several weeks to work this out, and it wasn't until I became aware of Dave's growing frustration (facial expression and banging of fists on something hard) that I realised that I was no longer wearing Superteacher's underpants over my tights. Dave needed logic. If what he was being presented with didn't compute to his brain through logical sequencing and staging, he simply shut up shop.

And this presented different challenges because the one thing the English language lacks – or often appears to lack – is logic. For example, before we go anywhere near phrasal verbs or metaphors, there are so many words that have several totally different meanings. The horror of homonyms ... right? Is that a direction, the opposite of wrong, or something you're entitled to? And that's before we get to rite, wright or even write. For all its richness, colour and diversity, the English language, the words we take for granted, is just a form of etymological encryption until we have sufficient understanding to crack it. Where's the logic in this?

And how do we get that understanding?

This was when I realised that my makeshift methodology had taken both Dave and me as far as it could go, and to hammer on with this would risk compromising the relationship between us.

I was way out of my depth – an enthusiastic hacker who now needed a miraculous intervention.

And then, two weeks ago, that miraculous intervention arrived in the form of Trish.

SIXTY-THREE

DAVE

I just heard this song on the radio sung by someone called Rod Stewart.

It's called 'Maggie May', which is an odd name for a song because you're not sure whether May is her last name, or whether it means that someone called Maggie *may* do something ... or then again, she *may* not?

Actually I know the answer to this, because after the song, the singer was interviewed and he said that it is about something that happened to him when he was sixteen. He said he was 'deflowered' by a much older woman, whose name wasn't actually Maggie May, but he named the woman who 'deflowered' him in his song after a famous prostitute called Maggie May – I know a prostitute is a woman who does sex for money – from Liverpool, who lived in the eighteenth century, and there was also a folk song written about her.

This was quite a lot of information for me to take in, but this evening – as it turned out – was going to be one of those evenings when I had to process a massive amount of information. And not all of it was going to be good, or even trivial like this.

I'll come to this in a minute, but back to Maggie May first.

If I'd had to answer a question on the meaning of 'deflowered' on a quiz show – *The Chase*, for example – I'd have had to have taken a guess; but I'm pretty sure from the context of the song, and what he said about the prostitute, that it means the first time he had sex. I can't work out what flowers have to do with it, though – maybe he had to buy her flowers first and then steal them back before he did sex? That's the trouble with language – unless you understand the relevance of a word or a phrase it's just a meaningless code, like a metaphor.

Anyway, the reason this song caught my attention was because he sang about it being late September and that he should get back to school. That was what you might call a coincidence, because today was the day that I went back to school.

I can't tell you how glad I am because – as I've already told you – my other options are quite limited. Well, I don't have any other options, other than to stay at home all day and do nothing. And as I do enough of this when I'm not at school, it would just be really boring, even though I can see now, and what's even better is that we finally had a letter saying that my tumour isn't going to kill me, so I can stop worrying about that.

Staying at home and doing nothing would be worse now that I can see, actually, because there is so much of the world out there I want to get to know and to understand by seeing it, and I'm not going to do that from a beanbag in my bedroom.

The best thing about being back at school is that Molly is my personal assistant. I'm just so happy that Molly is going to be with me every school day; that really is a dream come true. I hope that she doesn't feel she has to do this because she feels bad or maybe disappointed about trying to teach me after my accident. I *did* learn a lot of stuff from her ... I know about eight different words for penis (I did know some of them before, to be honest), I know about colours, I can read numbers up to ... well, probably a trillion if I ever needed to, I know the alphabet, and I know a lot of other stuff from what she taught me with the picture cards. The cards were really helpful and I learned a lot more than she thought, because I was able to relate a lot of this to what I already knew and also things I've seen on the TV.

I had a swimming lesson (hydrotherapy) today and I also had some physio. I don't think that the swimming teacher was very pleased to see me, but Molly changed me and I managed not to get so excited that I would need to poo in the pool. The physio was the one I like called Lucy, and Molly stayed while she worked on me, and they talked about me and not about wankers, which was nice.

So today had been a really good day until about half an hour ago when the mother came to bath me.

The mother used to bath me every night, and I enjoyed it because she talked to me, even though she thought I couldn't understand. Sometimes she would talk about the father, and stuff she'd say made me wonder why they ever got married. And sometimes she would sing, and I remember this as being a happy time ... especially when I was younger. She never used to talk on her phone, so the whole time she would pay attention to me, except when she had to go into the kitchen to shout at the ginger twats or get Scooter out so he couldn't do anything gross.

Then a while ago – I'm not sure how long, but I think it was a few months before I had the accident – she started talking on her phone while she was bathing me and she stopped talking or singing to me. It really upset me because, like I said, this was one part of my time at home that I actually looked forward to.

Then it got worse.

This was when I realised that she was talking to the same person every night, and that some of the things she said weren't the sort of things you would say in a normal conversation to somebody who was just a friend, or maybe someone you worked with. For example, when Lucy and Jane, the physios at school (well, I don't think Jane's a physio just yet but that's splitting hairs), have a conversation, they talk about other people – mainly wankers. But the mother and this person were always talking about stuff that was really, like ... personal? I mean, I'm not going to go into detail, but if you were talking to a friend and you were arranging a shopping trip or something, you wouldn't say stuff like 'I'm counting the hours until I can feel your fingers caress my breasts again', because you'd hardly do that in Sainsbury's, would you?

Sorry ... I've probably gone into a bit too much detail here, but I didn't have to be JFH or Gary O'Donoghue to work out that she must be doing stuff like sex – which she should only be doing with the father, although it's fairly obvious that she doesn't want to do sex with him any more (and I know this cos she said this on the phone once) – with whoever it is she talks to.

The name of her lover is Ali.

I know this cos when she answers she says things like: 'Ali, darling ... good timing, just bathing Dave, so we've got twenty minutes.'

I dislike Ali cos this is twenty minutes that should be for me and not for anybody else.

Anyway, this evening Ali rang and the mother said, 'Look, darling ... bad timing – Dave's just had a poo in the bath,' which I had, but it was unintentional. 'I'm going to put you on speakerphone, as I'll need both hands to clean it up. Hang on a sec ... don't know why I haven't done this before; no one ever comes in here when I'm bathing Dave anyway. There ... that's better, can you hear me, darling?'

And this was when I got the biggest shock of my life.

'Yes, sweetie ... loud and clear. Poor you.'

It was a woman's voice. Ali is a woman ... like, as in *female*.

I was stunned. The mother is doing sex with another woman. As Molly would say: 'Oh ... My ... God!'

'Aren't you worried that Dave may be listening, poppet?' the woman – Ali – asked, and then she laughed.

'Yeah, it's a secret, just between the three of us ... you, me and Dave.' The mother laughed at this, not in a nice way. 'Isn't that right, Dave?'

It was at that moment that I think I began to hate the mother.

'Even if he could hear and understand, who's he going to tell?' the mother asked, and they both laughed.

And that made me hate her even more.

Just you wait and see who I'll tell.

I could never forgive her for what she'd said to Molly, but Molly was still part of my life, so the memory of that had faded a bit. But this was ... I don't know ... it just meant that she had absolutely no time for me at all. And that meant that Molly was the only person in the world who cared about me.

Maybe you remember I said that I had never wanted to kill myself, even if I could? Well, at that moment, if I'd had a gun with two bullets and had been able to shoot it, I probably would have shot the mother first and then shot myself.

But because I didn't have a gun or any bullets, and if I had, I wouldn't have been able to use it anyway, I had to listen to them talking about what they were going to do to each other the next time they were in bed – which was gross, and, in fact, what the mother herself would have referred to as an 'inappropriate conversation'.

It sounds like they've gone well past the 'deflowering' bit.

SIXTY-FOUR

MOLLY JOHNSON

MSc RESEARCH PROJECT NOTES
NOTE 12: Friday, 20 December 2019

Today was the last day of term.

We had our class party at Dave's school ... deck the halls with boughs of holly, fa la la la la, la la la la.

I'm not a big fan of Christmas, especially since Mum died. This is our second Christmas without her, so there'll just be Dad and me again, and neither of us are looking forward to it.

There are four other children with a variety of disabilities in Dave's class, and Beverley has three classroom assistants to help her. Sometimes I wonder what she actually does because she never seems to get very close to any of the children. She spends most of the day in her office. One thing I did notice, though, was that while we were all sipping our non-alcoholic punch, she went into the kitchen, took a small bottle of brandy from her bag and tipped it into her punch. A sackable offence – not that I give a damn.

Anyway, I've got a vested interest in Beverley because at the start of term, I managed to get her to agree to a sort of trade-off whereby – unofficially – she has nothing to do with Dave and he is totally my responsibility, but ... and this is the best bit, Dave gets two hours a day with Trish, one of Beverley's classroom assistants.

Dave has made fantastic progress over the last three months ... no, astonishing progress – I'll annotate the details from my records later, and this will form an appendix in my thesis – but his progress is all down to Trish.

Trish adores Dave, and she's the miraculous intervention I'd prayed for.

She worked as a speech therapist for around thirty years before retiring. A couple of years later, her husband – a successful businessman – left her, and she decided to go back to work. She didn't want the level of commitment of her previous job, so she applied for the post of special needs classroom assistant at Dave's school. Technically, she should have had a qualification in nursery nursing, teaching assistance, childcare or play work, but because of her experience of working with special needs kids in the past, all she needed was a DBS check. She was the only applicant in any case.

Anyway, she's absolutely brilliant with Dave, and she seems to be really enjoying the challenge. I've had to be a bit careful, though, because I don't want Gill to know anything about this, so I've taken Trish into my confidence about the lack of parental enthusiasm for developing Dave's communication skills. Beverley, of course, has shown zero interest in what we're working on with Dave.

Her two hours a day have been fantastic because – unlike me, back in the summer – she knows exactly what she's doing.

Thanks to Trish, Dave can now use the alphabet board to communicate. His spelling is amazing, and we're both astounded at how quickly he's developed quite advanced literacy skills. I knew he was highly intelligent, but it's just incredible that he's got to this point so rapidly.

But communicating is still a slow process because he has to point his eyes at the first letter of a word, then the second and so on. Trish introduced a much more sophisticated Perspex alphabet board; details of all this will also be in an appendix, but I just want to objectively benchmark where Dave is, going into the Christmas break.

If Dave wants to ask a question, he points at a question mark first, as you do when you write in Spanish.

So, for example:

'Dave, do you want some more punch?' I asked.

'? ... D ... o — I — f ... u ... c—'

'We'll take that as a "no" then, Dave,' I laughed, and pinched his cheek ... probably a sackable offence too. '" No, thanks" is a more polite reply, young man.'

'What do you want for Christmas, Dave?' Trish asked.

His face contorted into a deep, almost troubled frown. I still can't differentiate whether this is his 'I'm trying to have a poo' face, or an expression of intense concentration. It was the latter.

'I — w ... a ... n ... t — t ... o — h ... i ... r ... e — a—'

'You want to hire a ... what? A Ferrari?' I jumped in and was rebuked by Trish.

'Don't interrupt him, Molly.' She smiled at me as if feeling guilty for the reproach. 'I know it's tempting, love, and really hard not to jump in or to anticipate, but you've just got to let him finish. Otherwise he'll just get frustrated.'

I nodded. She was right, of course. I just want everything to happen so quickly; the impatience of youth, I suppose.

'A — h ... i ... t ... m ... a ... n — t ... o — k ... i ... l ... l — m ... y — f ... a ... m ... i ... l ... y.'

Trish and I looked at each other, at first wide-eyed with shock, then we both exploded with laughter.

'If I win the lottery, Dave,' I said, 'I'll pay for him myself. That's a joke, of course.'

I think we're almost ready to move on to the next stage now.

But that's going to need a hell of a lot of both money and diplomacy.

SIXTY-FIVE

DAVE

It was Saturday, and we were sitting around the thing that the parents call the island in the kitchen, having lunch.

There was Christmas music playing and, as usual, I had a stupid Christmas hat on. Now that I can see, I know who it is that does this to me every year – Boris, of course. If I couldn't afford to pay a hitman to kill my family, maybe if I could get all my money out of my Post Office Savings Account, I might just manage to pay for someone to smash his teeth in. In my dreams.

Anyway, talking of money, all this was about to change.

I knew the parents had gone to a big court in London last week for the judgement on my compensation claim for the hospital fucking up my life. They'd not said much about it, but I could tell that there was what you might call an air of excitement – particularly coming from the father, who had been almost as nice to me since the hearing as he'd been when I was his lucky mascot at the casino.

Scooter started barking like a mad dog. There was a 'plop' as something dropped through the front door and the father said that it was probably the postman.

No shit – as Boris says – Sherlock.

So the father got up, went to the front door and came back holding a lot of letters. He held them in his right hand, slapped them against his other hand, sat down at the table, picked out one and said, 'Right ... here we go then. Christmas has come early. I think this calls for a drink!'

I happen to know that it's not Christmas for another four days yet, so I really hope he's wrong cos that would just make it go on even longer.

'Any excuse,' said the mother, who was shoving baked beans that had once been warm into my mouth. Actually, I don't mind baked beans. Occasionally I can manage to use my tongue and lips to spit one out, and once I managed to hit Boris in the face, but he was sitting really close to me. 'I would open the letter first before celebrating, if I were you.'

The father ripped an envelope open, pulled out a letter and started reading. I could tell from his face that it was what he'd been expecting, and while he was still reading it, he walked to the fridge and got a bottle out. He unscrewed this bit of wire and twisted the thing at the top, and then there was a really loud pop as the thing flew out of the bottle and almost hit the mother.

'For Christ's sake, Roger!' she said.

He poured two glasses, gave one to her and was about to take a drink from his when he came round the island, put his hands on my shoulders and gave me a kiss on the bit of my head above my eyes, where Molly had kissed me. I don't count that as a proper kiss, thank goodness.

'Here's to you, Dave.' Then he started singing. *'We're in the money ... We're in the money ... We've got a lot of what it takes to get along ... We're in the money ... The sky is sunny ...* Cheers, everyone. Here's to the happiest Christmas since ... well, since before you were born, Dave.'

'I'm not sure that's really an appropriate comment, Roger,' said the mother, 'particularly in the circumstances.'

'Oh, it's appropriate all right. Here, read this.' He handed the mother the letter. She stopped feeding me and began to read it out loud.

"Dear Roger and Gill,

Further to the hearing last Tuesday, I enclose a copy of the sealed Order.

The Order provides that Dave has been awarded a lump sum of £5.5m for retrospective damages, with annual periodic payment set at £375,000 per annum.

In addition, you, as Dave's parents and primary carers, will receive compensation in the sum of £2.8 million reflecting expenses accumulated on Dave's behalf over a sixteen-year period. We will transfer the sums set out above to you by BACS as soon as it is received from the defendants. We anticipate that this will be before the New Year.

I draw your attention to the following clause, the inclusion of which you requested and to which the defendants raised no objection:

'If, following the date of this Agreement, the Claimant's needs are reduced at some point in the future, the periodic payment – but not the lump sum and the compensation payment to the parents of the Claimant – may be reassessed, for the reason that the Claimant may consequently require a reduced level of care.'

I would be grateful if you could call my paralegal, Dominic, to arrange for a meeting to set up a trust fund and to appoint a deputy from our office to take charge of the administration of this fund. I would particularly recommend the services of Miriam Davison, who is vastly experienced in the field of trust administration.

May I take this opportunity ..." blah-de-blah ...'

Gill put the letter down, smiled, and took a sip of her drink.

Nobody said much for a while after that. They were probably all thinking about what they were going to spend the money on.

The mother had stopped feeding me and had started opening the other letters. They were Christmas cards. She would read one, say who'd sent it and then make a comment. I could tell from what she said that she didn't like most of the people who'd sent the cards, but I suppose that they probably felt the same about the parents. I think people only send Christmas cards because they feel they have to send them, and I've heard people say things like "*he* won't be on my Christmas card list", which means that they don't like them, but they probably still send a Christmas card anyway. I get a lot of Christmas cards – probably because people think they should send them, and cos the mother sends them cards saying they're from me – and this is the first year I've been able to see them and even read them. Actually, they're not all that exciting, and I don't even know most of the people who sent them.

'Ah ... here we go,' said the mother, 'Lucy's annual round-robin letter telling us what a wonderful year they've all had and how fantastically well the kids are doing with the Duke of Edinburgh, cycling proficiency, grade one piano or whatever.' I looked at her while she read it. She's got quite a nice face when she's not angry, and she's not so skinny now since she started going to the gym as well as running. She just wears old jumpers and things she calls slacks at home, but when she has her hair done, wears a dress and puts stuff on her face and perfume on, she looks totally different. I suppose she only does this when she's meeting Ali.

She stopped reading and looked at the father, who was pouring more drink from the bottle. The father is definitely not good-looking. He's not very tall – in fact, he's a bit shorter than the mother – and he's not exactly fat, but he's probably what you might call chubby. He's got small eyes that don't open fully and a fat nose and he has this thing ... a sort of big spot, on his neck and there are hairs growing out of it. He hasn't got much hair left on his head but he has some around his mouth and on his chin and it's ginger, which is the same colour as Boris and Axel's hair – which is obviously why he calls them ginger twats. If I had to describe the father with one word, it would probably be 'scruffy'.

Anyway, the mother looked quite upset.

'Jerry's got cancer,' she said. I don't know who Jerry is, but he's probably Lucy's husband. 'It's in his liver.' For a moment I thought she might even cry. 'Apparently he's only got weeks to live ... a month at most.'

'Poor bastard,' said the father, taking a drink. 'Better make a note not to put his name on the Christmas card next year.'

'For God's sake, Roger!' said the mother.

'Yeah, for fuck's sake, Rog,' Boris added, in a way that sounded like he was what's called 'jumping over a band-wagon' – I think – rather than taking offence at the father's comment. 'What're you going to spend it all on, anyway? All Dave's money?'

'What have I told you about bad language, Boris? And it's not all Dave's money in any case. I might just spend it on sending you to a boarding school as far away from here as possible. China sounds like a good bet, but I suppose, because of this bloody coronavirus thing, we'll have to settle for Sedburgh.'

Boris stood up, pulled a face behind the father's back and walked out, raising his middle finger as he left the room.

'Ah … the strong, silent type,' said the father, pointing his own middle finger at the closing door. 'What's in that other letter?'

Gill picked it up and flung it across the island to him.

The father opened it and read without saying anything, then he started to sing again. '*We're in the money … We're in the money …*' He stopped singing, poured more drink into his glass, then flung the letter back towards the mother. 'You can go and get yourself another ring now, dear. It's the cheque from the insurance – seventeen thousand smackers. Think I might just take a little trip down to the Aston Martin shop this afternoon. Fancy it, Axe?'

Axel stood up, narrowed his eyes and stared at the father. I don't think Axel likes the father much and, to be honest, I don't dislike Axel as much as I dislike the rest of my family. In fact, if I could hire a hitman, I'd probably tell him just to shoot Axel in the leg, but not to kill him.

'Not really,' he replied. 'But if I were you, I wouldn't drink any more champagne if you're going to drive. Lose your licence, and you'll not be able to drive an Aston, will you? Unless, of course, you want to break even more laws.' He then left the room as well.

For a few minutes the mother and father didn't say anything to each other, which was a surprise cos if I were the mother, I'd want to know what that was about. Then Axel came back in; he had a pile of money in his hands. It looked as if it was quite a lot. He slapped it down on the island in front of the father.

'Here, you can have this back. I don't want it.' He sounded really angry. Maybe he's going to take after the mother? 'I don't want any part of it, or any part of any other dodgy schemes either.' Then he walked out again and slammed the door.

'What the hell was all that about?' asked the mother.

Yes, I'd be interested to know what it was all about too.

SIXTY-SIX

GILL

DIARY ENTRY: Monday, 6 January 2020

Once again, I've not written my diary for ages.

Time's flown and I've just been too busy.

A lot seems to have changed but I can't put my finger on precisely how, or even why.

For example, Dave seems different.

I know Molly believes that the procedure to remove the tumour somehow magically led to a restoration of his sight. I think she also believes that Dave is able to make some sense of what she thinks he sees and probably also what he hears. And I'm beginning to wonder whether she might be right. I've no evidence for this ... he just seems, I don't know ... more switched on than before.

Take the Saturday before Christmas, for example. We were having lunch when the confirmation of the compensation arrived. I couldn't help but notice that he seemed to be following the conversation in a way I'd not noticed before. Maybe it's just my imagination.

What if he *can* understand what's going on around him?

Just supposing he's got locked-in syndrome, how could I possibly not have noticed it before? For sixteen years? Or maybe this was a side effect of the operation? All the experts, going right back to Dr Sullivan with that wretched Glasgow scale, have been convinced that Dave's brain was irreversibly damaged. And all these experts were required to give evidence for the medical negligence claim. Surely they couldn't all be wrong ... could they?

Just supposing they *were* wrong, and Dave can see, understand what he hears and have an informed view of the world, what happens then? As parents, morally we have a duty to help him to communicate, haven't we?

But on the other hand, this would mean a total reassessment of the compensation claim. Thank God I insisted on that clause, the one whereby should a miracle happen, only the periodic payments would be reassessed. But that's still a hell of a lot of money, and should we (he) lose that – or have it severely reduced – it would mean we'd need to dip into the lump sum just to cover his living costs. And at a base cost of almost half a million a year, it wouldn't last that long.

Even if it did transpire that Dave had confounded the experts and has a functioning brain that allows visual and auditory awareness, he's still a quadriplegic – nothing's going to change that – and the cost of his care will remain the same. Doubtless the NEHA would try to dispute this, so who knows what the result would be?

No, Dave ... if a miracle has occurred, you and Molly are going to keep this to yourselves. I have plans for that money, and no miraculous recovery is going to get in the way of that.

Unpalatable as the thought may be, I'm going to have to work with Roger to ensure we can manipulate the trust fund deputy when it comes to distributions from the trust fund.

When I leave Roger, my half of the two-point-eight million – particularly after he's wallowed his way through it – isn't going to last that long. But it won't take much to convince Roger that we need to syphon off funds from the lump sum and the periodic payments, as and when we can.

And there's another thing.

I never got to the bottom of the money that Axel gave Roger. What was that all about, I wonder?

He refused to go into detail about it; all he would say was that it was a sort of investment project he had been working on with the boys, and Axel had decided he'd rather put the money back into his bank account.

Bullshit.

Whatever it was, he called it a 'dodgy scheme' and that set my alarm bells ringing.

I don't trust Roger, and I'd really like to insist that we split the money to stop him wasting it on cars and whatever else he gets up to. I still have my suspicions, but I'm convinced that his other clandestine leisure pursuits don't involve another woman, unfortunately.

But if I insisted on that, he'd want to know why.

Roger isn't stupid, at least when it comes to being shafted by anyone other than himself.

No ... I need to work with him until I've got enough squirrelled away to get the hell out of here.

I know it means that I might even have to fuck the bastard, but if that's what it takes, it's a price I'll have to pay.

SIXTY-SEVEN

MOLLY JOHNSON

MSc RESEARCH PROJECT NOTES
NOTE 13: Monday, 17 February 2020

I've just had my monthly meeting with Josh.

Well, it's supposed to be once a month, but January's got cancelled.

I'd been looking forward to this for ages, but this time it wasn't just because I fancy him. I mean, he is totally hench, but I'm now so much more focused on discussing Dave's progress and getting his advice than trying to cop off with him, lol.

I had so much to tell him about Dave's progress, and I had one big question I needed to ask him. And, of course, one big proposal I needed to put to him.

So we grabbed a coffee, and first, I updated him with how Dave had progressed since Christmas. It's half-term at the moment, and Dave is at home. I'd imagine that he spends his days lying on his beanbag with the radio on, but Gill was happy to let me visit to bath him and get him ready for bed every weekday evening, so at least he gets some meaningful contact most days.

I told Josh about the daily programme that Trish and I had worked out for Dave at school. Before Christmas we had used a lot of BBC School Radio modules. These included myths, legends and traditional stories, and we tried to make connections between these and other stories that we knew Dave was familiar with.

These were aimed at Key Stage 1 children, and although Dave enjoyed them, he found them quite basic.

The trouble was identifying what Dave already knew and what he needed to learn. Trish decided that the best way to do this was to concentrate on the BBC Bitesize programmes and present Dave with a bespoke curriculum. This was a combination of what Trish thought he should study – we took this from the Key Stage 3 and 4 curriculums – and what Dave actually wanted to study. Dave selected English (he's told us that he wants to be a journalist), mathematics, history and geography.

Trish spent hours and hours streamlining this curriculum into something that was going to be appropriate for Dave's needs and interests, and prepared copious lesson plans and materials for me to use. For someone who'd applied for a part-time job in a support role with low commitment, Trish said that she was working harder than she had done for years – possibly ever – but that she loved it and was totally committed to the challenge.

So I would work with Dave, using Trish's lesson plans and materials, from nine until eleven-thirty every morning. After this, he would either watch a video (comparative religion seemed to float his boat, for some reason) or listen to an audiobook for an hour, then have lunch before Trish took over for a two-hour session in the afternoon. Trish's sessions would be purely focused on language development and assessment of his literacy skills. After a few weeks, Trish decided that a two-hour stint was challenging for Dave; she noted that after an hour he would begin to demonstrate the usual signs of frustration with which we were familiar, so we adjusted his schedule to punctuate Trish's session with hydrotherapy and physio, and this worked much better.

It was a long day for Dave, but the feedback he gave us was staggering.

His brain was like a sponge; after a month of history lessons, he could name every king or queen of England from Harold to the present day, the dates of their reign, how they died and where they were buried.

The guy was becoming an encyclopaedia.

He was particularly interested in a module on The Islamic World in the Middle Ages; he said that it illustrated the sociocultural differences between Christians and Muslims and had great relevance to contemporary problems. Wow. It took a bit of time for him to spell that out, but I didn't intervene.

He also demonstrated the ability to solve complex mathematical problems and equations that I couldn't even copy down correctly.

It was as if his brain had just been booted up and was now running on full capacity. And that full capacity was spectacular.

The only trouble was that communication with Dave was agonisingly slow. The alphabet board was okay for the basics, but once Dave's language skills had developed a sophistication way beyond what either of us had imagined possible, he became frustrated.

And this was when I did some research and came up with my breakthrough idea.

Time to put it to Josh.

I took a deep breath and laid it out.

'What Dave needs now,' I began, 'is to have his own voice. He needs to be able to talk.'

'Enlighten me?'

'Well, you know Stephen Hawking?'

'Not personally,' Josh laughed. 'I think you'll find he's dead anyway, so he won't be able to help.'

'Obviously,' I replied, slightly irritated by his frivolity. 'Did you know he had a nerve sensor in his cheek that allowed him to type, and a text-to-speech computer? And this was his primary mode of communication for four decades? This could work for Dave.'

I let this sink in.

'Go on.'

'I've been in touch with the team from Cambridge who refined and adapted the old system that Hawking had used from the late eighties. They later developed something called a Raspberry Pi, which he used from January 2018 until he died. The original was called' – I looked at my notes – 'DECtalk CallText 5010. Apparently, augmentative and alternative communication systems are quite common. A lot of them use eye movement on an alphabet board, but this would be way too slow to improve Dave's communication.'

Josh said nothing.

'Well ... what do you think?'

'How could this work for Dave?'

'The Cambridge guys ...' I looked at my notes again. 'I spoke to a Dr Simon Cipriani, who said that it might be possible to implant the nerve sensor in Dave's right eyelid so that the movement of his eye would generate the text for the computer to convert into speech.'

'I'm noting the word "might".'

I felt deflated by Josh's lack of enthusiasm.

'Well, he couldn't guarantee anything. Not until he'd met and assessed Dave. But it's really hopeful, isn't it?'

'How much is this going to cost?'

I sensed more negativity.

'Ah ... okay, that's the downside. He said we are looking at, for the installation and set-up cost, somewhere in the region of seven hundred and fifty thousand ... and an annual "subscription" of about a hundred grand—'

'Holy shit! Good luck selling that to his parents.'

'The compensation money's come through. Dave told me. He's got a lump sum of around five and a half mill and a yearly payout of just under four hundred grand. They can afford it.'

'They may not want to afford it.'

I could see what he meant; I'd told him about Gill's attempt at bribery and blackmail.

'In fact, if they're worried about having the payout reassessed, this is probably the last thing they'd want. Sadly, it's not up to Dave. Or you.'

He was right. I knew that it would be a massive challenge to convince Gill. To do this, I'd need to bring her up to speed with Dave's learning progress, and I was pretty sure that she wouldn't share the same enthusiastic optimism as Trish and me.

'I know. But we can't just let him vegetate, can we? I mean, unless he has the ability to express himself to the level of his potential, he might as well be back where he was when I first met him.'

There was a lengthy silence while Josh considered this, and that was when it occurred to me that perhaps there was a tinge of jealousy clouding Josh's vision. Maybe his initial enthusiasm for my collaboration with Dave would cast a shadow over his own research work. For sure – if this worked – everyone was going to know about it. It would almost certainly fire Dave into a media spotlight, and that would undoubtedly have an implication for me and my research – not that this was my motivation.

'It's your call, Molly.' He sat back and folded his arms. 'I can't really advise you on this one.'

You're my fucking supervisor, I thought. It's your job to advise me ... even to comment on the ethics of what I'm suggesting.

And that was it.

Meeting over.

It was left to me to decide whether to put this to Gill, a course of action which may well result in a very negative outcome (not least for my research), or just to carry on as we were, with Dave acquiring knowledge at a meteoric rate but with an increasing frustration at not being able to use that knowledge or develop the skills which would help him achieve his ambition to become a journalist – however challenging that might be.

Dave needed a challenge. Like most of us, he needed the stimulation to rise above where he was right now; he didn't need platitudes, nor stagnation.

'Tell you what, Molly,' Josh said, and he flashed his Jake Abel-slash-Alex Pettyfer smile at me. 'Why don't we discuss this over a drink later?'

I think I'm beginning to go off Josh. He may be totally gorg, but I'm not so sure that he's the man I thought he was.

'Tell you what, Josh,' I replied. 'Why don't we just keep our relationship on a professional basis?' I got up and walked out, tears of frustration streaming down my face.

SIXTY-EIGHT

DAVE

I've been back at school since September, only this time it's very different.

I'm actually learning something.

Well, not right now cos I'm at home as it's half-term and so I just have BBC Radio 4 to listen to all day, but at least Molly's going to come to bath me and have a chat every evening.

I really like Trish, my new teacher. She's kind and never gets upset when I have a poo – sorry – or bang my fists, so I now have two people who care about me. Trish helps me with linguistic skills – see how much I've improved already since I've been back at school? She's quite old and plump, which means fat but in a nice way, and she has a kind face and short blue hair, which is quite unusual for older people. I know that sometimes younger women have short blue or pink or purple hair or even hair that has a lot of different colours, but from what I've seen, if older women have hair that's blue, it usually looks like the sort of wig that someone in a pantomime might wear. Except for Katy Perry. She's an American singer and she's almost as beautiful as Molly, and sometimes she has blue hair and it suits her. But I'm glad Molly doesn't have blue hair.

Sorry ... I'm digressing.

Trish makes me work really hard, and sometimes I think she pushes me a bit too much, but I try not to show this cos I don't want her to get disappointed with me and leave.

To be honest, the best bit of my day is probably when I get to listen to audiobooks. My favourite is *Robinson Crusoe*, and this is because he was stuck on a desert island, one like my metaphorical desert island where I would have been left if it hadn't been for Molly and Trish. It's made me think about a lot of other stuff too, so I suppose in a way it's changed my life, or at least how I think about things.

If you don't know, *Robinson Crusoe* is a book by Daniel Defoe, and it's not just about someone who gets stuck on a desert island. There are five different themes to it. The first theme is when he runs away to look for adventure but gets shipwrecked and has to survive on a desert island for twenty-eight years. So this theme is about survival, looking after himself, and hard work. He sets himself goals and he doesn't just lie in the sun all day like most people would. This was, in fact, the second time he was shipwrecked – the first time, he was rescued, but then he was captured by pirates.

The second theme is about fear, and Robinson Crusoe works out that if he can get over his fears, he can be happy on the island, although he only has a dog and two cats to talk to. He also works out that that there's no point in wishing for things that he can't have, and that he should be happy with what he's got.

So one day, when he's on the (second) desert island, he finds out that other people live on it too; they're prisoners, but it's not clear who's keeping them prisoner or who's looking after them. Whoever it was didn't do much of a job, cos sometimes cannibals come to the island to kill and eat them. Anyway, Robinson Crusoe's about to kill the cannibals on what's called 'moral grounds' but then decides that he shouldn't do this because they don't know that eating people is wrong. So he just tries not to get eaten himself.

Then one of the prisoners escapes, and Robinson Crusoe takes him in and calls him Friday, and he basically slaves for him – which was quite normal in the seventeenth century, but people get very upset about it now – and Robinson Crusoe teaches him English and also about Christianity. I'm not so sure that Friday got such a good deal out of this, but I can understand the importance of learning English cos this is what I'm doing.

The third theme from the book is about what's called 'spiritual development'. During this part of history, everyone was taught that if you didn't go to church, you would burn in hell, and priests were like modern-day drug lords. Robinson Crusoe decided that you didn't need priests or rituals or even churches to be a good Christian. This was what was called being a Dissenter, and Dissenters were not very popular with the Church; in fact, the Church did everything it could to ban them, including sometimes having them killed, which seems a bit harsh to me. I think some of them – for example, a group called the Muggletonians – were probably what you might call nutters. This group was started by two London tailors who said they were the last prophets from the Book of Revelation, which is a part of the Bible. There are a lot of Dissenters – like the Puritans or the Quakers – who were better known than the Muggletonians – but one of the things I liked about them is that they believed that God doesn't bother too much about what's going on in the world, and doesn't intervene until something happens that could actually cause the end of it. I happen to think this is right, cos even though footballers look up at the sky and point at it every time they score a goal, I doubt very much if God really cares whether they've scored or not. The father says this as well, and this is one of the few things that I agree with him about. It annoys him that rugby players have started doing it too. Also, God could stop things like plane crashes or earthquakes if he wanted to, but he obviously can't be bothered. But then, God could have had something to do with Molly discovering that I've got this locked-in thing. Who knows?

I'm not sure about God. I find all religions really interesting and what I think is that until someone can prove that there is no God – or gods – then it's probably best to believe that there could be a God, cos if you believe this, it might make you a better person for the simple reason that if there is a God and there is a heaven, if you've not done much wrong to upset him, then he probably won't give you such a hard time when you die. This is something the father calls 'hedging your bets', and as betting is something he knows a lot about, it sort of makes sense.

I don't know – it's very confusing, but I know that religion has had a lot to do with most of the wars that have ever been fought.

Anyway, coming back to *Robinson Crusoe*, the fourth theme from the book is about racism. It's really bad to be a racist now, or even to look like you *might* be one. There's this coronavirus thing right now, which is called a 'global pandemic'. Someone on BBC Radio 4 said that a lot of people secretly hoped that it would wipe out the population of China, and that wouldn't be a totally bad thing because the world – particularly China – is over-populated, and it could be one solution to climate change. I think that's a bit extreme, but I'm not sure how this person on BBC Radio 4 knew this if the people who believed or hoped for this did it secretly. And another thing: people who wore masks in places like Manchester, where there are a lot of Chinese people, were accused of being racist, and I think that's a bit extreme too.

And some people even said that the Americans caused it by introducing the virus to China so that it would wreck their economy. I'd say that's racist too, because I'm pretty sure that there's no actual evidence for this.

Anyway, the way Robinson Crusoe treated Friday was an example of how English people treated the people in the countries they took over at that time in history, and I think the father still agrees with this because he was a big supporter of Brexit.

There's also supposed to be a mini-theme about Robinson Crusoe and Friday doing sex, but I don't think Defoe would have written about stuff like that.

The last part of the story is where an English ship appears and Crusoe helps the captain get control of it again, cos some of his crew had taken it over and were going to leave the captain on the island – which, by the way, is becoming a bit crowded now, what with all the prisoners and the cannibals.

The captain takes Robinson Crusoe and Friday back to England, and Robinson Crusoe finds he has no money, cos everyone thought he was dead years ago. But then he remembers he has a lot of money in Brazil, cos he sold a boy called Xury into slavery. Xury had helped him escape from slavery by the Moors, so selling him to the captain of the Portuguese ship they escaped on wasn't much of a way to repay him.

Robinson Crusoe used what he got from selling Xury to buy some land in Brazil, and this made him a lot more money, so the book ends with him being rich.

The last theme is also about money, which is useless on the island but is really important everywhere else.

That's *Robinson Crusoe*, and it made a really big impression on me. In fact, I've listened to it three times, and each time I've learned something new from it.

So why is it so important to me?

It sort of sums up my life – so far – and there are a lot of lessons you can learn from it ... apart from the obvious one: he wouldn't have been shipwrecked twice if he hadn't gone back to sea after the first time.

Before Molly rescued me from my 'desert island', I'd had to learn to survive, learn not to be afraid and learn to set myself goals; okay, I'll admit that some of these goals – like killing my family – were things I knew I was unlikely to do, but this at least helped me get over the fear of never being able to break out of this locked-in thing. Crusoe was a bit like me; okay, he could walk and build things and feed himself, but he was every bit as locked in as I was, and *he* didn't give in to it.

And the more I thought about Robinson Crusoe not killing the cannibals, and his 'spiritual development', the more I thought that killing my family – even if I could – wouldn't achieve anything, cos ... and I know I'm being really generous here, like the cannibals, they probably don't know what twats they are.

And the last theme that's about money ... I know how much money means to the parents – the father in particular. After Christmas he bought a new Aston Martin and last week he bought a new Range Rover. He can only drive one car at a time, so I don't get why he needs two?

And the parents still have the Davemobile, so that technically makes three.

I don't really care about money, so I don't waste time wishing for things I don't need or can't use, like two cars. Crusoe managed to survive on the island by working out what he really needed – of course that changed when he finally got back to England and got his money back. I suppose if cars had existed in the 1700s, he probably would have bought two as well.

All this has helped me work out what I really need. Before half-term, I heard Molly and Trish talking about something that could be fitted to my eyelid to help me to talk. Molly called it a 'text-to-speech computer' and said that Stephen Hawking had had one for years but they're much better now, and this would help me to actually talk and to talk quite quickly. I don't think Molly wanted me to hear her telling Trish about this – maybe in case nothing happened and I'd get really disappointed – so they talked about it in the kitchen at school and she probably forgot that I've got really good hearing.

Anyway, this is what I want more than anything else in life. And now that I've got all this compensation money, I don't see why I can't have it.

Having this would allow me to achieve my goals: winning something like *The Chase* and becoming a journalist.

But if the mother and father don't agree to it, I may have to find a way to kill off a few cannibals myself.

SIXTY-NINE

MOLLY JOHNSON

MSc RESEARCH PROJECT NOTES
NOTE 14: Friday, 21 February 2020

I've agonised over this all week.

In fact, I've had sleepless nights.

I didn't sign up for this burden of responsibility, and it doesn't seem fair that this decision has been left entirely to me.

I suppose there was never any doubt about what I'd do – it was just how to do it that I kept running over time and time again, an infinite loop coursing pointlessly through my brain.

So this morning, I borrowed Dad's car, drove out to Hillcrest, parked outside the Spar and waited.

Just before nine, a brand-new Range Rover drove through the gates and sped off towards Hull. Roger was driving, and I breathed a sigh of relief when I saw the twins squabbling in the back. I didn't want any interruptions.

Satisfied that Gill was alone in the house, I drove in and parked outside the front door.

I knocked on the scullery door and waited.

Nothing.

I knocked again and heard Gill yell from upstairs, 'Who is it?'

'Molly,' I replied. 'Can I come in?'

'What do you want?' She didn't sound friendly, but I'd already experienced Gill's mood swings.

'I need to talk to you, Gill.'

'I'm busy. We'll talk tonight when you bath Dave.'

I knew about her affair – Dave had told me. I wasn't surprised; I'd noticed how she looked at me. For a moment, I wondered if her lover could be upstairs, but then I remembered that Roger had just left. Maybe she was on the phone to her?

'It's important, Gill. There's something I really need to discuss with you.' My heart was beating fast. This hadn't got off to a good start, and I have to admit that I was slightly … maybe not scared, but apprehensive about Gill.

At last she replied.

'You'd better come in. Put the kettle on, I'll be down in a minute.'

We sat at the island in silence for a moment. She was wearing an expensive-looking gold sequin floral midi dress, heels, and she reeked of more than a subtle squirt of Chanel Chance; from this, I deduced at least part of the reason why I wasn't welcome. Clearly she had plans for today.

'Okay, so what's so urgent that it can't wait till this evening?'

I was reluctant to just dive right in and wanted a few more seconds to allow her to mellow.

To my surprise she got up, went to the window, opened it, sat down again and lit a cigarette. My astonishment seemed to prompt an almost triumphant smile to slide across her face.

'Want one?'

I shook my head.

She exhaled deeply and seemed to relax a little.

Well, here goes, I thought. It's now or never.

'I need to talk to you about Dave.'

'Really? I'd never have guessed.' She studied me disparagingly and in a way I assumed was meant to undermine me.

I didn't even know how best to open the conversation. What was going to annoy her least? Telling her that yes, Dave could see, he could communicate, or, in an attempt to appeal to her motherly instinct, telling her

254

straight out what Dave needed? But from what I'd observed, there was little evidence of a maternal bond, and certainly not one sufficient for her to dig deep into the compensation money. This wasn't a 'for three pounds a month you can change a child's life' sort of appeal.

Fuck it, I thought.

'I was right about Dave,' I began.

She took another drag from her cigarette.

'As in?'

'As in he can see. And he has a brain that functions fully, other than to overcome his quadriplegia. In fact, he's highly intelligent and would almost certainly get four A Levels if he were able to sit them. And probably grade As.'

Gill said nothing, stubbed out her cigarette and lit another one.

I continued.

'He learns really quickly. Trish – that's one of Beverley's classroom assistants—'

'I know who Trish is.'

'Okay, sorry. Anyway, Trish and I have been working with him, and he's made fantastic progress.' I smiled. 'You should be very proud of him.'

Another silence. Oh well, in for a penny …

'Look, Gill, I know I probably should have said something about this before, but we really had no idea how quickly he was going to learn. His brain's like a sponge. The thing is, we've gone almost as far as we can go with Dave. He needs to communicate better, or he won't be able to fulfil his true potential.'

Still she said nothing; she just sat there smoking with this utterly blank expression on her face.

At last she spoke.

'Yes, you're right. You should have said something about this before.'

'I'm sorry,' I mumbled. Be strong, I told myself, don't let her bully you. 'But the reason I didn't was that we really had no idea what Dave could be capable of.' I knew this sounded lame. What I really meant was that I didn't want to give Gill an excuse to pull the plug. I took a deep breath and continued. 'And now he needs … I mean, he

255

would benefit greatly from the adaptation of some technology that could help him to talk … I mean, *actually* talk. At present we're using this alphabet board, and it's effective for basic communication, but it's painfully slow, and Dave's outgrown it to the point that it's stunting his progress, and he's becoming frustrated by—'

'Who else knows about this? Beverley, I assume?'

'No, Beverley doesn't know anything. She doesn't care what we're doing as long as it doesn't increase her workload. Only Trish and me. No one else knows.' I'd conveniently forgotten to mention Josh.

'You've broken your word, Molly,' she said calmly. 'You gave me your word that you wouldn't mention your presumptions about Dave to anyone. We had an agreement. Do I need to remind you? The day after his operation, in the hospital?'

'I've only told Trish,' I said feebly.

'And how many people might she have told? She's an old woman, abandoned by her husband, and old women who've been ditched tend to become gabby.'

I had no answer to this, but I persevered anyway, although I knew I was wasting my breath.

'Don't you even want to hear about the text-to-speech technology? It could really change Dave's life. It could—'

'No, I don't want to hear about it, Molly. And I'm sorry, but I don't believe it could change Dave's life either. No matter what happens, Dave will live the rest of his days in a wheelchair. Only a miracle could change that. What I care about is finding a suitable home where Dave can be looked after, and when I do, that's precisely where he's going, and I can get my life back.'

I was too stunned to say anything. There was nothing I *could* say that would change this, in any case. I couldn't believe that she could almost flick a switch and turn into such a cold, uncaring bitch … and cold, uncaring bitches cannot be reasoned with.

'But what I *do* want is to put a stop to your interference with Dave. You gave me your word and you broke it. So from now on, I'm withdrawing my permission for you to have anything to do with him.'

She sat back, lit another cigarette and glowered at me.

'But what about his school?' I asked. 'I've agreed to be his primary carer for the remainder of the year.'

'Fuck his school,' she replied coldly. 'And fuck your uninvited interference, Molly. Now, if there's nothing else, I have things to do. You can see yourself out.'

SEVENTY

DAVE

I've lost track of time.

I think it must be about a month since the mother threw Molly out.

Okay, she didn't throw her out physically but she might as well have done. I know that she has a really bad temper but I've never seen ... well, heard – because she'd left me in my room – the mother as angry as that before.

And all Molly was trying to do was to help me get this technology that would mean that I could talk.

I'm pretty sure that this is against my human rights but, even if it is, there's absolutely nothing I can do about it. In fact, there's absolutely nothing I can do about anything.

I don't think I'm ever going to see Molly again, and sometimes I just lie awake at night and cry. I try not to think about things during the day and I don't cry cos I don't want the mother to know how upset I am. Not that it would make much difference anyway.

The mother and father have been talking a lot about where they're going to send me. The mother has found a residential home in Cheltenham where people like me live, and we're going to see it this weekend. Well, the mother and the twins and I are going to see it – the father says there's stuff he's got to do and if the mother's happy with it, just sign the papers and get me in.

Although Cheltenham is a long way from Hull, it sounds nice. The father said he might even come and visit me cos there's a racecourse there. I wish that Molly could

258

come and visit me, but the mother has already said that the home will be getting what she called an 'approved visitors' list' and Molly's name won't be on it. In fact, there probably won't be any names on it.

I've gone past caring, cos I'm back on my desert island and I was totally, totally stupid to even think that I could ever escape from it.

I've tried to think about what Robinson Crusoe would do and I've also tried really hard to stay positive and not to be afraid, but I can't find much to be positive about apart from the fact that I *will* be getting away from my family, but it's only slightly better than being sent to Mars on a one-way mission. In fact, it could be even worse.

I'm afraid. Really afraid.

What if the people who run this home or work there are even more horrible than my family? At least the mother feeds me and gives me water and makes sure I'm changed when I poo, and she's usually around when the carers come to bath me. I've heard stories on BBC Radio 4 about carers who are horrible to people like me, and sometimes they even hit them. It's called physical abuse and there's nothing that people like me can do about it. Although my family have done some pretty horrible things to me, they've never hit me ... well, not deliberately anyway.

And as far as goal setting goes, I can just forget about that.

I've even got to the point that I don't even listen much to the radio. It's always on, but most of the programmes just sort of slide over me. There's no point in listening and learning stuff that I'm never going to be able to use.

If the mother had agreed to let Molly help me, maybe I could have been on *The Chase* or something like it, and maybe I could even have become a journalist. I really do believe this. But all I'm going to be, for the rest of my life, is a blob that lies on a beanbag and makes irritating noises, probably next to other blobs who also make irritating noises but don't even know they're making them. I don't want to sound snobbish here, but I doubt they'll be able to think like I can. Maybe they will, I don't know, but

I don't think there'll be much what Molly called 'social interaction' to look forward to.

I have tried to communicate with the mother, but she doesn't know what to look for, and even if she did, I already know she wouldn't be interested, cos she just wants to get rid of me. Sometimes I've tried blinking – like it all began with Molly – and I think she does notice, but she just tells me to stop gurning or asks me if I'm trying to have a poo.

She probably still doesn't believe Molly, although I think she suspects that she could be right and that I *can* see and that my brain does actually work. Whatever she believes, she doesn't care, though, and once I become someone else's problem, she'll be able to go off with Ali. I really hate Ali cos ... well, I'll be blunt; if she hadn't come along, the mother probably wouldn't have stopped looking after me the way she used to. I'm not saying that she would have tried harder – or even tried at all – to communicate with me, cos I know she's worried that if the lawyers of the health authority who fucked me up find out the truth about me, it would mean that she wouldn't get a lot of my money.

I don't know how people can be so greedy, but I've heard enough stories on BBC Radio 4 to know that money is more important to most people than anything else.

Oh yeah ... talking of BBC Radio 4, I've had some more bad news: JFH is retiring from the *Today* programme.

He's not retiring completely cos he's still the question master for a quiz called *Mastermind*. I saw it a couple of times and I think I could do quite well on it, but I'd need text-to-speech stuff that worked really quickly. Actually, I'd need this for *The Chase* as well, but there's no point in even thinking about this now cos it's not going to happen.

I still listen to the *Today* programme; I haven't given up entirely – well, not yet anyway.

I also worry that the mother won't tell the carers at this home in Cheltenham to put BBC Radio 4 on, even though JFH won't be there for much longer. I quite like Martha Kearney, who's one of the other presenters, and I don't mind Nick Robinson, although I saw him once on the TV and he looks like a robot, but neither of them are nearly as good as JFH. I don't think many people know this, but I happen to know that JFH once got paid between £600,000–£649,999 a year, but then he took a pay cut and went down to £290,000–£294,999 in 2018–19 cos he thought he was getting too much money. That's the sort of person he is.

Anyway, back to me.

You see how much I have to worry about?

I know that life could be a lot worse than it is right now, but I'm really scared about the future.

I'm frightened that I could end up living somewhere where the carers hit me and swear at me, as well as not letting me listen to BBC Radio 4.

I'm sorry if you're reading this, but right now is probably the worst time of my entire life, and it's also the only time that I've felt that I might be better off being dead. There used to be two people who cared about me, and right now there are none.

And instead of just being left on my desert island – which is bad enough – I could soon be drowning in a sea that's full of sharks.

SEVENTY-ONE

GILL

DIARY ENTRY: Tuesday, 24 March 2020

I've finally got something on Roger.

I'm going to make the bastard pay. This is my way out of here, my ticket to freedom, maybe even happiness.

And of course, as usual, it's his own fault; as I said, there's no one better at shafting Roger than Roger himself. But even I didn't see this one coming.

Yesterday morning I was in the study wading through all the paperwork that has to be completed to get Dave admitted to Ravenscroft. We visited last Saturday and it looks ideal. The grounds are lovely, Dave will have a large en-suite room, and the staff all seem terrific. But the best thing about it is that they have room for him, so once the admissions' procedure is complete and Wendy, his case manager, signs it off, that's where he's headed. Toby, the manager, seemed professional, said all the right things, and was enthusiastic about welcoming Dave. Who wouldn't be, with his care package?

Anyway, it eases any my conscience; I'll sleep easier in the knowledge that I've done everything that could be done for Dave. All the medical evidence stacks up against any possibility that he has locked-in syndrome, and who am I to challenge it?

Then the weirdest thing happened ... well, two things really.

First, I noticed that Roger's antique mahogany partner desk had gone.

It's been replaced by something vile that looks as if it's come from Ikea. How could I not have noticed? I'd not been in here for ages, and I supposed I was so absorbed with tackling the mountain of paperwork that I didn't spot it straight away. And Roger's papers were all over it.

Why would Roger replace it with something like this? He loved that desk. He'd inherited it from his father, and it was the only possession that didn't have an engine and four wheels that he raved about.

And at the precise moment I was pondering this, the doorbell rang. I went to the front door to find an elderly couple I didn't recognise standing there.

I opened the door – we've had it fixed after the break-in. This piece of maintenance has only taken Roger thirteen years to get round to.

'Can I help you?' I asked. I assumed they'd got lost and wanted directions. This happens from time to time, and Roger says that people asking for directions are almost certainly casing the house.

I thought this unlikely as they looked as if they were in their late seventies, so satellite navigation would probably have passed them by. The man was wearing a stylish herringbone double-breasted overcoat and a trilby, and the woman wore a duvet coat, which struck me as a little excessive for a delightfully warm spring day.

'Mrs Hempsall?' the man asked.

'Yes, that's me.'

'We have something we think may belong to you.' I detected a soft Scottish accent.

'Really?' I replied.

'Yes,' he said. 'It's a bit of a long story. May we come in?'

It always is with old people, I thought, but my interest got the better of me, so a little civility wouldn't hurt.

I ushered them into the kitchen and offered tea while Scooter growled at them from his basket.

We sat at the island as they ponderously sugared then sipped the anaemic brew I'd plonked in front of them.

'Look, I don't wish to be rude, but I have a very busy day,' I said.

'Of course,' the man replied. 'Oh, sorry, I know who you are, but we've yet to introduce ourselves. My name is Harold Brown, and this is my wife, Edith.'

I acknowledged this with a curt smile.

'Well, what it is, you see, is that a few months ago ... sometime before Christmas ... I'm sorry, I can't be sure of the date, but it probably doesn't matter, I purchased an antique mahogany partner desk from a shop in Hull called Westmorland Antiques Reclaimed.'

Okay, this is getting interesting, I thought.

Edith piped up.

'You see, Harold's a wee bit of an armchair expert when it comes to antiques—'

'Well, a wee bit more than just an armchair expert, my dear, if you don't mind. Otherwise I would never have found them.'

'Found what?'

'Harold watches these programmes,' Edith continued, 'you know: *Flog It* and *Celebrity Antiques Road Trip* and the like. And so he knew where to find the secret drawer in the desk, and that's where he found them.'

'Found *what*?' I repeated, feeling a frisson of excitement, heightened by frustration at the length of time it was taking to find out what this was all about. People didn't put trivia into secret drawers, and whoever had done this – Roger's father or Roger – hadn't intended whatever it was to be discovered.

'We got your name and address from Mr Westmorland ... Zachariah Westmorland. He was a bit cagey about disclosing this information, but he said that if we were just returning something, it wouldn't be doing any harm. Besides which, he said, if he had to give back everything he found in furniture he bought, he'd never—'

'And what was it you found?' I interrupted impatiently.

'I found these.' Harold slowly withdrew two discs enclosed in semi-transparent sleeves from his inner pocket. 'We haven't looked at them, of course. That would be an invasion of your privacy. But we thought we'd like to return them because they could contain valuable photos or videos ... maybe of when your children were young? Or maybe of something else ... perhaps an event that was really important?'

I instantly knew exactly what they were, or what one of them was anyway. One disc had nothing written on it, but the other had the inscription ' 22/7' in Roger's handwriting.

My heart beat faster – much faster. If Roger knew nothing about the break-in, then why on earth would he have locked the security disc from the day it happened in his desk? I just wanted rid of the Browns so I could see what was on the discs.

Eventually they finished their tea and prepared to leave.

'Look, thank you very much,' I said. Should I offer them money? I wondered. 'Can I give you something for your trouble?'

They declined the offer and left. I raced into the study and put the first disc into the DVD player, my heart now beating like a drum. This was the disc with the date on it.

It showed nothing, so I decided to keep fast-forwarding until I got to around the time the burglary occurred. Then about an hour before this, I saw a flash of colour and a blurred frenzy of movement. I rewound the disc until I reached the point that had caught my attention and froze it.

An orange ball shot through the stained-glass window, then Boris put his hand through the broken pane and turned the key. Both the twins entered the vestibule, opened the front door and left the house, leaving both doors open.

I continued to wind the disc forward at the slowest speed. It took fifteen minutes to reach the point – one hour later, at 16.15 – where the disc stopped. After that there was nothing.

I felt a wave of disappointment surge over me. This hadn't proved what I was hoping it would: that Roger had some connection with the break-in. But it did suggest that the twins could have contributed to it by leaving both doors wide open. An opportunist thief could just have happened to be in the right place at the right time. Unlikely, I thought, but if that's what had happened, maybe that's why Roger hid the disc – the insurance company would have refused to pay out had they been able to access security camera footage that showed, well, a total lack of security. And even if Roger had hidden the disc, it wasn't exactly the hanging offence I'd hoped it might be.

I ejected the disc and inserted the second one without any real optimism. But this was security camera footage as well, so who knows?

The first thing that struck me was the time the recording began: 16.22 on the same day. That's interesting, I thought. Why eject one disc then insert another pretty much straight away? I forwarded the recording at the slowest speed.

And then, when it got to 17.13, I almost squealed with delight.

It showed Roger briskly exiting the front door carrying a long, thin iron bar that was curved at the end. He stopped, pulled the door shut, then attacked it with the iron. There was a splintering of wood, and shards went everywhere. Eventually the door conceded and he kicked it open. He then looked at the camera, swung the iron, and everything went blank.

Bingo.

I've got you, you bastard.

I think I can safely say that sex will be off the agenda.

No need to fuck you now … you've fucked yourself.

SEVENTY-TWO

MOLLY JOHNSON

MSc RESEARCH PROJECT NOTES
NOTE 15: Thursday, 9 April 2020

It's almost seven weeks since I last saw Dave.

There's a huge void in my life, and my master's is on hold.

No data, no thesis.

Never mind that; I miss Dave like hell.

I had a meeting with Josh a few weeks ago. I should have told him straight away, but I couldn't believe that Gill would actually go through with her threat and pull Dave out of school. I don't know why, but I kept hoping that she'd call me and at least relent about school, and maybe even allow me to have contact with him again. Silly me.

I mean, what sort of mother consigns their child to a life of isolation and solitude when there's even a glimmer of hope? The sort of mother who just wants shot of him and channels as much of his compensation money as she can into her own bank account; the sort of mother who wants to abandon her family and start a new life with her lover.

Oh, as I mentioned earlier, I knew about this because Dave had told me.

It was shortly before Christmas, and one of the most complex pieces of communication he'd achieved with the alphabet board. I remember it really well ... it took ages for him to spell it out, and he was clearly upset about it.

But I realised that this was something he desperately needed to share with me.

One afternoon – he'd just had hydrotherapy – he started to bang his fists with a look of anguish, bordering anger, on his face. No way could this be confused with his pre-poo animation.

I grabbed the alphabet board.

'M ... o ... t ... h ... e ... r — i ... s — d ... o ... i ... n ... g — s ... e ... x — w ... i ... t ... h — a ... n ...o ... t ... h ... e ... r — w ... o ... m ... a ... n,' he said.

OMG! I was shocked, although, if I'm honest, it didn't totally surprise me.

'How do you know?' I asked.

'T ... h ... e ... y — t ... a ... l ... k — o ... n — p ... h ... o ... n ...e. — N ... a ... m ... e — i ... s — A ... l ... i. — A — s ... h ... r ... i ... n ... k, — n ... o ... t — h ... e ... r — s ... h ... r ... i ... n ... k. — I — h ... a ... t ... e — A ... l ...i. — M ... o ... t ... h ... e ... r — h ... a ... s — n ... o — t ... i ... m ... e — f ... o ... r — m ... e — n ... o ... w.'

He then went on to tell me that he felt abandoned and that I was the only person who cared about him.

So I set about a little detective work. I figured that finding out exactly who this Ali was could come in useful at some stage,

Information is power, and I wanted to be well-armed for my last resort. If Gill could play dirty, so could I.

Of course, I'd thought about trying to appeal to her again, but as the weeks went by, I realised how pointless this would be.

I knew that Gill's therapist was called Martin, and it took me less than five minutes to find her – there are only four psychotherapy practices in Hull. Strange, you'd think there would be more with the number of nutters I've come across roaming the streets – particularly my ex.

Dr Ali(son) Carter is one of the top psychotherapists in the country. She's written countless self-help books as well as having a research track record culminating in having some pretty heavy academic papers published which attracted favourable peer reviews.

The Blue Sky Thinking Consultancy – probably so named to conceal the connotation that anyone consulting them may have less than 'blue sky' thinking – advertises therapeutic treatment for anger issues, self-esteem and confidence, stress, panic attacks and depression. From what I knew about Gill, that probably ticked all the boxes. Their website told me that there are two practitioners: Dr Martin Maynard and Dr Alison Carter, and detailed their qualifications, experience and areas of expertise. She's a good-looking woman, Ali. I've never even been slightly attracted to women but I could understand why Gill was.

A good-looking woman who would be sure to resent any publicity regarding her sexuality or her private life.

I filed this information away for later.

Anyway, coming back to my master's, Josh didn't seem at all surprised or – and I actually found this quite upsetting, after his initial enthusiasm – all that disappointed that my research with Dave had come to an abrupt end. Maybe Josh's enthusiasm had purely been at the prospect of getting into my knickers, which was a two-way street right up until the point that he put his cards on the table and more or less refused to advise me until we were between the sheets.

He told me, quite coldly, that in the circumstances, there was a good chance that the department head would agree to an extension of six months, possibly a year. But I'd already decided that I wasn't going to put myself through all of this again, risking another emotional attachment with a vulnerable young person.

***

And then yesterday, the weirdest thing happened.

I got a text from Boris.

It read: *Dave's goin into a home. Want to know more? Boris*

He had never liked me; I knew that. There was bound to be a catch, but I was intrigued, so I replied:

Yea thanx Boris. Plz call to discuss?

I was right:

Tell u evrythng for £200. Agree?

Two hundred quid was a lot of money but a small price to pay if it gave me even a slender chance of a link to Dave. If nothing else, at least I'd know where he was going, although what that information on its own would achieve, I had no idea.

Ok I agree

He replied straightaway:

Meet in McD's Boothferry rd 5PM cum alone or no deal.

I don't know who he thought I was going to bring along; maybe someone from Special Branch or perhaps Dave's case manager? From what I knew of Boris, I would imagine his mind had already acquired the sophistication of hardened criminal guile.

I got there early, but he was already seated in a booth near the door with a good line of vision.

'I'll have a Happy Meal – McNuggets – and a Diet Coke, thanks, Molly. And that's not coming out of the two hundred squid, by the way.'

I placed his order and a coffee for myself and sat down.

'Money first,' he said, a lopsided half-smile that reminded me of his father etched across his face. Chip off the old block.

My order number was displayed. I grabbed the tray, sat down and passed an envelope containing the money to him beneath the table. He counted it and put it in his schoolbag.

I sipped my coffee as he ate his Happy Meal in silence. When he'd finished, he shifted in his seat, lifted a cheek and farted noisily. The whole ... I don't know – and I'm not being snobby here because I do eat the odd Big Mac myself – but do we call Maccy D's a restaurant? Well, anyway, everyone within range looked round. Thank God there's not such an obvious age difference that I could be mistaken for his mother.

'Okay,' he said, taking a slurp of Coke and burping loudly, 'time to spill the beans. He's going to this place in Cheltenham. It's called Ravenscroft, and he's going there on Saturday.'

He handed me a slip of paper.

'Here, I've even written it down for you. And the website. Aren't I kind?'

I looked at it blankly.

So this was it. End of the road.

'Mind you, don't make any plans to visit cos you're not going to be allowed in. Gill's made a list of approved visitors and your name isn't on it. Actually, I don't think there are any names on it, so don't take it too personal.'

Boris leaned forward and lowered his voice to a whisper.

'Tell you what, Molly. I know something else that *could* get you in.'

How much was this going to cost? I wondered.

'For another two hundred smackers, I can let you into a bit of a secret. It's actually worth a lot more than two hundred – in fact, put a nought on it and that's what it's worth.'

'I haven't got any more money on me,' I replied.

'Not a problem, Molly. I know you're a good sort ... a diamond, as Rog would say.' Bloody hell, I thought ... you really ought to audition for a part in Bugsy Malone. 'You give me your word you'll pay, and I'll let you in on it.'

'I don't know, Boris. Your mother was very determined that I would never see Dave—'

'Nah. You don't know Gill. Someone could go to jail for a long time over this, and that could really fuck up her plans. I mean *really* fuck them up. So if I was her, I wouldn't want this to get out.'

My brain was in overdrive. I didn't have any moral scruples about paying for a potential bargaining chip that would connect me with Dave once again; after all, I had been prepared to blackmail her myself over her affair with Ali. It was just that I didn't trust the jumped-up little ginger weasel sitting opposite me who clearly has no moral scruples about anything, particularly if he's willing to sell information that could result in one of his parents going to jail.

And what was it about, anyway? Surely it couldn't be anything to do with Gill? However scandalous her affair might be, she certainly wasn't going to face jail for it.

But I was never going to pass it up.

'Okay, I'll owe you the two hundred.'

Boris scanned the building to see if anyone was listening. Satisfied that he had no audience, he continued.

'Thing is, Molly ... you know that break-in we had the day Dave had his accident?'

'Sure, I remember it. Your mum lost her ring.'

'Yeah. Well, it wasn't really a break-in. It was more of a break-out.'

'I don't understand.'

Boris glanced around the room again.

'Roger fixed it. He set the whole thing up ... trashed the house, jemmied the front door, smashed the security cameras and removed the discs.'

I couldn't believe it ... well, actually, I sort of could. If anyone I knew was capable of this level of criminal deceit, Roger would be top of the list.

'Then when me and Axe walked in on him and found him wearin' rubber gloves and holding a bag with all the loot in it, he made us swear not to say nothin'. He even tried to bribe us; offered us two grand each to keep schtum. Course we didn't take it.'

Boris sat back and was silent for a moment, a distant look of innocence in his eyes, and for an instant I really thought he was going to cry. Shakespearean.

He leant forward again.

'But I can't live with it no more, Molly. Every day I just feel guiltier by sayin' nothin'. I mean, he could go to jail for ages for faking the burglary and for defrauding the insurance company. I don't know how long he'd get ... maybe ten years?'

'Why don't you go to the police instead of selling me a confession?'

'I'm not confessin' nothin', Molly. Axe and me had nothin' to do with it. Roger bullied us into promising to stay silent, but I can't live with it no more.'

I can scent more than a whiff of bullshit in the air.

'And you'd be prepared to give evidence against your dad? Because if you're not, then what you've just told me would be totally unsubstantiated.'

'Of course. Once I've got that other two hundred in my hand, you have my word. You go to the cops, tell them what I've told you, and I'll back it up. Even stand up in court, if I have to, although I don't think kids are allowed in court but they've got some other way of taking evidence.'

'What about Axel? Would he give evidence?'

'He feels even worse about it than I do, Molly. He even gave Rog the two grand back.'

'I thought you didn't take the money.'

'Err ... well, he sort of forced it on us.'

'And you've given yours back too?'

Pause.

'I gave it to a charity, actually ... the RSPCA. Thought it was a way to make some good come out of this.'

I thought about it. This would be a bigger stick to beat Gill with than her affair with Ali. If only I could rely on him ... on them.

'One question: why do you want to see your dad go to jail?'

'Cos he's going to do the same to us. He wants to send us to this boarding school in the middle of fucking nowhere. Sedburgh, it's called.'

'I've heard of it.'

'Yeah, well, just imagine what it would be like for us, a pair of ginger twins. I don't want to be called Ron Fucking Weasley or Ron Fucking Weasley's Fucking Shadow until I'm big enough to do them some serious damage. It's okay at school at the minute cos we're top of the food chain. In fact, I'd rather swap with Rog and go to jail than go to fucking Sedburgh. So, if he isn't around, we can convince Gill that it'd be better to save seventy grand a year and send us to the local comp.'

'And you wouldn't be bullied there?'

'Nah. A lot of the kids there know us already. And those we've had run-ins with stay out of our way and warn others to do the same. It's all to do with reputation, Molly, building a brand. And going to a new place means starting all over again and right at the bottom of the food chain.'

We sat in silence for a moment. Much as I detest this family, going to the police would be seen as an act of war. And if Boris refused to give evidence, I could see some counter litigation coming my way for harassment or blackmail. It was a mess. But then, leaving Dave trapped in his locked-in world in the isolation of a distant residential home was something I'd do practically anything to avoid.

'Okay,' I took a deep breath. 'I'll go to the police and tell them what you've told me. You promise me that you'll back it up?'

'Like I said, once I've got the two hundred squid, you have my word. Oh, sorry … nearly forgot … that'll be two hundred for Axe as well.'

I sighed and nodded. This was going to virtually clear my bank account out.

'Oh, and, Molly?'

'Yes?'

Boris stood up and grabbed his bag.

'You *have* got really nice tits.'

SEVENTY-THREE

DAVE

Today is my last day here.

The only home I can remember.

I suppose Robinson Crusoe would be looking for the positives in my situation, but the only one I can find is that I'll finally be getting away from this family.

I've already told you how much I'm bricking it about my new carers, haven't I?

But now there's something even worse than that to worry about.

Coronavirus.

For all I know, by the time this gets published ... actually, it may not even get published at all, if the worst-case scenario happens. And if that does, there might only be a few million people left alive in the world, and they'll all live in really remote places where nobody wants to go – like Scotland or Papua New Guinea – and reading won't be that important cos they'll be spending all their time trying to survive. I don't suppose that Robinson Crusoe would have read many books on his desert island, even if he'd had them to read.

Personally, until this evening, I'd thought the whole coronavirus thing was something politicians call 'media hype' when they don't like something. I mean, for most people, it's no worse than a bit of flu ... probably what the mother calls 'man flu' when the father says he's ill. And his 'man flu' only seems to last about the same length of time as when he drinks too much beer, so it's hardly life-threatening, is it? So far, about ten thousand people have died from it, but they are mainly old people who would have died pretty soon anyway.

I know that Spanish flu killed around fifty million people between 1918 and 1920, but lots of things have changed since then; this is a different type of virus and most people recover from it.

Most people.

Apart from old people who are sick anyway.

Oh ... and people like me. People who have – and I'll quote from BBC Radio 4 – 'respiratory problems and complex medical conditions and are vulnerable to lung and chest infections'.

So people like me should be kept in something called isolation and not sent to some fucking residential home which will become a fucking funeral home when the virus gets in.

I'm sorry about the language, but I'm really angry about this, cos there's nothing I can do about it. I've just listened to the *Six O'Clock News*, and if I wasn't totally cacking it before ... well, I am now.

The news was about coronavirus; it always is at the moment.

In a way – well, before this evening – I didn't think this was a bad thing cos the news always used to be about Brexit. I wonder what would have happened if coronavirus had happened last year, right in the middle of Brexit? That's the only thing I wouldn't like about being a journalist – there aren't real news stories any more; news is just updating people about one story over and over again until another more important story comes along.

But I don't have to worry about the negative things about being a journalist cos I'm never going to be one. In fact, I'm not going to be anything except a name on a gravestone soon cos of what I've just heard on the news.

'The spa town of Cheltenham is the latest region to register fatalities from the rapidly spreading coronavirus, with fifteen deaths reported within the last twenty-four hours. Eleven were believed to be elderly victims with ongoing respiratory conditions who needed frequent hospitalisation. The other four fatalities are believed to have been severely handicapped victims in their mid-twenties, in residential care.'

Residential care?

Cheltenham?

WHAT THE FUCK?

That's where I'm going tomorrow, isn't it?

Fucking hell. This is a death sentence! I have as much a chance of surviving this as a Jewish person on a train to Auschwitz.

Just when I'd thought things had got as bad as they could get, they've just got even worse. There's a singer called Morrissey who writes songs about stuff like this, and even he would struggle to make this sound as miserable as it is.

Surely the parents – well, the mother – will have heard the news and stopped this madness?

Surely the person who manages Ravenscroft won't be accepting any more people?

Surely Wendy will tell the mother that I've got to stay here until this stops spreading?

But then, just after the news, the mother came into my room.

'Right, Dave,' she said and sounded really cheerful about it, 'time to pack a few things for your new home. Actually, time to pack everything for your new home.'

'YOU CAN NOT BE FUCKING SERIOUS!' I shouted; but of course she couldn't understand.

'Aw, you're really excited about your new home Dave, aren't you?'

Excited?

That's a fucking understatement!

SEVENTY-FOUR

GILL

DIARY ENTRY: Friday, 10 April 2020

Molly turned up out of the blue after I'd crammed Dave's stuff into the spare suitcase.

One suitcase was all it took; in fact, it was only half full. I thought about including the 'Only in it for the parking' T-shirt Roger had bought him years ago, but in the spirit of responsible parenting, I put it in the bin.

The cheek of the little bitch.

Not only did she try to blackmail me over my affair with Ali – although I don't know how the hell she found out about that – she also seems to know about the faked break-in and said she's going to go to the police unless I relent and agree not to send Dave to Cheltenham. Not only that, she demanded that I send him back to school and approve the funding for this text-to-speech thingy.

Fat chance of any of that.

She seems to know quite a lot, and I suppose I have a grudging respect for her research, although she has yet to learn how to manipulate people with the information she obtains. That's the number one rule of blackmail: when you dig up some dirt on someone (like I have on Roger), you need to build the tension ... to create the scenario as to how this information is going to wreck that person's life. You have to be a bit creative – show, and don't tell, how your victim's life will become a living purgatory; lead them along a path that takes them to the ledge of a high building, a downturned empty bottle clutched in one hand, suicide note in the other.

You don't just blurt it out or put all your cards on the table at once; you need to be totally convincing. Whatever cards you're holding, you must persuade your victim that you know exactly how to play them and that you have the confidence to drive your threats through.

I can't see Molly going to the police. I can tell how much she hates controversy; if she'd had to rely on a neighbour to go to the police over a boyfriend that had tried to kill her, she certainly wasn't going to get mixed up in something where she'd have to rely on someone else's testimony.

'I know that you and Alison Carter are having an affair,' she'd said.

I sat down at the kitchen island and lit a cigarette, wondering why I'd been so foolish as to let the stupid cow in. She'd threatened, Violet Elizabeth Bott-style, to scream and scream and scream until I let her in. I was half-minded just to leave her to scream, but wrongly assumed she only wanted to see Dave and then would disappear out of my life and into obscurity. I can't work out how she'd got to know where and when he was going, though. Only five people know this: Roger, the twins, Wendy (Dave's case manager) and myself, so I assume that Wendy must have spilled the beans; another gabby old woman.

'So?' I replied. 'Where did you come by this dubious piece of information anyway?'

'Dave told me.'

I laughed – or tried to make it look as if I was laughing.

'How'd he tell you? Did he "moo" it to you? Or was it communicated telepathically?'

'I told you, Gill. He *can* communicate. If you had even the slightest shred of interest in him, you would see that this is why he so desperately needs the text-to-speech technology, and not to be interned in that bloody residential home. You've no idea what harm that will do him.'

I went to the fridge and found a third-full bottle of Pinot Grigio – unlike Roger to not to finish that, I thought, and where the hell was he anyway? I poured a large glass, sat down and lit another cigarette. He'd gone out an hour or so ago, and the last thing I wanted was him bursting in when she was here. God knows what the little bitch might say. It could ruin everything.

'Let's just say, for a moment, that that I *am* having an affair: a) so what? and b) who's going to believe you? It'll just come across as a spiteful, fantastical rumour drummed up by a resentful ex-carer who wants to get her grubby little paws on some of his money. Maybe you think Dave is able to tell you things, Molly, but that's just your overactive imagination at work. As far as everyone else is concerned – in particular, the medical experts who gave evidence – Dave cannot communicate. End of.'

She had no answer to that, at least not for a good thirty seconds.

'That's rubbish, Gill, and you know it. You don't believe it yourself.' Her eyes began to fill, and I almost felt sorry for her.

'Now, if there's nothing else, Molly—'

'Yes, there is something else. What about the break-in? I know that Roger faked it. Do you really want him to go to prison?'

Actually, I did, but not through any intervention of Molly's.

'There are two people who will testify against him.'

Shit.

The bloody Browns must have looked at the discs after all. On reflection, there was something almost too syrupy nice about the way they declined my offer of 'something for their trouble'. But that was almost three weeks ago. Surely they would have made demands already? Maybe not ... a good extortionist's skill set includes both patience and timing. And how would Molly have found out about them? Perhaps she knew them and they were planning some sort of collaboration? I still had the discs, but of course, they would have made copies.

Double shit.

This meant that I would have to change my plans, to bring forward my own particular blueprint of extortion on Roger, before either Molly or the Browns, or perhaps an unlikely coalition of the aforementioned, could launch that particular ship.

I needed to get her out of here, but she wasn't done yet.

'Have you heard the news today?'

'No,' I replied. 'I don't listen to the news.'

'Well, you should do. Five people have died in Cheltenham today from coronavirus. And two of them were young disabled people like Dave, who lived in a residential home. Like the one you're sending him to.'

'Well, sorry as I am to hear that, Molly, it's not going to affect our plans for Dave. The residential home manager would have contacted me by now if he considered that there was even the slightest issue over Dave's admission. So you're grasping at straws, Molly. And Dave won't be going anywhere or having any visitors when he's there, so don't even think about making the journey to Cheltenham.'

A heavy silence descended. I went to the fridge and tipped the rest of the Pinot into my glass.

'Look, Molly ... I know you care about Dave, and I respect that. But you overstepped the mark, and Roger and I have decided that Dave's interests will best be met in Ravenscroft. I'm not heartless; of course you can say goodbye if you'd like to. You can have five minutes, but no longer. I need to prepare for tomorrow, and he needs to get a good night's sleep.'

Five minutes later, she left. She walked out of his room and through the kitchen, set-faced without so much as a glance at me. She stopped when she reached the scullery door and turned to face me.

'I don't know how you can live with yourself, Gill. I hope you enjoy your new life with Ali and I hope you enjoy Dave's money, but most of all, I hope that every day that passes, you think about what you've done to Dave. Because deep down in the depths of your soul, I know that you believe me, Gill, and beneath it all, you know that you have sentenced him to a life of solitary confinement.'

Fuck you, Molly.

Just fucking fuck you.

Saving Dave

SEVENTY-FIVE

MOLLY JOHNSON

MSc RESEARCH PROJECT NOTES
NOTE 16: Friday, 10 April 2020

What a waste of time and breath that was.

I'm a lousy blackmailer. Gill didn't even bat an eyelid at my pathetic threats.

She knows I'm neither going to go to the police over the break-in, nor the media over her affair with Ali.

She's right. What would be the point?

It may compromise Ali's reputation, but nothing worse than that; after all, she wasn't even Gill's councillor – and she's right: who cares? And if she did feel threatened, I could end up facing all sorts of litigation. And what would it achieve anyway? It's clear that Gill isn't to be deterred from taking Dave to Cheltenham tomorrow, no matter what threats I make.

And I'm not sure that she even gives a damn if Roger goes to jail for the burglary. Perhaps I'd even be doing her a favour.

I could ring Wendy and try to persuade her to at least delay Dave's admission to Ravenscroft. I could plead with her to carry out some sort of environmental health and safety audit, but if the home – which, I'll have to concede, is highly accredited – is still accepting residents, it's unlikely that she'd intervene.

I had five minutes with Dave.

282

I've never seen him look so forlorn, and the whole time I was trying not to cry and to push the thought that this may be the last time I see him to the back of my mind.

'You know what's happening, Dave?'

Stupid question. The suitcase stood by the door like a beacon guiding the way for his imminent departure.

I looked around the room. This was his space; within these four walls, he'd lived, listened to the radio, absorbed and assimilated what he'd heard into his rapidly expanding understanding of the world, and recently had even dreamt of a future full of promise that was about to be whisked away from him.

Within these four walls, he'd slept, been bathed, overheard conversations that would ultimately taint his future, and shared his first meaningful communication with another human.

He blinked twice.

Of course he knew where he was going.

I squeezed his hand, then I leant forward and hugged him ... and then I kissed him. This time on the lips.

I stood to go.

'I don't know how, Dave. But I'm going to help you. I'm not giving up, I promise.'

There was nothing more to say.

SEVENTY-SIX

DAVE

Molly tried her best for me.

She tried to get what murderers on something called Death Row in America call a 'stay of execution'.

I heard the whole conversation with the mother. My hearing isn't as fantastic as it used to be now that I can see, but I can hear everything that's said in the kitchen really clearly.

I think the mother has become a totally different person now. I'm not sure when this started, but I think it must have been about the time she started to do sex with Ali. Molly told her that she knew stuff about her and Ali and that she knew the father had done the break-in himself – that was news to me, and I wonder how Molly found out about it and who the other two people who know about it are?

She even told her about the coronavirus in Cheltenham, which, by the way, is now by far my biggest fear, but the mother just said that I was going anyway.

At least Molly tried ... she didn't have to.

The mother let her say goodbye to me, and it was all I could do not to cry, and I think she felt the same. Then she gave me a kiss on my actual lips, and it wasn't just her lips brushing against my lips; the kiss lasted for longer than it takes for the mother to try to put a spoonful of baked beans into my mouth and it was a lot nicer. I even got a bit of an erection – I've told you before that I have some sensation there – and it felt fantastic.

I'm going to think about this a lot when I'm in Cheltenham – that is, before I die from coronavirus – and I'm going to use this memory as a positive thing ... maybe even as a sort of goal, like Robinson Crusoe might have done.

What Molly said to the mother before she left was really brave. It won't make her change her mind, and I know I'll still be going to Cheltenham tomorrow, but it may make her think a bit, but probably not that much cos even though she might secretly believe that my brain actually works and that I can communicate, she doesn't want to admit it. She thinks that they'll take some of the money – which is actually mine – away so that she can't spend it.

She's what's called a denier. She's like people who refused to admit that Hitler murdered around seventeen million people during the Second World War in the Holocaust, even though there's loads of evidence that he did.

Anyway, before I could think too much about this or anything else, the father came home and they had this massive row.

The parents don't usually have big rows; what normally happens is that the mother loses her temper with him and he doesn't really say very much. And sometimes this makes her lose her temper even more – she might throw things at him, and once she threw a mug of tea that she'd just made over him, so that must have hurt a lot cos tea's made with boiling water – so if this happens, he just walks out and drives off somewhere. I don't really blame him, although if he'd not done stuff to annoy the mother, it wouldn't have got to what Boris calls 'Defcon Two' in the first place.

Anyway, they've just had the worst row I've ever heard, and I actually felt a bit scared.

And after there'd been some stuff thrown by the mother – well, I presume it was the mother – the father left. I could hear his car starting, and he drove off really fast so that the engine, which I can hear from about five miles away anyway, sounded even noisier. He normally drives much too fast, even when he's driving the Davemobile, so I'm always bricking it when he's driving, but usually it's driven by the mother. He never takes the Davemobile if he can avoid it; mostly he drives his new Aston Martin, which is much faster and much louder than the Davemobile.

I hope the mother'll be driving to Cheltenham tomorrow, cos that would be one less thing to worry about. She probably will, cos he'll probably not want to come unless there might be horse racing on.

Anyway, I heard the car make a screeching noise when he reached the gates, and then I heard the engine for about three and a half more minutes until it faded into the night, and there was silence until the mother threw something else that shattered in the kitchen and she yelled 'fuck' and something else and then there was silence.

I thought of Molly's kiss again and felt slightly better, but I also had this feeling that something really bad was going to happen.

SEVENTY-SEVEN

GILL

DIARY ENTRY: Friday, 10 April 2020

Peace at last.

I sat at the island, went through the deep breathing rigmarole Martin had taught me, and gradually I calmed down.

The bastard's driven off, so I opened the bottle of Pinot I'd stashed in the freezer before this kicked off, poured a large glass and went to the study to write my diary.

I'm alone in the house – oh, apart from Dave. The twins have gone for a sleepover with the one family who will still have them. I'll pick them up on the way to Cheltenham in the morning.

Driving off is Roger's answer to everything. But it's fine by me, as I just wanted him out of the house so I could plan what I'm going to do next.

I didn't handle that very well, I'll admit.

In fact, I didn't handle it much better than Molly's attempts at blackmail. My temper gets in the way too much to make me a good negotiator, I know that, and he knows which buttons to press.

Not that it really matters. I've got him where I want him ... well, apart from one thing, which I will deal with. He *will* agree to my demands because – unlike Molly – I *will* go to the police. I'm not sure about the Browns, though, which is why I couldn't delay this. I have the strength and resolution to carry through my threats, and

I also have the evidence, so I don't need to rely on witnesses to corroborate his guilt.

Molly had only been out of the house for five minutes when he rocked up with a stupid big grin on his face which told me that he'd already had a couple of pints. I hadn't time to plan how I was going to handle this, so I just dived right in.

But I did have the element of surprise, because this would be the last thing he'd have been expecting when I told him there was something we needed to talk about.

'Not Dave again?' he said, opening the fridge and grabbing a bottle of Stella. 'Don't tell me they're not taking him now because of this bloody ridiculous coronavirus thing? If you ask me, it's totally overhyped. It'll all blow over in a few weeks. Anyway, the world's population needs a bit of a cull, doesn't it?'

'I'm not asking you, and it has nothing to do with coronavirus or Dave, Roger. It's to do with you,' I said calmly.

'Me?'

'Yes … you. I had a visit from an elderly couple two weeks ago.' I pulled an envelope holding the discs from my handbag, took them out and held them so he could see what they were. 'Recognise these?'

His eyes, rarely fully open – which adds to the general seediness of his appearance – were like the proverbial organ stops.

'The old man who bought your antique mahogany partner desk – remember it? Well, he found these in a secret drawer.'

He lunged at me and tried to grab the discs, but I was ready and I deftly moved to one side so that he collided with the island unit, banging his knee heavily.

'Fuck! And fuck you, Gill.'

I pulled my self-defence anti-attack spray from my bag and pointed it at him.

'I wouldn't try that again, unless you want this sprayed in your face.'

'Fucking hell, Gill, what's got into you?'

'I could ask you the same question, Roger. What on earth got into *you* to stage a burglary?'

'I have absolutely no idea what you're talking about. What's on those discs anyway?'

He was panting heavily and starting to sweat.

'Don't play the innocent, Roger. It's a bit late for that. You know bloody well what's on the discs.'

Stalemate. See how good at this I am? Up until the point when I lose it, that is. But I was enjoying myself. I held all the cards. Husband: fucked.

'Okay ... so just what are you planning to do with them?'

'That very much depends on you, Roger. But what I'm going to do with them right now is to keep them under lock and key.'

I went to the study, locked the door behind me, and stowed them in the imitation double plug socket wall security box I'd had installed after the 'break-in'. Roger doesn't know about it, and I have the only key in any case. But if I'd had the sense to install the bloody thing before he ransacked the house, I'd still have my ring.

I returned to the kitchen. He was seated at the island, beer bottle in hand, looking mawkish.

'There,' I said,' and don't even think about trying to find them. And unless you agree to exactly what I want, I'll take them to the police. A Detective Constable Bragg was the officer in charge, if I remember correctly? I never did give him the statement he requested. Oh well, better late than never.'

Silence.

'So, what exactly *do* you want?'

This I had planned for. After the Browns' visit, I knew this moment would come, so ... forewarned is forearmed ... I'd typed out my demands, printed them, and then deleted the file from the computer. I handed it to Roger.

He read it aloud:

"I, Roger Hempsall, being of sound mind and body, do hereby agree to accept the following conditions, in consideration of which the police will not be informed about my staging a faked break-in at Hillcrest, Rising Bucklebury, on Wednesday, 24 July 2019, and my subsequent fraudulent insurance claim of £17,235.67, which was paid out on Saturday, 21 December, 2019."

'Fucking hell, Gill ... what is this? Have you totally lost it? I think I'd better call your shrink—'

'Just read on, Roger.'

He continued. Reluctantly.

"'I hereby resign as co-trustee of the trust fund set up to administer both the proceeds from the medical negligence compensation and the annual periodic payment on behalf of my son, David Nigel Hempsall.

"'I agree to make payment of my half of the Primary Carers' compensation – a sum set at £2.8 million; the minimum value of this will be one million pounds – to my wife, Gill Hempsall.

"'I agree to move out of Hillcrest immediately, and accept the generous offer of a period of one calendar month to remove all my possessions from the former family home. The house will undergo an immediate valuation and will be placed on the market forthwith. I agree to accept twenty per cent of the net profits (after deduction of all costs and the outstanding mortgage) following the sale of the property.

"'On grounds of the irretrievable breakdown of our marriage, I agree to the commencement of divorce proceedings from my wife Gillian Margaret Hempsall (née Smith).

"'Following the decree absolute, I agree to pay fifty per cent of all maintenance costs for my sons, Boris St Johnstone Hempsall and Axel Rudi Pell Hempsall, and I agree to be liable for their ongoing private boarding education."

'Jesus Christ, Gill ... divorce? What the—'

'Fuck, Roger? That's right, I'm not going to fuck you again. Ever.'

He just stood there looking pathetic. I almost felt sorry for him.

'I realise it's not a professionally drafted legal document, but I think it gets the message across as to what I want. And if you analyse it, I think I'm giving you a pretty good deal. You still have four hundred grand – or what's left of it after you've gorged yourself on cars – twenty per cent of the net proceeds from the house sale, and I'm only demanding fifty per cent for the twins ... well, apart from the school fees, of course. I could ask for a lot more.'

290

His mouth flapped like a dying fish's, and irritating squeaky noises escaped his larynx. He actually made Dave look intelligent.

'Or perhaps you'd prefer to go to prison? I've been told that you'd be looking at somewhere in the region of ten to twelve years behind bars.'

Eventually he managed to speak.

'I don't want a divorce. What do you mean "irretrievable breakdown" of our marriage? Okay, we've had our ups and downs like every other couple I know, but – at least as far as I was aware – we don't have any major issues.'

I took a large gulp of wine and lit a cigarette.

'Do you have to do that in the house?' I ignored him.

'There is one. And you can cite it as the reason for divorce, if you like.'

I could see the cogs in his mind circling, clicking and ultimately coming up with blanks. He didn't have a clue, and for an instant I hated myself for enjoying my position of supremacy so much.

'I'm having an affair.'

SEVENTY-EIGHT

DAVE

This is when I started to feel scared.

The mother had just told the father that he had to leave home. She seems to want to throw everybody out, and she's throwing me out tomorrow as well. I suppose the ginger twats will be next. Maybe this is what she means by spring-cleaning.

She'd told him to read out some sort of agreement – it sounded a bit like the letter they'd had from the lawyer about my compensation just before Christmas. At first I thought it was something that the father had written, but it soon became obvious that the mother had written it for him, cos he wasn't very happy about it.

The last part of it was about them getting a divorce. That was what seemed to upset him more than the money stuff. To be honest, that surprised me a bit; I'd have thought he'd have been more upset about the money. But I suppose he could always refuse to agree to the mother's demands and just go to prison.

Then she told him she was having an affair, and he went really quiet.

I could tell that this was news to him.

'Who the hell *is* he?' he asked after taking a long time to think about it.

'Not that it matters,' the mother replied, 'but "he" is a "she".'

'Fucking hell, Gill. You're … a … a muff guzzler? How long have you been seeing … her? Jesus!'

'A year; it was a year ago today, actually, that we slept together for the first time. And you can keep your pathetic little homophobic and misogynistic rants to yourself.'

There was another long silence. I heard the mother light a cigarette and smelt the smoke. I don't really like the smell of cigarette smoke, and the father hates it, so I suppose she was just doing it to annoy him.

'A woman? You're having an affair with a woman? I just don't get it. Why?'

I'd like to know the answer to that as well.

'You don't need to "get it", Roger. You just need to sign the papers when my lawyer sends them and accept the terms of this agreement. That's all you need to do.'

He didn't say anything to this. The father usually has an answer to most things, so this conversation was really unusual.

'Why do you think we've not had sex for ages?' the mother asked. 'The last time we did it ... remember? I do. It was eighteen months ago. I was physically sick afterwards. Feeling you inside me made my flesh creep. Thank God you were in and out in less than twenty seconds.'

'But with a ... *woman*?'

'I don't have to justify myself to you, Roger. It's the twenty-first fucking century anyway. You know all you need to know. Just put your signature on that document, pack some of your stuff and leave. You can start to get the rest of your shit together on Monday.'

'Jesus Christ, Gill. Can't we at least talk about things? I don't want a divorce. I'll change ... I'll try to be more sensitive and, I don't know ... considerate. I'll leave the toilet seat down and try not to do whatever else pisses you off. And we don't need to have sex ... not if you don't want to. Please?'

I think this is the first time I've ever felt sorry for the father. He was doing what's called grovelling, but it wasn't getting him anywhere. Maybe it *was* just about the money cos I really didn't think he actually loved the mother. Maybe I was wrong?

And then he seemed to remember something.

'Oh yes,' he said, 'I almost forgot,' and then he seemed to change and he sounded confident and even happy, like he did in the casino when he was winning all the time and I was his lucky mascot. 'Look what I found?'

'My fucking ring, Roger. You fucking stole it, you bastard. Give it to me.'

'Oh, I don't think so, Gill. If you want this ring back, you're going to need to rip up that piece of paper and hand over the discs. I think that's a fair swap, don't you?'

Clearly the mother didn't, cos the next thing I heard was something that was probably made of pottery or china crashing loudly into something that was probably made of brick.

'Fuck you, Roger.'

'That was Dave's christening plate, Gill. My parents gave him that.'

'Fuck Dave's christening plate. And fuck your parents. Now give me that fucking ring.'

I've never heard anyone as angry as this, not even on the TV or in plays on BBC Radio 4.

Then there was a bit of a silence before something that sounded like glass was thrown and shattered really loudly.

'Jesus, that nearly hit me, you stupid cow. I think I'd better ring Martin, see what he'd advise to calm you down. How about taking some of your Prozac? Huh?'

'Just give me my fucking ring, Roger.'

Then there was this sort of swishing noise, like the sound of something solid flying through the air followed by another, much louder, shattering noise.

'Christ, Gill, that was a perfectly acceptable Pinot. And I think it was the last bottle.'

'My ring, Roger, give me my fucking ring. Or I call the police – right now.'

And then there was another silence for a bit until the father started what the mother used to call his 'rat laugh'. Only, when she'd called it that, it was years ago and she'd thought it was quite funny. Obviously, she didn't now.

'Take it out of your mouth, Roger. You swallow that ring, and I'll fucking kill you!'

The father laughed again and made this weird sort of exaggerated glugging sound.

'If I were you, I'd want to be around whichever toilet bowl this reappears in with my Marigolds on. So I think it's in both our interests that we continue to live together … don't you? Now, I'm going for a drink and I'll try my best not to have a shit in The George.'

I heard the back door slam and his car start, and the mother threw something else that smashed, and then she started to cry really loudly.

'Fuck you. Fuck the whole fucking lot of you. You've no idea what's coming to you!'

I think I do pretty much know what's coming to me; but suddenly, having carers that might abuse me, or maybe even dying of coronavirus, doesn't seem nearly as frightening as the mother when she really loses her temper.

SEVENTY-NINE

ROGER

Roger sat at a table in a window corner of The George, nursing a pint.

A double scotch sat beside it.

He twiddled with Gill's Van Cleef & Arpels Sweet Alhambra ruby and diamond-encrusted effeuillage ring with the thumb and forefinger of his right hand, then placed it on the table, picked up the scotch and consumed it with one gulp.

The easiest of deception tricks – one he'd learned in his first year at prep school – was to convince a punter that you'd swallowed an object, and then produce it from wherever you should choose.

But, on this occasion, it had brought him little solace.

The George was quiet for a Friday night almost dead in fact, with only a murmur of muted conversation from those souls brave or stupid enough to defy the recent government social distancing recommendations urgently configured in the blitzkrieg that the COVID-19 virus had become.

The place will probably be closed tomorrow, Roger thought. Every pub, club, gym or other social hub had been closed for weeks in almost all European countries. But Britain stood alone; a fact that had delighted Roger – a confirmed Leaver – until this evening when his world had turned upside down in the blink of an eye. He had basked in the fact that post-Brexit Britain was an island in the truest sense once more, free to self-legislate, free to be different and free to do whatever we bloody well want, for no better reason than because we're British.

Happy days, or so they had been until Gill dropped the bomb … well, several bombs, he reflected.

But now Roger didn't give a proverbial flying fuck whether the pubs would close, or whether every man and his dog would face months of quarantine, because – from where he sat – he was looking at the prospect of at least a decade of extreme social distancing behind bars at Her Majesty's pleasure.

Roger downed the remainder of his pint, sidled to the bar and ordered the same again.

'Thirsty tonight … *sir*?' the barman quipped.

Something about the way the youth pouring his pint stressed the word 'sir' made Roger hold back from telling him it was as much his business whether he was thirsty or not as it was Roger's to enquire about whether his wages covered his weekly budget for Clearasil.

'You don't recognise me, do you, *sir*?'

Roger had a closer look.

'Nope'.

'You used to teach me, *sir* … SMSC Education, including careers. Can't even remember what it stands for, so you can't have done much of a job. Bells, wasn't it, *sir*?'

Roger nodded, still trying to place the youth, not that it really mattered. But the quicker he could get the encounter done with, the sooner he could return to his corner and try to figure out what he was going to do about the shitstorm his life had unexpectedly become.

'Spiritual, Moral, Social & Cultural Education,' he replied. 'That's what it stands for.'

Then the proverbial penny dropped.

'Actually, I do remember you. Briggs, isn't it?' Roger also remembered an incident in which the head's car had been vandalised when one of the semi-literates had rammed potatoes into the exhaust pipe. Briggs had been heavily tipped as the most likely culprit, having had form for other such misdemeanours, but, as was normal at Wiley Hall, nothing was ever proved. 'Well, done Briggs … good to see you've got a job. I wouldn't have put money on that.'

297

Querulous as to the sincerity of Roger's comment, Briggs placed change from the twenty-pound note on the counter, scowled at Roger and went back to examining his latest crop of spots in the mirror.

Roger sat down, sipped his pint and considered his options.

First, he supposed, he could concede to Gill's demands. This would leave him with about two hundred grand in liquid assets before the house was sold, insufficient for him to escape from Wiley Hall and another cohort of Briggs-like Neanderthals. And the cars would have to go. Even figuring Gill's ring into the bargaining equation, this was really not an option.

He could always go to prison, he supposed. That would at least protect his assets. And, as he was unlikely to spend much money in jail, he'd have a tidy little nest egg when he came out. But ten years was a long time, and the more he thought about it, *if* he came out seemed more likely than *when* he came out. With the spread of the virus, jail, he imagined, would be one of the worse places to be. And that was before he'd even considered the probability of being buggered even more senseless than he'd been at prep school. No … this was an even worse option.

What about murder? Not such an unattractive option, he pondered, as that would neatly remove Gill and her threats from the equation, thus avoiding the ignominy of a divorce, particularly when it came out that she was a lesbian. It would also potentially leave him much better off. But the word 'potentially' anticipated several assumptions that to a gambling brain offered very poor odds.

Roger took a large pull from his pint and considered this. How would he do it? Oh, that would be easy enough, he thought. After all, he'd done it before, and had even kept the bottle of Sitagliptin that had mysteriously disappeared on the morning his father had taken the fatal overdose. In fact, it sat in the glove compartment of the Aston – the safest place to keep it. He would only need to find the Prozac Martin prescribed for Gill's anger management and make a switch. But she rarely took her

298

medication, so this was an imperfect solution. Anyway, he thought, that had been months in the planning. If Roger knew anything about himself, it was that he wasn't good at spontaneous crime. The burglary had taught him that.

And time was against him; he would need to put the Sitagliptin into something that Gill would drink, and – as things stood – they were a very long way from enjoying a social drink without Gill throwing the literal kitchen sink at him.

No ... murder needed much better planning. He would be looking at a damned sight longer than a ten-year stretch if he got caught. Still ... let's not rule this out entirely, he thought, as the ghost of an idea tapped him softly on the shoulder.

But the cops would be sure to sift through Hillcrest and would undoubtedly find the discs. Game, set and match. Unless, the ghost goaded him ... unless there were no discs.

Still, he'd be staring down the barrel of a murder charge banged on top of what the judge would dish out for fraud and a faked break-in. Yes, he would have a tidier nest egg when he came out, but that would go straight to the nursing home he'd be transferred into directly from clink.

No, murder certainly wasn't a practical option, particularly given the timescale.

Or was it?

There was no telling how soon Gill would go to the police, but he figured pretty soon, if her mood had been anything to judge by. He estimated he had twenty-fours, at the most. Maybe, due to her plans to take Dave to Cheltenham tomorrow, he would have until Monday ... no longer.

But something in his voyage of deliberations had jarred him like an unseen speed bump. Trouble was, he couldn't pull it back, and the harder he tried to trace it, the more elusive it became. There was an answer somewhere ... he just couldn't access it.

He looked into his whisky tumbler for inspiration; none came, so he downed it and banged the glass on the table rather louder than he'd intended so that the few people left in the pub turned to look at him. Roger looked away self-consciously, and his eyes landed on a spot above the door.

Bingo.

A security camera.

That was the solution. He knew exactly what he had to do.

He needed to find and steal the discs.

Shouldn't be that difficult, he thought. She'd locked them somewhere in the study, and with the departure of his desk, there were only two other secure hiding places, one being the double plug socket wall security box Gill thought he didn't know about. Five minutes with either a screwdriver or the tyre iron should be sufficient.

Problem solved.

EIGHTY

GILL

DIARY ENTRY: Friday, 10 April 2020

I'd almost finished writing up this evening's episode, which calmed me down considerably, when I received a text.

I've actually enjoyed writing my diary recently, and I think that as well as being therapeutic, it's revealed things about me that would otherwise have just passed me by.

Sometimes I don't even recognise myself; it's almost as if I'm writing about another person. Martin said that it would only help if I were completely honest, and I've done this so successfully that sometimes I really detest the person I'm writing about.

Who is she?

When I flick back to when Dave had his 'difficulties', I seemed to be a much more caring, less selfish person. Those entries may reflect a depth of something perhaps bordering resentment, but they still come across as com-passionate. And there's no evidence of compassion inside the woman writing this now. And the lack of warmth I wrote about on the day Dave was born was more of a premonition than an absence of love. And I was right, wasn't I?

I suppose this is a reflection of my psychological is-sues exacerbated by stress from all that's happened re-cently. Martin refuses to label my disorder, but I have a feeling, from my own research, that Bipolar isn't far off the mark.

Maybe I'm just making excuses for her ... well, for me, because what I seem to have morphed into is – let's be honest – this vile bitch who's blackmailing her husband (although he does deserve it – I could kill him for stealing my ring), who pulled her handicapped son out of school, and who is about to send him to a home so she can run off with her lover. And, to tell the truth, I'd never even examined Molly's claims. I just treated them as some form of heresy. I hid behind the weight of medical opinion that said Dave is as Dave appears because it's more convenient – and, of course, financially beneficial – to do so than to examine what Dave might be ... maybe might have been.

Is this really me? It appears that it is. Well, we all change, don't we? That's an easy cop-out, but I'll buy it.

It'll soon be over, and I'll be with Ali and well away from this bloody family. Dave will be cared for in Cheltenham, the twins will board at Sedburgh from September, and Roger? Well, Roger will be in prison.

Family ... sorted.

And glancing into the conscience of the person I used to be through the spyhole of my diary will only have been a momentary blip.

I opened the text. It was from Roger. There were two pictures.

The first was of my ring sitting next to a pint of beer, and the second was a selfie of a smiling Roger sitting at a pub table with two drinks in front of him and the ring placed in the middle. For a second, I wondered who the other drink belonged to, and then I remembered that on rare occasions – usually when he wants to get pissed quickly – he abandons his high horse about drinking spirits and has a whisky chaser. And it's often a large one. I suppose he'll drive after that too.

Then a WhatsApp voice message arrived.

'Gill,' he slurred. 'Look ... I'm really shorry. I didn't *shwallow* your ring. Remember, that's an old trick of mine? Ha! Anyway, I've thought about what you said, and you're right, Gill ... I *have* been a complete twat ... I really have. You can have what you want, Gill ... look, I'll shine that bloody paper, if that's what you want.'

302

Then the message stopped. His finger probably slid off the button. I don't think I've ever heard him that drunk. I could see another voice message being recorded.

He sounded even drunker.

'Gill, I don't want to go to prison. Look ... I don't want a divorce either *but* ... if you're *not* in love with me any more ... if you're in love with ... whatever *her* fucking name is ... then, I'm short of happy for you. Maybe we can shtill be friends? I don't know. I'll tell you what? Let's just settle this now, why don't we? You've got to take Dave tomorrow and I jusht ... want ... this ... shettled. Fuck knows ... you might even go to the cops ... but I *do* want it shettled, so here's what I'm going to offer: come to The George ... now ... letch have a drink together ... you know, one where we don't throw things at each other' – he laughed at this, or it sounded more as if he was making an attempt to laugh – 'and I'll give you your ring and shine whatever you bloody well want me to shine. Can't say fairer than that, can I? And I'm going to shtay here tonight, they've got a room ... cos ... cos I've had a wee bit too much to drink. What d'you say, Gill? Huh?'

I thought about it.

The sensible thing would be to let him stew. Leave it until Monday. But if the Browns decided to stick their oar in before I got my ring back and got a signature on my agreement, that would totally scupper things. Yes, Roger would still go to prison, but I wanted the money.

What harm could it do?

One drink, and I'd be out of there, he'd be out of my life – or well on the way out of it – and my 'happy ever after' with Ali could begin much sooner than we'd anticipated. Should I call her? No ... wait until it's a done deal.

The thought struck me that I was probably over the limit, but it's less than a ten-minute drive to The George on a three-car-a-day road. And I'd just have an orange juice when I got there. What could go wrong?

So I texted back.

Ok. I'll be there in 15.

I closed my laptop, had a pee and grabbed the keys to the Range Rover.

EIGHTY-ONE

ROGER

Roger sensed the merest flicker of a smile flush his face, finished his pint, placed Gill's ring in his trouser pocket, stood up and made for the door, a look of grim determination having now replaced what might have been construed as a smirk.

Clever, that, he thought, pretending to be drunker than he actually was. And so convincing that Gill would be taken in by it. He'd had a lot to drink, but he felt far from inebriated, such was the jeopardy of his situation.

As an afterthought, he stopped at the bar. The recalcitrant Briggs reluctantly dragged himself away from his phone and asked if he would like the same again, *sir*?

'No, *sir* would not, thank you, Briggs,'

He pulled a twenty-pound note from his wallet, ripped it in half and handed one half to Briggs.

'What's that for ... *sir*?' he asked.

'A small favour, Briggs, and one for which I will give you the other half, once completed.'

Roger took out his wallet, opened it and showed him a photograph.

'This is my wife. She'll be joining me for a drink in ten minutes or so. I need to pop down to the ATM to grab some cash—'

'We *do* cash back here, *sir*.'

'Not for the amount I need,' Roger replied testily. This was wasting time. 'When she arrives, just tell her where I've gone and get her a drink. I'll pay for it when I get back. Oh ... and there'll be another twenty in it for you if she's still here when I return.'

Leaving Briggs holding one half of a twenty-pound note, a look of dazed confusion on his face, Roger exited The George, started the Aston, and drove off with speed and undue care inexpedient for someone who had consumed a significant amount of alcohol.

EIGHTY-TWO

MOLLY JOHNSON

MSc RESEARCH PROJECT NOTES
NOTE 17: Friday, 10 April 2020

After I left Gill's, I drove around aimlessly for a bit.

I couldn't face going home to Dad … well, not yet anyway.

The adrenalin from my pathetic parting shot at Gill had worn off, leaving me feeling weak and mentally exhausted. My failure to rescue Dave from being sent to Cheltenham hadn't really sunk in yet; I still couldn't accept that there was nothing else I could do for him, and I felt defeated. I'd tried reasoning and I'd tried blackmail, albeit not very convincingly. What else could I have done? This thought didn't make me feel any better.

With nothing else to do, I drove into Hull. I had absolutely no plan. Maybe I'd pick up a takeaway and buy a bottle of wine to take home? I don't drink a lot, but I felt this was probably as good a time as any to get pissed.

It was a beautiful, warm spring evening, and scores of young people – mainly students, I'd imagine – were wandering the streets without an apparent care in the world. They're saying that all pubs, bars, restaurants and everywhere else the public gathers will be closed from tomorrow. So this is probably the last chance to party.

I bought a burger and a bottle of Chardonnay and drove home.

Dad had gone out, to my relief; he'd left a note saying that he'd gone to the pub but wouldn't be late – the last chance saloon, he'd called it. There was a curry in the freezer I could microwave. He keeps forgetting how much I hate curry. Bless him.

I opened the wine and turned on the telly. The national news was on. All the stuff about the coronavirus was coming to an end and the 'news where you are' followed, with scenes of hoards of young people partying, ignoring the government's advice to stay at home, and the local MP saying what a disgrace this was and telling people to go home and not to clear out the supermarkets as there's no need to panic buy.

Whatever.

I was about to take a bite of my burger when I froze.

I didn't notice I'd dropped it till it bounced off my lap and landed on the floor.

The cameras had cut to footage of a road traffic accident. Two cars were involved, and instantly I knew two things: the first was who owned them, and the second was that no one was going to get out of either car and walk away. The number plates were blurred out, but my conviction wasn't. I prayed I was wrong.

A young reporter, with a jaundiced look on his face that suggested he might have just thrown up, stepped in front of the camera. He stood about twenty metres from the scene of the wreckage, now lit with emergency services arc lights and blue flashing lights from ambulances and police cars. I knew the road well; it's called Beverley Lane and it links Rising Bucklebury with South Cave. There's a particularly nasty bend about a mile from South Cave, and that's where it had happened.

'*A man has died and a woman in a critical condition has been airlifted to hospital following one of the worst road traffic accidents in the East Riding of Yorkshire for many years.*

'*It is believed that both vehicles were travelling at considerable speed when a head-on collision occurred on a bend in Beverley Lane, a notorious accident black spot that has witnessed fatalities before.*

'*The driver of one of the cars, a grey Aston Martin Vantage, was an unnamed forty-six-year-old man who was pronounced dead at the scene.*

'*The woman, also at this stage unnamed, was driving a new Range Rover and is believed to be in her early forties.*

'*Beverley Lane will remain closed for an unspecified period of time as police look for clues to the probable cause of the crash, and emergency services work to clear away the wreckage of what can only be described as a scene of utter carnage.*

'*I spoke to Detective Constable Bragg of the East Riding of Yorkshire Constabulary, and he told me that this is the worst traffic accident he had witnessed in his time on the force, and added that the lead investigator already had evidence to suggest that the Aston Martin had been travelling at a speed in excess of eighty miles an hour at a point in the lane barely wide enough for two vehicles to pass.*

'*DC Bragg told me that he had arrived at the scene by chance. He was on his way to Rising Bucklebury to follow up a lead into a burglary in the village that had been reported several months ago.*'

I felt sick.

I sat down, raised the bottle to my lips, and drank as much as I could before I dropped it and vomited.

I wiped my mouth, still staring at the image of sudden death on the screen, and through the fog of my fractured consciousness, became aware that my phone was ringing.

Mechanically, I picked it up and answered.

'Molly?' A voice I recognised but couldn't immediately place. 'Molly, is that you? It's Wendy ... Dave's case manager.'

'Oh,' I replied.

'Molly, I've got some bad news, I'm afraid.'

'I know,' I replied, 'I've just seen the news.'

Silence.

'Roger's dead, isn't he? And Gill? How bad is she?'

'She's in intensive care. It's hard to get any information out of them, but I don't think her chances are terribly good.'

'What about Dave?' I asked. 'Who's looking after him?'

'That's what I was going to ask you, Molly. I know there was some sort of fallout between you and Gill a while ago, but in the circumstances—'

'Of course, Wendy, I'll look after him.'

I did my best to clean up my own particular scene of carnage, brushed my teeth, packed a few things into a carry-on case and drove to Hillcrest, taking the long way round and trying not to think about what had just happened on the route I'd normally take.

A state of shock didn't come close to touching it, but at least I had something to do.

***

And someone who needed me.

Someone who certainly wasn't going anywhere near Cheltenham tomorrow.

Nor on any other day.

EIGHTY-THREE

DAVE

The father had his funeral today.

It was cold and wet and the priest who made the speech at the grave did it really quickly so that we could go home. Or probably so that he could go home. He'd made a long-enough speech in the church anyway, although I don't think he knew the father very well cos he said what a 'pillar of the community' he was and that he was a 'devoted family man' and a 'popular and committed teacher' at Wiley Hall Academy. Maybe he was getting him mixed up with somebody else? There are probably a lot of funerals at the moment cos of this coronavirus.

There weren't many people there anyway. Most people probably used the coronavirus thing as an excuse not to go – like, for example, Mr Cant, the head at Wiley Hall. But more likely there weren't many people there cos the father didn't have many friends. In fact, I don't think he had any.

There was just me and Molly, the twins and Viv, an aunt who I'd never met. She's the mother's sister and she lives in Palma, which is a city on a Spanish island called Majorca. She owns a lot of businesses – I know one is an English school – and I think she's quite rich. I don't think that her and the mother got on at all, which is probably why I'd never met her.

She's really nice, and I liked her straightway cos Molly told her all about me and showed her the alphabet board and we had a really long chat. She told me that I am amazing – I don't think that I am but it made me feel really good. She's going to speak to Miriam Davison – she's what's called a deputy and she's now the only one left in charge of my money – and tell her that I need this text-to-speech thing, once this coronavirus has gone. She said that once Miriam sees what I can do, she'll have to allow it to go ahead, especially as I'll be able to tell her myself how much it's going to change my life. And she's not interested in my money cos she said that she doesn't care if the compensation has to be reassessed.

That's really good news, isn't it?

I mean, I *could* get a place on *Mastermind* and maybe become a journalist someday, if it works as well as Molly thinks it will.

The bad news is that nobody knows how long this coronavirus is going to last or how many people it might kill, and of course it's much more likely to kill people like me, so after today Hillcrest is going to be like a fortress and we're not allowed to go to the hospital to visit the mother.

The mother is still in a coma and she's on a thing called a ventilator. This is not good news, cos there is a big shortage of ventilators and doctors have been told that if someone on a ventilator is unlikely to recover, then they have to give the ventilator to someone with coronavirus who has a better chance of getting over it.

They're going to give her another week then will probably switch the thing off, and that'll mean that we'll have to go to her funeral too.

I feel really sad for the mother.

And apparently Ali hasn't even bothered to visit or even ring up about her either.

Anyway, Viv told Molly that she must bring me to Palma when things get back to normal ... if they get ever back to normal. It was lucky that she was staying in a house she owns near Kendal or she wouldn't have been able to get to the funeral.

I feel really guilty about the mother and the father.

I've never felt guilty about anything before, not even when I vomited on the father and his instructor on the parachute jump.

But I feel really terrible for saying that I wanted to kill my family because now the father is dead and the mother probably will be soon. So now it's just the ginger twats and me who are left; they're staying with Viv at her house until they can go to Majorca with her.

Viv and the ginger twats seem to get on really well. She's going to be what's called their guardian, and that will mean that's she's sort of stuck with them. Axel seems to have changed a lot, and even Boris has stopped swearing (well ... almost) and was actually quite okay with me at the father's funeral. I think what's happened has affected all of us, one way or another. And if ... I know it's a big maybe ... but if *maybe*, someday the twins and me have a better relationship, then some good will have come from it. Look ... I've stopped calling them twats, so I suppose that's a start.

Another reason they like Viv is cos she's said that they're not going to board at Sedburgh. They're going to go to a normal school in Palma where they can swim in the sea every day and they won't even need to wear a uniform.

Anyway, Molly talked to Wendy yesterday and she said she was going to put it on speakerphone so that I could hear. Molly has agreed to become what's called my 'de facto' primary carer, but apparently there's a long process that she needs to go through for this to be official. Wendy told her that she would start the paperwork, but as there was a team of carers in place already, it was just a procedural thing.

You've probably worked out that I'm not going to that home in Cheltenham. I'm sorry that the father and probably the mother had to die, but if there's any good to come from that, it has to be me staying here with Molly.

***

So, that's about all there is to tell.

Oh ... Molly has introduced me to someone called Sarah who is a ghostwriter and she's agreed to write my story. She's going to do this by interviewing me, with Molly helping, using something called Facetime. I think it's going to take ages, unless coronavirus ends soon and I can get the text-to-speech technology.

If you're reading this, then she'll have finished writing it and you'll know everything about my life so far. Of course, I could be dead by the time you read this, either from coronavirus or because it just took so long to write.

But I hope not, and this brings me to something really important I'll like to tell you before I shut up.

Maybe you remember at the beginning I said that when you've finished reading this, you could make your own mind up about whether I've been lucky or not?

Well, I think I've been lucky. Really lucky.

Not only did Molly come into my life and save me, but I don't feel bitter or resentful about what happened to me any more.

I'm happy with my life.

Yes ... read that again. Happy. With. My. Life.

But who knows what the future holds?

Do any of us?

The End

Coming Soon...

DEAD BRIDES

#2 in the Richie Malone series

one

It may be over-simplifying matters to say that it began at the precise moment that Elvis and Kojak stole the pig.

But it had to start somewhere, so this is probably as good a place as any to begin the story.

Besides, it was like a jigsaw puzzle with only one piece, to which others would attach themselves over time.

And, in any case, it wasn't just *any* pig.

It was a pig that had been spit-roasted almost to the point of perfection – a pig that was about to be consumed by a gathering representative of the wealthiest, the most powerful and – with a few exceptions – the most corrupt residents of the Costa Del Sol.

And it was also a pig – although Elvis and Kojak were ignorant of this fact at the time – that belonged to the host, Alexei Nikolaev, the godfather of the Andalucían Bratva.

Nikolaev is one of most evil bastards I have ever come across and also a good friend of mine. He is certainly someone from whom one should not steal a pig, particularly at his daughter's wedding.

ACKNOWLEDGEMENTS

I would like to offer my grateful thanks to those who gave their time, expertise and support with my research and during the writing of *Saving Dave*.

In particular, I'd like to express my gratitude to Dr Maria Lyko, who advised me as to the credibility of Dave's brain injury, and talked me through the medical processes that would, or could occur.

I would like to thank my editor, Nicky Taylor, whose highly professional work and enthusiastic support for the project has guided me from the developmental stage.

I'd also like to thank Laurence and his proficient team at BooksGoSocial who picked up the ball and got Dave across the line. As Arnie said: "I'll be back".

Thanks also to the host of Beta readers who gave helpful feedback on *Saving Dave*, especially my good Borough Road amigos.

Particular thanks go also to my good friend Graham Downey for providing inspiration with the plot. Without Graham's suggestions, Roger would be considerably duller and would almost certainly never have entered a casino.

I'd also like to thank my good friend and fellow scribbler, Cec Lowry for his support and enthusiasm throughout.

Saving Dave is dedicated to my son Jake, who sadly passed away in 2015. Without Jake, Dave would not exist, and the lives of those touched by his short life would be so very different. Thanks also to Jake's siblings, Rosanna and Cameron for their support and opinions.

Finally, a huge thanks to my wife Monika for her unwavering support and tolerance of my prolonged but productive writing spells in Marbella.

About The Author

Richard Grainger was born in Belfast and has worked as a teacher, personal trainer, rugby coach, restaurateur, reluctant wedding planner, and journalist.

His first book, *The Last Latrine*, is an account of his experiences in Nepal running the world's highest marathon. *Losing The Plot*, the first in the Richie Malone series, was his debut novel and he is currently working on the sequel.

He is also planning more adventure for Dave.

Richard divides his time between Marbella, where he writes, and Wroclaw where he enjoys Polish beer and teaches English part-time.

Visit www.maverick.co.uk for more information about Richard's writing, blog, and future projects.

Printed in Great Britain
by Amazon